The Heart of
Karameikos

Atlan Tepes Mountains

Castellan Keep

Duke's Road Keep

Castellan River

Wulfholde Hills

Threshold

Castle of the Three Suns

Highreach River

High Forge

Hillfollow River

Penhaligon

Verge

Ford

Ford

Kelvin

The Moor

Bywater Village

Lake of Lost Dreams

Riallian River

Windrush River

Duke's Road

Dymrak Forest

Rugalov River

Ruins of Krakatos

Rugalov Village

Speculanim

40 miles

Rugalov Keep

Gulf of Marilenev

Sea of Dread

"What is this place?" she asked. Her voice sounded loud in the hall, and she winced, not wanting to seem irreverent.

The monk did not answer at first, but sighed loudly. In time, he said, "This is the Corridor of the Fallen."

The word *fallen* made Jo think of the first time she had seen Flinn, surrounded by children shouting, "Flinn the Fallen, Flinn the Fool!" She wondered if he would be found in the Hall of Heroes, as Donar had called it, or in this place. Making sure to quiet her voice, she asked, "Where is the statue of Fain Flinn?"

The monk stopped, but did not turn. He bent his head even lower, and Jo wondered if he were going to cry. She grew uncomfortable in the heavy silence as she waited for an answer. She did not think Flinn a failure, but nor did she think this corridor held failures, only those heroes who had fallen before they could fulfill their ultimate glory. Flinn had achieved glory, but only in his death.

"I am sorry, Johauna Menhir," the monk whispered. "I do not know that name."

Books

The Penhaligon Trilogy
D. J. Heinrich

Book One
The Tainted Sword

Book Two
The Dragon's Tomb

Book Three
The Fall of Magic

DUNGEONS & DRAGONS™
Books

THE FALL OF MAGIC

D. J. Heinrich

THE FALL OF MAGIC

Cover art by Sam Rakeland.

Map by David C. Sutherland III.

First Printing: October 1993

Printed in the United States of America

Library of Congress Catalog Card Number: 92-61102

9 8 7 6 5 4 3 2 1

ISBN: 1-56076-663-8

TSR, Inc.
P.O. Box 756
Lake Geneva, WI 53147
United States of America

TSR Ltd.
120 Church End, Cherry Hinton
Cambridge CB1 3LB
United Kingdom

To M

Acknowledgments

Most of the time the acknowledgments page sounds like the Academy Awards, so I'll keep this brief.

My thanks goes to Margaret Weis, my mentor and confidante; to Bill Fawcett for waking me at 9:00 in the morning; to all my friends who knew me when; and especially to Jon, Mike, and Andrew. They know why.

Prologue

here are many reasons to write an account of one's life. The journals of statesmen always provide excellent histories. Sometimes it is important to leave behind a written record for children. Sometimes it is important to honor friends.

Flinn the Mighty was the greatest hero of Penhaligon. He embodied the spirit of the Quadrivial: Honor, Courage, Faith, and Glory, the four corners of knighthood. I began his training fully expecting that he would one day inherit my position as castellan of the Castle of the Three Suns. He did not.

Everyone knows of his final fight with Verdilith, the Great Green. Though he maimed Verdilith's foreleg with Wyrmblight, Flinn was struck down before he could kill the beast, and his body was given up to the flames in the manner befitting a knight. His sword, Wyrmblight, was taken up by his squire and love, Johauna Menhir, a remarkable young woman.

Verdilith had an ally at the Castle of the Three Suns, a mysterious sorcerer whose real name was Teryl Auroch. Auroch had forged the abaton, a box that consumed magic. The wizard caused the havoc-wreaking box to be taken to Armstead, a village of mages.

Jo and her companions, Braddoc Briarblood, Karleah Kunzay, and Dayin the wild boy, traveled to Armstead to intercept the box, but arrived too late. The magical energy at Armstead had activated the abaton, now a dimensional gate between Mystara and the world of the abelaats—the world of Teryl Auroch's origin. By the time Jo and her friends had arrived, the abaton had already opened, destroying the town and everyone in it.

Verdilith dogged the heels of Wyrmblight's bearer. The Great Green slew one of Jo's companions, took his form, and entered Jo's company, whispering venom in her ear. The twisted heart and mind of Verdilith drove him in the end to assume the form of Fain Flinn, hoping to fool Jo. But Jo saw through the outward appearance of Flinn the Immortal to the beast that lurked within. With Wyrmblight, Jo struck down the dragon and avenged the death of Flinn, her only love.

As I have stated, Jo was a remarkable woman. She sacrificed more than any knight could ask, or hero could offer.

**From the Chronicles of Sir Lile Graybow
Ten Years After the Reconstruction**

Chapter I

ohauna jerked awake, her heart racing. She clutched the broken halves of Wyrmblight closer to her for protection, but the cold metal burned her skin. She panicked, realizing she had fallen asleep again, despite the cold, despite the pain, despite the urgency of her mission. She could not even remember having stopped to rest, but she was already covered with a thin layer of snow.

The wind from the Black Peak Mountains howled mercilessly around her, and Jo wished she were somewhere warm, somewhere safe. She had taken refuge beneath a shelf of black slate rock, hugging her arms so tightly to herself her shoulders were sore from the strain. She could tell she had attempted to start a fire, though she could not imagine where she had found the tiny twigs and branches that lay now beneath a slight layer of snow. She recalled using Wyrmblight to strike sparks.

Jo moved her arm to brush away the flakes, but the motion made her colder. She closed her eyes again, attempting to recall how she had arrived in the middle of the Black Peaks without any protection. The cold and wind were clouding her thoughts, but she was determined to stay awake and alive. Scattered memories of Armstead and the darkness that filled the sky flitted through her mind. Her dream-memories brought images of the abaton and the name Teryl Auroch, and the death of the green dragon, Verdilith. Fain Flinn's name stood out from the other recollections. But the darkness from the abaton and the need to kill Teryl Auroch—these two things seemed more important than even her dead love, Flinn.

"All right, squire," Jo murmured to herself, attempting to keep her eyes open against the frost. "Time to move . . . as soon as I rest a little while."

᪣ ᪣ ᪣ ᪣ ᪣

Jo awoke in a different world. Her limbs felt oddly warm, and she guessed that they had finally gone numb from the cold. But that didn't explain the smell of cooking food, nor the fact that she no longer held Wyrmblight.

As she quickly sat up, Jo's eyesight filled with darkness and stars, the sound of the ocean rushing in her ears. She felt her bandaged hands press against her face, against scabs from healing abrasions where the mountainside had scraped away her skin. She put her hands on her knees and realized she had no clothes. These and a thousand other strange sensations convinced her to lie back down.

The smell of food brought Jo slowly back to her senses. She saw she was inside some kind of pavilion tent, heavy brown canvas supported by a single center pole and numerous stakes hammered into the sandy ground. The food was arrayed across a nearby table, set with plates and bowls made from the finest gold and the poorest clay. Everything in the vessels appealed to her.

The down mattress beneath Jo was big and comfortable, the kind Jo had dreamed about sleeping on when she became a landed knight. The brass-rod frame was attractively crooked, the four rods at the corners ending in large brass spheres. The quilted spread that covered her weary form was a patchwork of hundreds of fabric squares, old and new, fine and cheap. She touched a piece of a dark, wine-colored weave and remembered seeing such cloth in a Specularum shop. She smiled at the memory, and a scab cracked on her face.

Squinting, Jo peered at herself in the shiny brass ball nearest her head. The distorted image showed cuts and bruises; her lips were covered with blood. Worried that she might ruin the quilt, Jo kicked the heavy blanket to the floor and searched about the bed for something to wipe away the blood. She found a small piece of white cloth covered with brown stains. She wiped her fingers clean, then held the cloth to her cracked lips until they stopped bleeding.

For some reason, her left leg was better tended than the

rest of her body. The bandages were reasonably fresh, though they, like the little cloth she held, were covered with brown stains. Jo found a small vial of a sweet-smelling salve that had undoubtedly been applied to the wounds. She scooped a small bit out of the vial and applied some to the cut on her lip. The pain instantly faded.

With the pain finally gone, Jo began to wonder where she had been taken, and by whom. Seeking answers—and clothes—she walked over to a large wooden trunk on the floor and threw it open. She found a chaotic pile of clothes so rich and varied that her eyes widened with delight. Like the variety of weaves of the quilt on the bed, some of the clothes in the trunk might have been worn by royalty, others by peasants. Without searching for anything in particular, Jo reached down into the pile and pulled out a shimmering blue gown covered with white lace and inlaid with delicate pearls. The cloth was so smooth that she almost had trouble holding on to it, and when it brushed her cheek, it felt cold, like a silk scarf she had once found in Eirmont's fall-season moonlight. Lovely though the gown was, it was not the attire of a squire.

Jo continued to pick through the clothes, at first placing them carefully on the ground, then becoming less concerned as the pile rose. She found fine silk blouses with matching vests and pantaloons, embroidered with heraldic designs she did not recognize—falcons and shields. There were sackcloth garments that made her arms itch as she touched them. She discovered great rolls of leather straps, alternating black and red, which she guessed were supposed to be wrapped around a body like bandages.

Eventually, she uncovered a shirt of mail with links so fine she knew it must have been fashioned by an elven smith with the purest of magics. The chain made a sound like tiny bells when she held it up, and she saw herself reflected a thousand times in the links. She smiled widely and clutched the shirt to her body in delight, then draped it over her shoulder as she continued to search through the trunk.

To her disappointment, Jo could not find another of the elven garments. However, she did find red-tinted metal greaves and bracers and shoulder-guards to match. She did not recognize the light metal, but it was too strong for her to bend when she tested its worth. Perhaps it was elven, too.

Jo found a pair of boots buried under more clothes. The boots fit better than any pair she could remember, including the ones she had worked so hard to make when she was an apprentice. She found it very odd that the boots and the armor fit as well as they did; it seemed her saviors had this trunk filled especially for her.

Jo removed pants and a matching shirt from the trunk. She looked carefully at the clothes; they were the same color and make as the garments worn by the knights of Penhaligon except that the tunic was missing the three golden suns. The stitching on the rich blue brocade shimmered, and Jo thought about the raiments that Flinn had stashed away, the same ones he had torn apart to use as bandages when Jo was injured. She smiled a half-smile, remembering how she had resown the garment so it was almost as good as new.

The bandages on her hands reminded her that Wyrmblight was gone. Jo left the trunk and sat back down on the bed, confused. The sword had been the only physical reminder she had of Flinn, but when it had cracked in two, her memories and feelings had seemed to shatter also. She had depended on Flinn, both physically and emotionally, looking vainly forward to his return from death, as the bards sang. But Wyrmblight's breaking had made Jo acutely aware of the false promise of this return.

With great deliberation, Jo removed all the bandages from her legs and hands, finding that there was little there except for some caked blood and scar tissue. She donned her clothing.

Jo looked at herself in the reflection of one of the bed's brass balls. Everything fit perfectly.

The smell of the food was too great for Jo to resist any longer; she rushed to the table, unsure what to eat first. She picked out one of her favorite dishes, duck roasted with orange sauce, and ate straight out of the hot dish with her fingers. It had a better taste than anything she had eaten, even when she had stolen from the best tables in Specularum. She drank fresh water from a clay cup and ate fruit and dried meats from a brass plate. She ate and drank, stopped for breath, ate more—all the while certain she had never eaten so well or been so comfortable or felt so safe her entire life.

As she ate another piece of duck, something in the clothes trunk caught Jo's eye. She finished her food and walked back to the pile of clothes. There was a simple robe inside the trunk, a tabard made from a cloth the same color as her brocade, but not as fine. She threw the tabard over herself to hide the display of her armor, tying it tightly around her slim waist with the attached belt. The robe covered the shoulder-guards and fell down just far enough to hide her greaves.

She hoped she might find the halves of Wyrmblight, but didn't bother to look, doubting they would be in the tent. She would have liked a weapon at her side, at least a dagger for protection. With a final look at the tent, Jo decided to meet her saviors. With a deep, steadying breath, Jo turned, pushing back the flap leading to the world outside.

れ れ れ れ れ

Jo felt herself dying. She was too tired to panic as the cold tore the life from her body. The wind howled loudly in her ears, like a pack of wild dogs. Wyrmblight had frozen to her hands. She wanted to start another fire until she realized that her wood was buried under half a foot of snow.

Jo pushed herself up slightly using the pommelled end of the broken great sword as a crutch, expending the last of her failing will. The moment she moved, her leg burned with agony, and she saw the reason for the pain. Something had bitten into her flesh and rended her calf open. She stared at the fresh blood as steam rose from the packed red flakes. Whatever had bitten her would be back soon.

Ice cracked and broke away from Jo's limbs and face as she slowly rose to her full height. Jo felt very little except the cold from the wind, and the pain. The very act of rising to her feet had exhausted her, leaving her unable to move away from the mountain beast's feeding ground. Jo leaned against the black shale of the mountain for support, blinking her eyes to keep them from tearing and freezing. A trail of bloodstained paw prints led off back to blasted Armstead. The beast had been alone.

Perhaps, she should climb onto the ledge to better defend herself. With a swing of her arm, Jo impaled the broken half of Wyrmblight into the mountain's flat, snow-crusted side. The metal hilt dug into her flesh. The additional pain cleared her head slightly, but she wasn't sure if a clear head was desirable.

Jo lifted her left leg and propped it against the mountainside. Ignoring the wind, the cold, and the pain, she pulled herself across the shale. Ice scraped her cheek and fell down her neck, further chilling her shivering skin. Wyrmblight dug into her hand again, and her voice carried above the wind's agony.

Jo was forced to halt. The blood from her hand trickled down her side and onto her wounded leg. With face pressed against the black shale, her breath came slow and ragged. She inhaled more ice-dust than air, and felt herself losing consciousness again.

As she slowly slid to the ground, Jo heard a wail above the incessant wind. She attempted to stand again, but could not lift herself.

The mountain beast had returned. It was a wild dog, a scavenger looking for easy prey. The dog snuffled around the blood, then stared directly in Jo's eyes. Jo could barely move as the beast stalked toward her, loping across the short distance, teeth bared.

A moment later, Jo awoke to find the dog lapping again at the blood on her leg. She had fallen unconscious, and the dog had taken her for dead. She batted at the beast with both halves of Wyrmblight, uncaring if she did more damage to herself than to the dog.

The pommel half of the blade sliced through the animal's right hind leg. The other half of the blade struck the pommel, creating a small shower of sparks. The dog howled in pain, then leaped at Jo, snarling its anger. Jo tried to roll the dog off her body, but she was too weak, and the dog too heavy. Its jaws snapped at her face and tore into her cheek.

Jo yelled in pain and sank her own teeth into the dog's muzzle, biting viciously from fear and anger. She battered the animal with the halves of Wyrmblight. She fought and bit and struggled and yelled, lapsing in and out of consciousness as she did. . . .

&a &a &a &a &a

What Jo found outside the tent shocked her. The place looked nothing like Mystara. She was surrounded by tents, she guessed hundreds, maybe thousands. Their number seemed to go on forever, forming grassy walkways and sandy paths. They seemed erected according to some kind of scheme, perhaps shading or color, and in the distance, the bright, flapping canvas looked like a field of flowers.

Jo turned in place and took in the view of the tents. A pebble-covered avenue caught her eye. She walked toward it, arbitrarily naming the direction east in order to keep her bearings.

Each of the tents seemed to be made of the same heavy canvas, like sailcloth for ships. They were colored with exotic dyes, and some were unevenly stained. The entire tent grounds had a smell of light oil, and the dyes possessed sweet and bitter scents of their own, making Jo's nose wrinkle as she walked past. It seemed she walked among the bands of a rainbow, separate and discrete, but a rainbow that also included textures and smells. She realized that her mouth hung open in wonderment, and she quickly closed it.

Each tent had a symbol above its entrance. Like the colors of the tents, the symbols varied in shape and form. The first tent she passed boasted a picture of two cubes made of smaller cubes of varied colors. The next had the same image, but she saw that the smaller cubes had fewer colors. By the time she had passed the tenth tent, the cubes had actually become dice. As she walked onward, the dice on the placards turned and seemed to roll, showing their pips in different combinations even as their backgrounds changed. The dice grew smaller, then multiplied, then spread out into patterns, triangles, and rough circles.

Jo was surprised to reach the end of the row of colored tents. The adjacent area was filled with white tents that stretched endlessly to the horizon. The placards on these tents were bare. Jo guessed they were empty.

She looked back down the avenue where she had walked, and the once-straight path now turned and twisted, eclipsing her view. She felt as if she were inside some great labyrinth, like the hedge-maze that surrounded King Stefan's castle, where she had once fled a baker after stealing some bread. But this place was infinitely larger than the hedges.

The last tent with any decoration was dyed in alternating squares of black and white, and the placard that held the symbol above the entrance was some kind of game board with black and white squares. Jo seemed to recall having seen one of her old sponsors in the bookbinders guild playing a game on a similar board. The playing pieces had been carved from yellowed ivory into the shapes of heroes and armies. She stared at the symbol, but couldn't remember the name of the game.

Whatever the name, the idea of diversion in this endless place interested her, and perhaps the contents of this tent could provide some answers.

Without another thought, Jo pulled back the tent flap and walked inside. She expected to find a tent much like the one she had left, with a bed, a table, maybe even some more food. To her surprise, she stood in total darkness, and the air was quiet and still. The oily scent of the canvas was gone, leaving only the light smell of pipe smoke. She tried to step back, but could no longer see the tent flap in the darkness.

"Come in," a voice said. Jo jumped with fright and her heart raced. She searched the darkness but could not see anything.

"Please, sit down," the voice added. Jo glanced around her, wondering why the voice seemed to come from everywhere within the tent. It was not an alarming voice, but a distracted one.

A white light flared down from somewhere above, illuminating a table with two chairs. The table was made of unremarkable wood, as were the chairs. The sudden, unnatural flash made Jo wish again that she had a weapon, even the broken halves of Wyrmblight. Unfortunately, the glaring light did not reveal the owner of the voice.

"Who are you?" Jo asked cautiously.

"Please, sit down," the kindly voice repeated.

Weaponless and dumbfounded, Jo gave in. With a sigh of resignation, she crossed the short distance to the table and sat in the nearest chair.

An old, balding man appeared out of the darkness. He had a long gray beard and wore clothes as black as the tent around them, revealing only his hands and face. He carried a small, flat box under his left arm and clenched a long pipe between his teeth.

Setting the box carefully on the table, the man sat down and pulled up his chair. Without glancing up at Jo, he nimbly released the two golden clasps on the box and opened it, revealing a similar board to the one on the tent's placard.

"Would you like a drink?" the old man asked distractedly. Without another word, he reached out and his hand disappeared into the darkness. When he withdrew it from the shadows, he brought back a number of small playing pieces, carved of blackened metal to look like statesmen and soldiers. He began placing the pieces on his side of the board, then reached out into the darkness a second time. He brought back a small golden goblet filled with a wine Jo could smell from across the table. He handed it to Jo without meeting her gaze.

"Thank you," Jo murmured, taking the goblet. It was engraved with hundreds of geometric images.

The board was soon filled with playing pieces on both sides. The color of Jo's pieces was red-tinted silver, much like the color of the armor she wore.

"This game," the old man said, finally looking up at Jo, "is called Wizards and Warriors. Do you know the rules?"

Too astounded by all that had happened—and a bit heady from the sip of wine—Jo did not answer.

"Do you know the rules?" the man asked impatiently.

Jo shook her head. "No."

The man pursed his lips and raised an eyebrow. He shrugged. "No matter. You move first."

Jo tried to find a relation between her playing pieces and those used by her guild master back in Specularum. Some had been called pawns, the least powerful and most plentiful pieces. Others—the sorcerers, clerics, and towers —waited behind the row of pawns. The only way to use the more powerful pieces, she remembered, was to move the pawns out of their way. Jo moved the pawn closest to the edge so she might reveal a tower.

The old man shook his head and put her piece back in its original position. "No, sorry. You lost that one," he said around the stem of his pipe. He leaned back in his chair, apparently waiting for Jo to start again.

Instead of shifting a piece at the end, Jo moved a pawn in the middle two squares, recalling a move her master had made with a similar piece.

"No," the old man said again. He put the piece back.

Jo considered the row of her greater pieces. They all seemed equally stately and powerful. She put her hand on a piece carved like a knight, watching the man's reaction. His face was blank and surrounding by a thin veil of smoke. She moved the piece in front of her line of pawns, as she had seen done before.

The old man leaned forward, and cocked his head to the side. Jo wondered if she had finally moved correctly.

"Sorry." The knight also was placed back at its starting location.

Jo tried a sorcerer.

"No."

A sheriff.

"No."

A prince.

That obviously surprised the old man, but didn't stop him from putting the piece back.

"What do you want from me?" Jo asked. "You won't tell me the rules, so how am I supposed to play?"

The old man leaned back in his chair again, and for the first time removed the pipe from his mouth. "That is a question we all must ask, Johauna Menhir."

If this man's sorcery can divine my name, Jo thought, perhaps it can divine where Wyrmblight is. "Can you tell me—?"

"Yes, but no," the man said as he began picking up pieces and cleaning off the board. Before she realized what had happened, both the board and the pieces were gone, leaving only the table, the chairs, and the two of them.

"You look very much like Diulanna," the old man said.

Jo skeptically cocked an eyebrow. "Are you toying with me, sir?"

"Of course I am, young lady. There will come a time when you must make a choice between us. My fellows hope that you will pick one of them."

"I don't understand, but if you are the one who saved me, I would like to thank you and—"

The old man held up his hand again, and Jo fell silent. "Of all the directions you could have chosen, you chose this one, whether it was a choice of the heart, the mind, or the will. That should help you make your decision."

"Decision for what?" Jo inquired, rising slightly from her chair. "What choice do I have to make?"

Jo stood up.

She was outside now, standing before a huge rectangular building constructed of rose-colored marble and granite. The dark interior of the tent had been replaced by a shimmering sky, beneath which lay the limitless field of tents and the enormous edifice.

The building was hundreds of feet wide, and its sheer size made it impossible to see in one glance. The long, flat walls were elegantly carved in regular patterns that crawled up the sides like ivy. Peering up, Jo saw two spires pierce the sky, positioned at either end of the megalithic structure. Their crenelated steeples were made of the same rose-colored granite as the rest of the place.

The architecture of the building told Jo it was a necropolis, a monument to the dead. She had seen one like it in Specularum, but that one was nowhere near as large. The necropolis's arched entrance was easily the height of the largest tree Jo had ever seen in any forest. The archway's two doors were smooth, shaped like those of a temple—flat at the bottom but tapering gracefully to a point above.

It would take the strength of a titan, thought Jo, to push back one of those doors.

Jo approached the portal, seeing that the natural grain of the oak was inset with myriad images engraved with the greatest skill. In one hand-sized area, Jo recognized a perfect carving of a battle between Traladaran forces and Thyatian armies. The battlefields were so perfectly sculpted that she could tell regiment from regiment.

There were thousands of other images, some like the first, portraying vast armies conquering nations, others of individuals overcoming incredible odds. Jo found an image of a single hero dying at the end of her own cursed blade, giving birth to a new world. She saw a similar image of a knight on horseback slaying a dragon with a spear. Jo looked for an engraving of Flinn fighting Verdilith on the open plain, but then she stopped herself; the past was gone and Flinn was avenged.

She stood back from the door and rubbed her eyes in fatigue. It would take a lifetime to read even the smallest portion of these great doors, she thought.

Gritting her teeth, she pushed hard on the door with her shoulder, expecting to meet resistance. The door swung silently open, and Jo was carried forward by her momentum, spilling to the cold, black marble floor. As huge as the necropolis had been without, it was even larger within.

Jo looked out past stately columns of white limestone to the wide rotunda that lay immediately beyond. Numerous colonnades spread spokelike from the round chamber and seemed to stretch on into infinity. The colonnades were lined with statues, armies of them—

ranked into the dim distance. Jo's eyes followed the rose-hued marble walls of the rotunda up to a vault that disappeared in blackness above.

Now she wished she had stayed in bed.

Chapter II

ohauna walked the corridors of heroes. That was the name she gave to that strange, infinite place peopled only with heroic statues . . . and herself. She could not imagine how long she had roamed the hallways, but she was beginning to tire. She would have left except that the entrance was now lost to her in the tangled intersection of colonnades.

The halls were very wide and very tall, at least five horses abreast and the height of a small castle's tower. The sheer scale of the necropolis was impossible: the building's inside could not possibly have been contained within the granite walls.

Jo's footsteps echoed through the necropolis; if anyone other than the statues knew she was here, he could easily find her. The hallway ahead of her, as dimly lit as the rest of the monument, stretched on farther than her eye could see. She glanced back over her shoulder and saw that she had apparently walked an equal distance. She turned her eyes away for a moment to quell the dizziness she felt.

Her gaze fell on one of the countless white marble statues of armed and armored men and women. Each stood in an alcove between columns, lit like the gaming table in the old man's tent had been. This particular statue portrayed a man holding a warhammer, bearing down on some unseen opponent, and was as finely crafted as all the others.

Jo had stopped at many of the displays to marvel at the skill of the sculptor or to wonder what battles had been fought with a given sword or lance. Despite her close scrutiny, Jo did not recognize any of the statues. There were hundreds of men and women of every description, many dressed in styles of armor that had not been seen on Mystara for centuries. In fact, many of the statues were not of humans or demihumans, like the elves and dwarves. Jo had passed one statue shaped like a man, but with legs and arms like those of some mechanical construct. There were sculptings of creatures that looked like great insects, and others that had obviously possessed no particular physical form.

Regardless of race depicted, each statue had some weapon or artifact next to it, displayed on a pedestal or mounted on wood, some even floating in the air. The more common weapons like swords and bows she easily recognized, but there were many puzzling things displayed as well. There had been abacuses held by stately men and women, ink quills, physiker's tools, musical instruments, and things Jo had not seen before.

Clearly, this necropolis was a monument to heroes of legend, heroes from every land and every race. But there was a similarity to them all, a noble expression in the eyes. These signs, coupled with the perfect carvings on the great doors and the impossible infinity inside and out told Jo that this monument had been erected by immortal hands. At one time or another, all these heroes had been the agent of immortal powers.

"The immortals, of course," a loud voice laughed from behind.

Jo spun on her heel and reached for her weapon, then realized she did not have one.

The man she faced was huge, the muscles on his arms and chest barely contained by his ancient scale mail armor. He wore a wide metal belt around his waist and heavy gauntlets fashioned apparently by the same armorer. In his right hand, he held a giant warhammer. His hair and beard were shades more red than Jo's.

"Please allow me to introduce myself," the man said, his voice booming through the corridors. "My name is Donar."

"Johauna Menhir," Jo returned, unsure if she should bow, curtsey, or remain standing. She opted for the last.

The huge man laughed at the reply. "Welcome to the Hall of Heroes, Johauna Menhir. How do you like our displays?"

Somehow he had guessed her name, or Donar had read it from her mind. Jo glanced back nervously at the statue with the hammer. It did not seem to be the same as the man who stood before her. Turning back, she said,

"They're magnificent."

"Yes, they are, aren't they?" Donar said, walking around Jo to admire the statue of the warrior with the hammer. He gestured at the display, saying, "This was Vardmer, a man of singular strength and character. He fell at the battle of Rospielheim, killed by a poisoned dart from his lover."

"I'm afraid I have not heard of him."

"Nor should you have."

Donar switched his hammer to his left hand and held out his right to Jo. She took it cautiously, wondering if this man were an immortal. She also wondered if the touch of an immortal would harm her. Her hand was dwarfed by Donar's.

The two walked down the corridor in the direction Jo had been heading. Unlike the distracted old man in the tent, Donar seemed cheerful and glad. He would occasionally peer into an alcove and smile, as if remembering some grand time.

"Excuse me, Donar," Jo said as she withdrew her hand and halted. "I have a question I must ask."

Donar seemed disappointed that the walk had been interrupted, and even more disappointed that Jo had removed her hand. "All right, then," he mumbled. "Ask."

"Did you save me from dying?"

A stunned expression crossed the huge man's face, then he burst out laughing in a voice so loud Jo's ears hurt. "Of course not!" he bellowed.

"Then who did?"

Donar continued to laugh, slowly calming himself and wiping a tear from his eye.

"Please tell me. I would like to thank him so I can leave."

Finally in control again, Donar held out his hand again and said, "It is to him that I am taking you."

He gestured ahead of them, where a set of normal-sized doors stood in a wall that had not been there before. Apparently of its own volition, one of the doors opened slightly, revealing a middle-aged man with hair shaved on the top like a monk's, but very long on the back and sides. His robes were shades of dark gray, and he wore a sash that formed a ring around his neck and extended to his knees. He stood a short distance from Jo. She tried to see past the man, but he only held the door wide enough for him to stand in the opening, and the area behind him was dark.

"Please, come this way," the man beckoned in a soft voice. Jo turned to Donar, whose lips were pursed together in concern.

"Is something wrong?" Jo asked, wondering what could possibly make this huge man seem uncertain.

Donar shook his head, then turned to her and smiled. "No, nothing at all." he replied. With a gesture, he added, "Please, follow this man."

"Aren't you coming?"

"No, I am afraid I have other things to do." The huge man paused, looking over Jo with an eye she guessed had seen hundreds of battles. "That armor suits you well. Good-bye, Johauna Menhir. Good luck."

Without another word, Donar turned on his heel, walked back down the corridor, and was quickly lost in darkness.

"Please," the man in the door insisted. "Come this way."

Jo wondered briefly why Donar would think it necessary to wish her luck, but she allowed herself to be led
past the doors into the corridor beyond. The man walked
before her, head bowed reverently, hands clenched
together. There was no sound except for the echo of Jo's
hard boots.

The hallway was much like those Jo had already seen,
except this one seemed sad, as if some great melancholy
hung in the air. The statues in the alcoves showed heroes
fallen in battle or other conflicts. The weapons and tools
displayed were broken or smashed, and some seemed
burned out, as if a flame had burst from inside and then
died. Swords were snapped in two, and maces' hafts shattered. The strings on a black harp were missing, and the
bow cracked at the base.

"What is this place?" she asked. Her voice sounded
loud in the hall, and she winced, not wanting to seem
irreverent.

The monk did not answer at first, but sighed loudly. In
time, he said, "This is the Corridor of the Fallen."

The word *fallen* made Jo think of the first time she had
seen Flinn, surrounded by children shouting, "Flinn the
Fallen, Flinn the Fool!" She wondered if he would be
found in the Hall of Heroes, as Donar had called it, or in
this place. Making sure to quiet her voice, she asked,
"Where is the statue of Fain Flinn?"

The monk stopped, but did not turn. He bent his head
even lower, and Jo wondered if he were going to cry. She
grew uncomfortable in the heavy silence as she waited for
an answer. She did not think Flinn a failure, but nor did

she think this corridor held failures, only those heroes who had fallen before they could fulfill their ultimate glory. Flinn had achieved glory, but only in his death.

"I am sorry, Johauna Menhir," the monk whispered. "I do not know that name."

"What does that mean?" Jo asked, feeling unsettled that she had not seen a statue of Flinn in either the Hall or the Corridor. She couldn't believe that Flinn would not be immortalized among the world's heroes, fallen or no.

"It means that I do not know that name," the monk replied leadenly. He raised his head and resumed his slow pace.

Jo clenched her fists but said nothing further. This man was apparently some kind of servitor or custodian, unlike Donar or the game lord, who had been masters. Like other custodians she had met in her life, either at the libraries of Specularum or the men who scraped barnacles off the hulls of ships at the ports, this man would probably know little beyond his duties.

Passing hundreds of other displays, Jo was surprised when the monk stopped in front of what appeared to be a new display. Her guide slowly gestured with a hand for her to step forward. Jo walked around the man and saw the display. She nearly fell as her legs buckled beneath her.

Wyrmblight floated in the air, both halves coldly reflecting the pool of light that illuminated them.

"What—what is the meaning of this?" Jo gasped. She felt suddenly weak.

"This is the monument to Wyrmblight, broken in battle fighting the foe it was created to destroy," the monk said in a low, reverent voice.

"What do you intend to do with it?"

"Keep it here for eternity, amongst the other weapons in the Corridor of the Fallen."

Jo stared at Wyrmblight, the sword that had represented the memory of her lover and the sword with which she had tried to spark a fire and protect herself against a common mountain dog. She had cut her hands holding the naked edge of the broken half and remembered the pain, though now she felt nothing but scarred skin on her palms. Jo realized that she had known nothing but pain since traveling with Flinn, pain of the flesh or pain of the heart.

The memory of her love for Flinn returned, and with it Jo felt weak, almost consumed. She closed her eyes and steadied herself, knowing that nothing would bring Flinn back from the dead, and not even the abelaat stones would allow her to commune with him again.

The monk drew closer. He whispered, "We are offering you the opportunity to be the custodian of Wyrmblight for eternity. You can be with it forever," the monk added, "and remember its greatness."

Jo looked at Wyrmblight and saw the edging of elven silver over dwarven steel. Flinn was dead, but her life did not have to end. Jo smiled grimly to herself. She knew that living would not be easy, that the quest would only become more trying from this point; but she was determined to battle on, as Flinn would have done. And she knew how to start.

Turning to the monk, she looked down on him and said, "I reject your offer, sir. I will not tend the memory of the dead forever."

The monk, his expression downcast and his demeanor still heavy, replied, "If that is your wish. You are free to wander the Hall of Heroes and Corridor of the Fallen as long as you desire."

"And then?"

"We shall return you as you will."

Jo stepped back and stared at a procession of other monks who had emerged apparently from thin air. They were each stooped and sad, such as her guide. She said, "You are the ones who saved me?"

The monk bowed low in confirmation and started to move away from Wyrmblight's monument. The other monks followed. Jo looked to the blade and thought of the elven armor she wore beneath her tabard and brocade shirt.

"Wait!"

The monks seemed loathe to stop, but as one they all turned to face her.

"Why must Wyrmblight be left here in the Corridor of the Fallen when it could still fulfill its purpose?"

The first monk appeared puzzled. He said, "It *has* fulfilled its purpose. The foe is vanquished."

Jo stepped forward excitedly. "You don't understand. Its purpose is to be whole, to be a weapon of heroes."

The monk looked into Jo's eyes, and she shuddered, feeling the depths of his apathy and melancholy. He shook his head and said, "What are you suggesting?"

"Reforge the blade!" she replied, gesturing toward Wyrmblight. "It still has a role to play!"

The monks glanced at one another but did not raise their heads. Jo's heart beat quickly as she waited for an answer, not knowing if the monks had the capability to reforge the blade, let alone the authority to remove it from the display.

Finally, the first monk shook his head again. "You do not know the cost." Without another word they all resumed their walk, disappearing into the shadows.

"Whatever the cost, I'll pay it. We could use its metals to forge a new weapon," Jo cried in frustration. "The world is in danger and needs another hero's blade!"

Jo stood alone in the corridor. She turned back to Wyrmblight and reached out to pull it from its display, but her hand could not penetrate the circle of light. It seemed that she was pushing against the might of a waterfall. She pulled her hand back and ran her fingers through her hair.

"Why should we destroy the blade in order to make another?" a voice asked from behind.

Jo turned. A different man, dressed much like the monks had been, stood before her, but his dirty robes were made of leather, and he carried large iron tongs and a well-worn hammer. He was tall and heavily muscled. There were a number of others with him, both men and women, dressed in much the same fashion.

"The abelaats are returning to destroy Mystara. I need something to fight them," Jo stated softly.

The man, who smelled like coal and fire, scowled and asked, "Weapons need heroes. Who will wield this weapon, then? You?"

"Yes, I will! I wielded Wyrmblight after Flinn was dead, and it was I who finally killed Verdilith. Since I know of no other heroes to stop the abelaats, that leaves only me."

The large man crossed his bulging arms over his chest and sniffed loudly, wiping some grime from his face with a hand. "Do you truly know the cost?"

Jo nodded. "Yes."

Without warning, the man reached out and grabbed Jo by the collar, pulling her forward. She found herself near the stifling heat of a forge, the hall and corridor gone. The smell of coke and coal made her gasp for air. The area was so bright with the glow of white-hot iron that Jo shielded her eyes so they could adjust to the light. In time, she saw that the cast of a long blade lay before her, a blade like Wyrmblight but shorter and thinner. Two crucibles waited nearby, both filled with bubbling metal: dwarven steel in one, she was sure, and elven silver in the other. The huge and soot-blackened man tended the crucibles, his eyes glowing red beneath fierce and smoky brows.

"This is to be your blade, Johauna Menhir," the large man yelled over the roar of the fire. Jo winced as sparks filled the air from the furnace before them. He held out his fist and opened it, palm up. Inside were Jo's three remaining abelaat stones. "These will be added to the hilt, which has been preserved whole from Wyrmblight."

The man reached behind him and revealed the hilt of the great sword, intact except for the removal of the blade. He placed it into the end of the cast, then passed his hand over the grip. To her amazement, Jo saw that the abelaat stones were now imbedded into the wire-wrapped hilt, as if they had been placed by a master artisan.

"Who are you?" Jo asked as loudly as she could.

"I am he who gives inspiration to the makers of weapons. In some places I am known as Vulcan," the man replied.

"When we are finished with this cast, I will appear to the master artisan at your castle so he might know how to complete the work we start. But first, you must be reforged along with your blade!"

"What must I do?"

Vulcan pointed at the furnace, glowing hot and showering sparks. "Enter!"

"What!" Jo asked with horror. "I can't go in there! I'll— "

"Enter!" Vulcan commanded again.

Jo heard the power of the man's voice and saw fury in his eyes. She could not resist his command. She turned and faced the furnace, walking as close as she could before the heat grew so intense she felt it burning her skin.

"Enter!" Vulcan commanded a third time.

Jo closed her eyes and stepped forward. She heard the rush of the fire and the scream of the steel as it was melted in the heart of the fire. She actually found the sounds comforting, and wondered how much longer she would live to hear them. She did not think of the heat.

Jo opened her eyes. She lived, standing in the furnace. Pools of molten metal bubbled around her, and orange light filled the room, which seemed as large as the hall of the Castle of the Three Suns. She stood atop a stretch of floor that wound its way through the seas of steel and silver, a floor that led to an altar.

Stepping forward, Jo experienced a strange sensation— not a physical impulse, but one of memory. She remembered her past, the time when she was put on the ship by her parents to be sold to the sweat shops. Another step and she remembered being turned away from the orphanage.

Every step was another memory. Some of them were painful, and Jo was not sure she could move forward. Some of them were pleasant, and Jo was not sure she wanted to go back. And all of them were sharp, clear, and, she felt, helping to reforge her soul, temper her mettle. The memories were as real as the experiences had been on the day she felt them. It seemed that she could stop whenever she wished, to stand in one place and relive a memory forever, but she refused to give in. When she was ten steps from the altar, she relived her love of Flinn, and though the tears ran from her eyes and the temptation to stop and live with him forever was great, she knew her destiny lay elsewhere.

The casting of the new blade, filled with the metal from the crucibles, rested on the altar. The hilt of Wyrmblight rested in its place, and the red abelaat stones reflected the light of the fires.

Vulcan's voice boomed in the furnace, above the heat and the sound of the forge: "When you return to your land, present this blade to Baroness Arteris, and tell her that as her father had blessed Wyrmblight, so must she bless this weapon. The master artisan will know how to complete the cast."

Jo nodded her understanding.

"This blade shall protect you, Johauna Menhir, and only you, from dying at the gate between the worlds. By what name shall it be known?" the great voice asked.

Jo nodded again, slowly understanding the question. There was only one thought in her mind, only one thing she knew a knight ultimately seeks. As she stared down, the Quadrivial raised itself onto the metal of the cooling blade. Above the four runes, a fifth appeared, combining elements of the previous ones but remaining separate. She knew the name of this rune.

"Peace."

Chapter III

o awoke to the choked light of the sun. The grass and leaves beneath her head crackled with dryness, and the chill air made her breath steam from her mouth. She blinked and slowly rose to a sitting position. The snows, if there ever had been any, were gone. Her wounds were mended.

Only then did she feel a bundle under her hand.

Peace lay next to her, wrapped in oilcloth, the hilt that was Wyrmblight's jutting out of the top. Jo dragged the sword onto her lap, slowly unwrapping the oilskin. She wondered if what she was feeling—the tension, the fearful hope—was what Flinn had felt when Braddoc returned Wyrmblight to him after all those years. Jo tried to put herself in Flinn's place as he had unlatched the catches of the beautiful wooden box, chased with silver at the edges. She had looked into his eyes and had seen his hope that the great sword might bring about his salvation, had seen his fear that the blade might have been completely devoured by the blackening tarnish.

Peace lay across her legs, nestled in the heavy cloth. Jo caught the reflection of her own eyes in the silver, the same tint as the armor she wore beneath her tabard. She saw the same hope of salvation that she had seen in Flinn, and the same fear. It was not fear of the Quadrivial; it was something greater, fear for the world, fear that the world might need a savior stronger and wiser and braver than she. She was not even a knight, but had the responsibility of a hero.

Jo thought about her ultimate foe. Teryl Auroch was a fearsome magician with a fearsome weapon—the abaton, the gate that led to the abelaat world.

Jo wished Karleah were still near to provide guidance and wisdom. The old woman was the only magician of import Jo had ever known, and she had expected Karleah to have been the one to ultimately defeat Auroch. Jo touched Peace, feeling the blade's cool alloy in the cold air. The edges were still rough, the metal ready to be finished and reveal its true purity of color. She recalled that Vulcan had said Peace would act as a shield against the soul-killing effects of the abaton. Just as the last true abelaat stone protected Karleah. But she had still died. Jo felt another surge of fear, wondering if anything could withstand the abaton.

But Peace had been forged by Vulcan, who Jo had little doubt was an immortal. She *had* stood in the Hall of Heroes and wandered through the Corridor of the Fallen, convincing the smith to use the metal of Wyrmblight for a new weapon to fight the world's greatest enemy. Peace could not fail.

"Do you truly know the cost?"

She blinked to clear her thoughts and craned her head back, relieving the tension in her neck. The air was cold, but the armor and clothes she wore were keeping her reasonably warm. Jo had been left to survive in the winter air many times in her life, most often when she had lived on the streets of Specularum. At times, she had given up hope for herself, believing she would never be able to leave the alleys and back roads and find happiness and stability. Other times, the happiness she sought had been found.

Jo remembered the words of the healer she had known in Threshold. He had told her that life was a balance, and that the balance always sways between hope and despair. Jo rewrapped Peace in its oilskin covering and stood, cracking the stiffness out of her limbs and muscles.

She had to return to Penhaligon and approach the baroness. With her help and the blessing of the people, Peace would become a part of the unborn war.

❧ ❧ ❧ ❧ ❧

The custodians of the Hall and Corridor had been true to their word. Judging from the familiar hills and rivers, Jo quickly discovered she was only about twenty miles from Penhaligon, on the outskirts of the Cilmari Woods. The sun was covered by clouds, the same clouds that hung over destroyed Armstead, but Jo did not have any trouble determining which direction was north. Holding Peace in both arms, she left the woods and entered the Cilmari Plains.

The sword was much lighter than any sword of similar size she had held. Though it was made from the same metals as Wyrmblight, it was much shorter and thinner, perfect for Jo's height and strength. It could be used with either one hand or two, what Jo had once heard called a bastard sword. She wished Braddoc would reappear and teach her the sword's technique, but felt little hope in seeing her old friend.

The Cilmari Plains were covered with rolling hills. Though Jo struggled in climbing some of them, her training as a squire had considerably increased her endurance and strength. While living in Specularum, she had been quick on her feet, but that speed had mostly been a matter of fear; she had always been left panting for breath.

Even so, the first five miles were difficult, and Jo briefly stopped to rest. She peered out over the plains, which were too hilly for farming and did not have enough green pastures for animals. Consequently, she did not expect to see anyone until she had traveled farther, to within ten miles of Penhaligon.

A small contingent of knights, however, were heading away from the castle at great speed, the horses' hoofs digging up clods of cold earth. Jo recognized their Penhaligon heraldry. Squires and other followers quickly came up from behind, attempting to match the speed of their masters.

Jo pursed her lips in thought. The only reason she could guess that the knights would be moving with such speed was to intercept some enemy, but there were not enough of them to form an effective contingent. Furthermore, there were no yeomen, archers, or other cavalry.

The knights and their followers quickly disappeared behind the hills, leaving nothing more than clouds of dust in the cold air. Jo wondered if the abelaats had been able to amass their forces quickly enough to begin ravaging Mystara. Filled with new energy, Jo trotted back down the side of the hill, determined to reach the castle before night.

᪐ ᪐ ᪐ ᪐ ᪐

Penhaligon was wreathed by flames.

Jo broke into a run, quickly discovering that the flames were not consuming the castle, but lighting it. Either the magicians had not been able to reignite the magical lanterns and torches that illuminated the castle, or the abaton's grasp had extended this far from Armstead.

As she approached, Jo saw many other contingents of knights rush out of the castle proper, though she noticed that a great number were heading off north, seemingly toward Armstead. Her pace quickened. She hoped the baroness already knew of the abaton and the invading abelaats.

Within a mile of the castle, Jo was forced to jump out of the way of horsemen several times. They all had looks of anxiousness. Even the squires' jaws were set in lines of unusual determination. She recognized several of the knights and almost called out as they rode past, but thought it best not to stop them.

Jo heard the preparations of war outside the castle walls. The sounds of horses being shod and barded, armor being pounded out, and orders being shouted created such a cacophony that Jo did not hear her name being called out. She hugged Peace close to her body and continued to walk through the bustling main entrance of the castle.

"Johauna Menhir!" a woman's voice cried when she had reached the courtyard beyond.

Jo turned and staggered back a step. Baroness Arteris Penhaligon herself was addressing Jo above the din of preparations. Several of the other council members stood near the lady.

"Now that we have your attention, Squire Menhir," the baroness shouted, moving forward in a manner Jo found to be particularly threatening, "we demand to know of your whereabouts for the past two weeks!"

"My—whereabouts?" Jo muttered. She could not understand why the baroness would care, then remembered that Wyrmblight was considered a treasure of the realm.

"Is there a problem with that, *Squire?*" Councilman Melios asked. Jo knew he had not been friendly toward Flinn and was sure Melios felt the same way toward her.

Jo looked into the councilman's eyes and thought about the tents and the necropolis. The smell of fresh oil-cloth rose from her arms, and she could not resist smiling; the man was nothing more than a petty noble. She had seen the Hall of Heroes and tasted the sadness in the Corridor of the Fallen. This man had no right and no power to be threatening her.

Jo stepped forward, never breaking her gaze. Melios, a few inches shorter than Jo, swallowed hard and clenched his jaw in an obvious attempt to maintain his stand.

"There is no problem, Councilman. I have much to tell you all."

❧ ❧ ❧ ❧ ❧

Jo ran her hand over her brow, wiping the sweat back into her hair. The domed council chamber, lit by dozens of torches, was extremely hot, and the room was grimy with ash and oil. The tapestries adorning the walls seemed heavy with soot. During the two hours of interrogatives and interrogations, Jo had looked at each of the members in the council except for the baroness, whose imposing eyes she did not want to challenge. She had already told the story of the abaton a number of times, but knew she was going to tell it again.

Sir Graybow, who sat next to Baroness Arteris, rubbed his hand over his new, short beard. He had apparently lost weight in the short time Jo had been gone. She wondered if this had anything to do with the recent events that had troubled Penhaligon and the Castle of the Three Suns.

"Now, Squire Menhir," Sir Graybow began, rubbing his eyes with ink-smudged fingers. "Tell us again of the location of the abaton."

Jo could not see any reason for pretense or preamble on this repetition of her story, so she simply started again. "The abaton is now in the city of Armstead— "

"Which you claim was destroyed by this—thing," Councilor Melios interjected.

Jo sighed. "It is not a claim, Councilman. The entire

city of Armstead—all its people—are dead. Their lives were drained by the abaton to create the gate between this world and that of the abelaats."

"And what are these abelaats, Squire Menhir?" Sir Graybow inquired officiously. "Some of us know you were attacked by at least one of these creatures, but most do not know their power."

"Or their origin," the baroness added.

"During our travels to recover the abaton from Penhaligon's messengers," Jo began, shifting in her seat, "we met a woman who was the keeper of sacred knowledge carried down from before the time of the birth of humanity."

"This, 'Keeper' Grainger, as you call her," said Councilman Melios. "Do you think that she might answer questions for this council, Squire Menhir?"

"I doubt very much that she is alive, sir."

"And why is that?"

"She knew that Teryl Auroch wanted her dead," Jo retorted.

"And this is because, 'the magician desires her death in his quest to purify this world of all that is not abelaat. Her impure life angers him,'" Sir Graybow said. "This Keeper is a half-sibling to Teryl Auroch."

Jo nodded.

"I don't think we need to hear the origin of the abelaats again, Squire Menhir," the baroness said, her voice rising above the noise from outside. She pressed her palms flat against the stone table around which the council sat. "You have told us that these abelaats are magical creatures whose crystals, created from their own blood, anchored their magic to this world?"

"Yes."

"And that Teryl Auroch, a man whose mother was wed to one these abelaats, is beginning a campaign to reclaim the magic from Mystara, returning it to the world of the abelaats."

"And in doing so will cause the death of every living thing. That is correct."

Councilman Melios stood and pointed an accusing finger at Jo. "And you want us to believe this preposterous story because you, a mere squire, claim it to be true?"

Jo's resolve snapped. She bolted up from her place, her elven chain ringing lightly. "I was the squire of Fain Flinn, Flinn the Mighty, the greatest knight this land has ever known! It was people like you who doubted his integrity, stripped him of his honor through deceit and treachery!"

"Squire Menhir, sit immediately!" Sir Graybow commanded as he stood.

Jo wanted to obey Graybow, the only one at the castle who had shown her any kindness, but her anger was too great. Jo stepped forward and Melios fell back into his chair, the expression of rage on his face changing to hatred. The chamber was silent, and even the noise from outside seemed muted.

"Squire Menhir, I understand your concern. Please, take your seat," the baroness said evenly. Jo was surprised to hear the baroness speak so civilly. She resumed her seat.

Baroness Arteris glanced at each member of the council in turn. It seemed that half the council members didn't believe the story. The other half were lost between doubt and agreement.

As the baroness was about to speak, the doors to the council chamber burst open, admitting a man covered with dust and sweat. The two guards posted at the door attempted to stop him, but he held up a saddlebag with an official seal from Threshold and shouldered them aside.

"A message, my lady," the man gasped, sinking to his knees in fatigue. With a great show of dignity, he stood again, using the council table as a prop, and pulled a note from his pouch.

Baroness Arteris took the note from his dirty hand and opened it. She read it intently, then stared hard at Jo. Jo, still angry, returned the gaze, uncaring about the niceties of court etiquette.

"Council members," the baroness began officiously, breaking Jo's stare. "I have here a report that strange creatures roam the land just north of the Black Peak Mountains. They have already destroyed two villages."

"Where are these villages, milady?" Sir Graybow asked.

"Near the town of Armstead."

Baroness Arteris motioned for the door guards to come near. She said, "Send messengers to the Barony of Kelvin, Specularum, and the Duke's Road Keep. Tell them I am calling a Grand Marshaling of Forces. Give them all copies of this dispatch. And see that this man be given food and a place to rest," the baroness added, nodding to the messenger.

The guards took the letter and the messenger, closing the great doors as they left.

"We must now thank Squire Menhir for her assistance in the upcoming campaign against the abelaats. I suggest that we convene after we have a full report on the strength of our—"

"Milady," Jo interjected without fear as she stood. "There is another matter of greater import." The baroness arched her eyebrow skeptically. Jo continued, "I have been given the means to survive the power of the abaton." She reached down next to her chair and brought up the bundled sword. "I have been sent by the one who created Wyrmblight. I was told that when I returned to my land, I was to present this blade to you. As your father had blessed Wyrmblight, so must you bless this weapon."

"And where is the much-vaunted great sword Wyrmblight?" Councilman Melios asked. His words were sharp, but the tone in his voice was weak, and he did not rise from his chair.

Jo pulled back the oilcloth and revealed the hilt of Wyrmblight. "Wyrmblight was destroyed in the final battle with Verdilith. It was reforged by an immortal into this blade." Jo let the rest of the cloth fall to the floor.

The council members rose from their seats to admire the weapon. Jo felt proud. She wished Flinn, Braddoc, and Karleah were here to see this moment.

"The finishing of this blade is the most important task, as it was at the time of your father," Jo said.

Instead of the scathing rebuke Jo expected, the Lady Arteris crossed her arms, lost in thought. "You are correct, Squire Menhir."

Baroness Arteris turned to Sir Graybow and demanded, "Call the master artisan! Tell the people to meet in the courtyard! We must tell them of the danger, and take their blessings for the blade."

"What is the name of this weapon?" Councilman Melios inquired weakly.

"Peace," she said. Ignoring the other council members, she leaned forward and addressed Melios, who slunk back into his chair. "And if there is any doubt of my skill in bearing it, *I* am the one who slew Verdilith!"

Chapter IV

ohauna walked with Sir Graybow through the corridors of the castle. She breathed deeply, taking in the light oil of the cloth. It reminded her of the ethereal smithy where she had seen the cast for the sword, where she had relived her life by steps, and where she and the sword had been reforged.

"Johauna?" Sir Graybow said softly, reaching out to touch her shoulder.

"Sorry. I'm just lost in thought."

The two walked past an open courtyard on their way to Sir Graybow's chambers. The air was cold despite the greasy heat of the torches mounted in the walls.

As they turned a corner, Sir Graybow asked suddenly, "Jo, what exactly did you see in Armstead?"

Jo blinked, many horrible memories flooding back at

the mention of the town. She had lost everything in Armstead, her friends, her sense of purpose, even her hope.

"I saw—I saw—" A tear ran down her cheek and dropped onto the oilcloth, creating a dark stain. She wiped the streak from her face with the back of her hand and took a deep breath. "I saw hundreds of people dead, their lives drained from their bodies. Men, women, and children littered the streets, their flesh turned to ash and dust. I saw a town laid to waste by a great conflagration from the damned abaton."

Sir Graybow led Jo through a short hall and down a flight of stairs. She barely noticed his concerned touch as she continued.

"Verdilith took the form of Flinn. He convinced me he had become an immortal and—" Jo could not stop her mouth from trembling, could not stem the tide of fresh tears. "I lost my faith, and allowed the dragon to crack Wyrmblight before I realized my mistake. I took the blade and ran him through, breaking it in two."

Stopping, Jo looked intently into Sir Graybow's ashen face. "I killed Verdilith with the halves of Wyrmblight, hacking him until he begged for mercy." Jo glanced away, unable to stare into the reflection of Graybow's eyes. "I did not give him mercy. I gave him justice."

Jo leaned against the wall with a sigh. The stone was cold and a little damp, and she found it comforting.

Sir Graybow held out his arm for Jo to take. "If you can make it a little farther, I'll get you some hot tea."

Jo looked up into the face of Graybow. His was a kind face, but one traced with lines of worry and of command.

He was the castellan of Penhaligon, his sole duty the protection of the castle.

"You don't like to politic in the affairs of Penhaligon, do you?" Jo asked quietly.

"Why do you ask?" the old man replied, obviously taken aback.

Jo shook her head and weakly smiled, reaching out to take his arm as they started walking again. "I have been lately involved in—things I do not understand, but they remind me of the—antics of some of the nobles against Flinn. The nobles have their own desires, which aren't always for the benefit of the people."

"Really?" Sir Graybow replied archly. He smiled. "I'm much impressed, *Squire* Menhir. Do you require any assistance, or perhaps some advice in these matters?"

"I might, if these are matters in which you have experience."

"The very word 'experience' implies lessons that can be applied to many situations." Sir Graybow paused and peered into Jo's downcast face. "If you can tell me something of your—troubles, I might be able to help. Just describe some of the things that concern you most."

Jo thought about the statement, then nodded her compliance. For a moment, the hallway through which they walked seemed to her to be much like the Corridor of the Fallen: dark, quiet, and still.

Before she could begin, they reached the door to the study chamber, and Sir Graybow produced a large key from his belt and opened the door. Jo was glad that she would have a few moments to let her frustrations die down.

The room was dark and comfortable, in the same clean state she remembered.

"What kind of tea would you like?"

Jo shrugged. "What do you have?"

"Let's take a look," Sir Graybow replied, walking up to one of the cabinets near the fireplace and tugging it open. "We've got a fine blend from the Achelos Woods near the Five Shires. We've got rare tea from the Emirates of Ylaruam, excellent for chasing away the cold."

Jo shook her head and took a seat near the table in the middle of the room. There was a book open to its title page, but she could not read the strange writing. She continued to clutch Peace close to her body, unwilling to let go of her protection against the abaton.

"Would you care for a brew from the Earl of Greymington?"

Jo looked up from the book and nodded. "That would be fine," she answered.

Sir Graybow nodded in return, taking a jar out of the cabinet and closing the door. He put the kettle on the fire and set the jar down next to two waiting mugs.

"That will take a while," the old man muttered as he took the seat across from Jo.

"Are you well?" she asked in concern.

"Why do you ask?"

"You seem so much—thinner."

Graybow smiled introspectively and peered up at the ceiling, saying, "There comes a time in every man's life when he finds he must take better care of himself, and that means no idling, more action— "

"And less shortbread with tea!" Jo interjected with a

slight laugh.

The old man smiled fondly. He leaned forward with a conspiratorial air and said, "I see you know my secret."

"Have the duties of the castle been wearing?" Jo inquired seriously.

Sir Graybow pursed his lips and glanced away. "Yes, you know my secret. But we're not here to discuss the castellan, we are here to help Johauna Menhir."

"Don't you mean Squire Menhir?"

The old man shook his head. "No, I mean you."

Jo nodded her understanding, glad for Graybow's warmth. She didn't feel deserving of any particular kindness, and never received any beyond a few lurid glances when she had lived in Specularum.

Jo pulled the oilcloth away from the wire-wrapped hilt of Peace and ran her hand over the abelaat stones. She shifted in her chair, uneasy with the thought of the abelaat poison in her body.

"What is wrong?" Sir Graybow asked.

"You knew that I was attacked by an abelaat when I stayed with Flinn," Jo replied. Graybow nodded his head. "It's true. I have some of its—poison running through my body, and Flinn dug these three stones from my shoulder where I had been bitten."

Sir Graybow rose from his chair and exclaimed, "That's where the stones came from? By the immortals, Jo! I had no idea! Are you ill, shall I call a healer?"

Jo smiled and put her hand on Graybow's shoulder, pressing him back down in his chair. "No, really, I'm fine. I guess poison isn't the right word."

"Taint, perhaps?" Graybow offered.

Jo shrugged. "Karleah told me that the—taint would protect me against the abelaats, though I am not sure how. I think she said it would make me difficult to detect through sorcery."

"Karleah died attempting to unlock the secret of the abaton?" Sir Graybow recalled.

"Yes. She had a stone from the last true abelaat on Mystara. Karleah thought the stone would protect her, but something went wrong."

"How does this relate to what you want to say?"

"I have been given this sword," Jo began, holding up Peace for emphasis. "The people that forged this blade were the same ones that created Wyrmblight—"

"I thought the master artisan at the castle did that," Graybow cut in.

"He might have finished the job. . . . " Jo gave a polite half-smile. "There is more to that story than most people know."

Sir Graybow nodded his understanding, saying, "But what is your ultimate question, then?"

"I have a mission—to kill Teryl Auroch and close the gate between Mystara and the other world. All of this is a matter of trust."

Sir Graybow looked confused. "All of what?" he asked.

Jo shook Peace in her hand, then indicated her elven armor. "This, these, everything that has happened between my time in Armstead and now. I have met strange and wonderful people who have power and wisdom beyond my own. How far can I trust my part in these events, and how much trust can I give to the ones who started me on this path?"

"You want to know that if, by being given this blade, you are a piece being played in a game?" Sir Graybow inquired in an open attempt to make sense of Jo's confusion.

She smiled and nodded. "That's exactly what I want to know."

Sir Graybow nodded in return, walking over to the copper kettle. He donned a heavy glove, took the kettle out of the fire, and poured hot water into the mugs. He put the kettle back in the fire and removed the glove, turning to make the tea.

Jo looked at the old man expectantly. She finally let go of Peace and leaned it against the table, stretching her arms.

Sir Graybow returned with the tea. Jo took her mug and put it on the table.

"That question, Jo," he began, interrupting himself with another sip. "That question is one that has been asked since the beginning of all things."

Jo started to pick up her mug, then changed her mind and clutched Peace with her hand.

"I guess I'll soon find out," she mumbled.

🐝 🐝 🐝 🐝 🐝

From the top of the steps of Penhaligon's ancestral temple, Jo stared out at the thousands of people who lived in the towns and villages of Penhaligon. They had gathered in the main courtyard and outside the open main gate to the Castle of the Three Suns—frightened and agitated, their voices a low rumble of doubt. The clouds that had choked the sun for days now, and the rumors circulating of horrible monsters were taking their toll on morale.

The baroness stood to Jo's right, and Sir Graybow was on her left; the rest of the council stood behind them, inside the temple entrance. They wore appropriate finery, though Jo continued to wear the armor and tabard from the other world.

Baroness Arteris glanced to Sir Graybow, who nodded solemnly. The baroness's eyes lingered for a moment on the oilcloth bundle in Jo's arms, but the woman's expression was unreadable.

With a final glance to the councilors, Baroness Arteris stepped forward, raising her arms to the folk gathered in the courtyard. She called out, "To the citizens of Penhaligon, I bid you listen."

The woman's voice was clear and strong and could be heard from outside the walls of the castle. The low droning of the people's voices grew still, and Jo could not hear a sound except for the expectant, fearful pounding of her heart.

"Dark times have come upon us, as they had in the times when my father ruled," she began, taking a deep breath after every pause. "Many of you have heard of the evil growing in the land beyond the Black Peak Mountains. Everyone, even those beyond the realms of Karameikos and its bounding territories, are in peril."

The baroness continued: "There was a hero once, knighted by my father, who brought evil to its knees wherever it was found. He was a man who embodied the four points of the Quadrivial: Honor, Courage, Faith, and Glory. He was inspiration to us all.

"Fain Flinn, Flinn the Mighty, has perished on the field of honor in his fight against the green dragon, Verdilith." Jo clenched her jaw tight against the pain of Flinn's memory. After the uncomfortable murmurs died down among the crowd, Baroness Arteris continued, "Before he achieved his final glory, he found one among us he felt worthy to follow after him, to learn the path to knighthood under his guidance. This honored soul has joined the ranks of our soldiers as squire, in the name of Penhaligon."

Jo suddenly felt the stares of the people upon her and almost collapsed beneath the weight. She was sure that everyone knew of her association with Flinn, and wondered if they were ashamed of having believed the lies of Verdilith. The recollection of their behavior kept her jaw clenched tight and gave her the strength to stand.

With a gesture toward Jo, the baroness cried, "This squire has proven through her actions that she walks the same path of glory as Fain Flinn. It was she who slew Verdilith in the name of the people of Penhaligon!"

Everyone in the courtyard cheered, obviously heartened by the news that the green dragon that had terrorized them for so long was finally slain. Jo was humbled by the attention she was receiving. She wished Graybow and Braddoc were nearby to give her support.

Baroness Arteris lowered her arms and spread her fingers in supplication. "People of Penhaligon, I tell you that we have the means to combat this and any evil that invades our lands. We are strong together, and nothing can dominate us. Take this time to pray for those who fight in the coming battles, not just for those of our home, but our allies, and those allies we have yet to know."

The baroness bowed her head and clasped her hands together. Sir Graybow also clasped his hands, as did the rest of the Penhaligon council. Jo, still humbled, watched as every face in the crowd bent down. She was overwhelmed at Penhaligon's unity and strength of faith.

After a few moments, Baroness Arteris raised her head. "Pray, citizens of the realm," she said, her voice seeming to Jo no louder than a whisper. "Pray. Give your trust to the defenders and the weapons they bear."

Turning, the baroness reached out and pulled the oilcloth from the sword in Jo's arms. Jo gazed at her own reflection in the fine silver of the blade. Her eyes were wet with tears and filled with inspiration.

Baroness Arteris raised Jo's arm. "As with the blessed sword Wyrmblight, wielded by our greatest hero, Flinn the Mighty, I call upon you to grant your blessings to this weapon. I call upon you to grant your faith to its wielder, she who walks on Fain Flinn's path." The baroness raised her free hand and cried, "I call upon you to pray for Peace!"

The silence was greater than any Jo had ever known. She stood, holding Peace aloft before the citizens of the realm, at last confident of the decisions that had led her to this point. The people continued to pray without words. Jo now felt what she thought Flinn must have felt upon receiving Wyrmblight from the Baron: responsibility. Responsibility to the people. Responsibility to herself.

Jo walked down the steps of the temple, looking out over the sea of silence. Her hard boots made the only sound in the courtyard, echoing off the high stone walls. She was moving on inspiration, without thinking about her actions. Her only thought was to her new duty; she was going to kill Teryl Auroch and close the gateway between the worlds. With Peace, she would accomplish this task.

Jo moved slowly toward the center of the courtyard. Wherever she walked, the people raised their heads in wonder. They looked to Peace raised above her head, a shining sword of hope. Within moments, the throng began to form a procession behind Jo, following wherever she went. They began chanting a name, and Jo, thinking only of her mission, slowly realized the name was Peace.

The whole of the courtyard chanted the name of the sword; the trees in the courtyard shook with the deafening sound. With deliberate steps, Jo moved in the direction of the castle's forge, ready to complete the ceremony.

The artisan waited at the doorway, and Jo could already smell the familiar scent of heat, iron, and sweat. The man was old but strong, and his face was covered with grime from the forge. Jo thought he looked very much like Vulcan, but many years older.

The master artisan took the sword from Jo's hand and expertly spun it in his palm by the hilt. With a nod, he walked back into the shop, inspecting the edge of the blade. He heaved open the door to the forge, revealing the furnace within, and plunged Peace into the depths of the fire, grabbing a hammer from a nearby peg.

The sword glowed with its own internal fire as the master artisan placed the flat of the weapon on his anvil. He raised his heavy hammer high above his head and struck. The metal rang, echoing around the courtyard; everyone fell silent. Jo was blinded by an aurora of sparks.

The man threw his hammer to the floor and handed Jo the blade, hilt first. The elven silver and dwarven steel had separated on the flat of the blade and melded at the edge. The four points of the Quadrivial and the final rune for peace continued to glow with the heat from the forge. With a single blow, the sword had been completed.

Jo turned to face the crowd and saw their expectant faces. With a smile she could not suppress, she held Peace aloft.

The magnificent cheer from the citizens of the realm echoed in Jo's ears beyond the closing of the day.

Chapter V

"I don't know about you, old friend, but my legs are tired."

Actually, Braddoc's legs were not tired, though he pushed hard to keep up with his companion, who had already mounted the crest of the last hill, which led to a dense forest of spruce and pine. The sky was gray with heavy clouds and the air was cold. Braddoc had made several attempts to evoke some kind of reaction from the man on the hill, without success.

The dwarf watched solemnly as Flinn surveyed the surrounding land. The silhouette of Flinn made Braddoc think about Jo and wonder if she was safe.

"What is the name of this region?" Flinn inquired with a sweep of his arm. The tunic and pants Flinn had magically clothed himself with luffed in the wind.

Braddoc considered saying nothing to see if Flinn might remember on his own, but changed his mind. Flinn had been blessed with new life, but obviously not old memories.

"This is Highreach Forest," Braddoc replied, stepping closer to Flinn. "You once lived here."

Flinn continued to stare out over the woods. Braddoc wondered what thoughts flowed through the mind of the once-dead Flinn. He waited for a response, then mumbled to himself, "Guess immortals don't seem to need their pasts."

Flinn slowly turned his head to look down, his motions almost mechanical. Braddoc shifted uneasily under that gaze.

"How do you know I am immortal?" Flinn asked, his words slow and exact in enunciation.

"Do not play games with me, Fain Flinn. You may be immortal, but I have lived a hundred lifetimes more than you," Braddoc said tersely.

Flinn turned and reached out with his hand. Braddoc felt suddenly afraid and stepped back, clutching his battle-axe.

With a half step forward, Flinn touched Braddoc's forehead. For a moment all expression left the man's face and eyes; then just as quickly, the light returned. Flinn's jaw clenched and relaxed, and he stated, "You *have* lived more than a hundred lifetimes."

Braddoc shrugged. "I told you. I wouldn't lie to a friend."

Flinn nodded introspectively. "I don't think I would, either."

"No, you wouldn't. And you never did." Braddoc pointed a finger at Flinn for emphasis. "I'm going to help you regain your memory, so you can do whatever it is you've returned to do."

"I am to close the gate between the worlds," Flinn said, turning back to his observation of the landscape.

"Then why don't we leave now, before something—"

"I do not yet have the power to perform this task," Flinn interjected with a threatening sweep of his hand. "There are places to which I must travel to gain this power."

Braddoc nodded and sighed. "The first place you must go is Rockhome. My ancestral land."

Flinn turned and regarded the dwarf with suddenly passionate eyes; Braddoc could not stop himself from stepping back, awestruck from his friend's power.

"Tell me how you know so much of my mission, Braddoc Briarblood," Flinn commanded. "Tell me how it is you have lived so long."

Braddoc had always kept the secret of his past a mystery from everyone, even Flinn. He had not been able to tell Johauna his origins, and he doubted that his dead friend Karleah had ever guessed what made him so special among dwarves. With a sigh and the impression that he was dealing with a demanding child, Braddoc sat crossed-legged on the ground, motioning for Flinn to do the same.

The man looked down, appearing confused, as if he were searching for a chair. Braddoc thought his friend might summon a divan from the air as he had done with his clothes, but Flinn slowly sank to the ground, his legs beneath him.

Reaching inside his leather jerkin, Braddoc pulled out
a long pipe and filled it from a pouch he removed from
his belt. He lit it from a tinderbox and puffed on the
stem, searching for a place to start.

"Before I tell you of myself, let me explain how you
arrived," he began slowly. "You know of your goal, but I
do not think you know much else."

Flinn's expression remained impassive. He nodded.

Braddoc gave a tight smile. He said, "On this world,
you were once known as Fain Flinn, Flinn the Mighty.
You wielded a sword named Wyrmblight and were a great
hero." The dwarf paused, hoping for some reaction, but
Flinn showed no expression. He continued: "Wyrmblight
was blessed to kill the green dragon, Verdilith. It was
because of Verdilith that you lost your name and your
faith."

"It seems I was a weak man," Flinn responded.

"No, not weak," Braddoc said, slightly angry. After a
pause, he added, "You wanted to believe your faith had
died because the one you loved lost faith in you. She was
poisoned by lies and died at the hands of her deceivers."

Braddoc pulled on his pipe and let out a great plume of
blue smoke. The taste was earthy and soothing. It cooled
his temper, allowing him to resume. "You fought Verdilith once but did not defeat him. You were destined to
fight him again, and it was there that you died."

The dwarf took another drag on the clay stem and
glanced through the curtain of blue smoke at the immortal sitting in the cold grass. He smiled to himself at the
remarkable absurdity of such a strange meeting. He said,

"Verdilith was not satisfied with your death. He desired to destroy Wyrmblight, and in his scheme he took your form."

"It allowed me to find flesh on this world," Flinn replied absently. " 'In the Land of the Dead can everything be found in perfection,' I was told. 'All things of the world are connected to these things in perfection.' "

Flinn paused again, then said, "I had no body there . . . "

"But on this world you found your form in perfection, thanks to Verdilith," Braddoc said. "In order to convince Jo that you had indeed returned as an immortal, the dragon used the most perfect form his magic could create. Verdilith became a model for your spirit's flesh."

The dwarf watched for a reaction, but Flinn said nothing. He stared off into the distance, and Braddoc wished that he had the ability to read an immortal's mind.

"You are correct, Braddoc Briarblood," Flinn said with a nod of confirmation. "I stepped from the Land of the Dead into this mortal identity."

"Helped by Diulanna and—"

"And guided by Thor and Odin the All Father. It was they who gave me this mission. But now, please tell me of yourself and how you understand so much."

Braddoc blinked in surprise. He almost laughed out loud, keeping silent by biting hard on the stem of the pipe. He, Braddoc Briarblood, had been asked to *please* speak by an immortal. He thought that there might be hope to rediscover his friend, after all.

"Finding a place to start might be difficult, but I'll try," he said around the stem. He peered up into the gray sky and wondered if Teryl Auroch had brought Dayin back to this world. He shrugged and looked back across to Flinn, who continued to wait patiently.

"The dwarves have two histories. The one best known is called Kagyar's Grace. It tells of the time when Rockhome lay under a thick layer of ice, infested by creatures suited to such an existence. Kagyar the Artisan ripped the curtain of ice away and altered the land to his liking."

"Kagyar is an Eternal of the Sphere of Matter," Flinn stated. "He is interested in art and artisans."

"And the dwarves are known to be his creation," Braddoc said with a nod. "The first creation he carved from the living rock of Rockhome using his magics and consummate artistry. This being was called Rockborn, or Denwarf in the dwarven tongue. He was the dwarves' first king, as well."

Braddoc shifted his weight to be more comfortable. "Kagyar gave the dwarves a desire to craft beauty from all things that come from the land, such as stone, gold, and precious gems. He also gave them abilities so they could thrive below ground as well as above."

Braddoc reached under his belt and pulled out his bag again, filling the pipe. The heady resin left from the gray ash was his favorite part. He used his fingers to tamp down the excess, staring over his work to see if his story had elicited any responses from Flinn. The man continued to sit as patiently as a rock, and Braddoc realized this lack of motion was beginning to have the strange effect of annoying him immensely. He told himself to be patient as he struck sparks from his tinderbox.

"In the ages that followed," he continued as he put the box back into his pocket, "the dwarves increased in population, explored the mountains, learned their craft, and eventually encountered other races—"

"Like the elves and the humans," Flinn interjected.

"And the orcs," Braddoc added with a nod. "There were wars, and great achievements, and wonderful tales." The dwarf paused a moment to let the resins add their flavor to the freshly filled pipe. He leaned forward conspiratorially, as he had done with Flinn many times in the past, and whispered, "But that is not the true story, is it?"

Flinn remained motionless, locking his gaze on Braddoc's blind eye. The man blinked twice as if in remembrance, then leaned forward and softly asked, "What is the true story?"

"How much do you know already?"

"There are gaps in my memory," Flinn said, deliberately placing his hand under his chin. The effect was almost comical. "I know my name, my mission, and what must be done to close the gate—"

"And you know other things as well," Braddoc said, pointing with the stem of his smoldering pipe. "For instance, you know you are an immortal."

Flinn dropped his hand and shrugged, his left shoulder falling before his right. "That is trivial," he intoned. "I am sent by Diulanna, Thor, and Odin the All Father to complete this mission. Otherwise, I do not believe I know much more than I did when I was merely a man."

"Yet you cannot remember anything of being a man," Braddoc retorted.

Flinn's face contorted into something that resembled irony, or perhaps nonchalance.

Braddoc put the pipe back into his mouth and said, "Why don't we continue our journey. I'd like to reach our destination before the sun—" Braddoc cut himself short. "That is, before it gets too dark."

The dwarf pushed himself up off the ground with a groan. He took a step forward and held out his hand to help Flinn rise.

Flinn stared at the hand and did not move.

"Are you thinking about my hand?" Braddoc asked.

Flinn shook his head. "No. I was thinking about what to do."

Braddoc shrugged in disbelief. Flinn was the only immortal he had ever met, and at the moment, he was not impressed. He reached forward and grabbed the man's hand, pulling hard.

Braddoc went sailing high over Flinn's shoulder. The dwarf dropped his pipe in midair so it wouldn't break when he hit the ground. Fortunately, the soil on the hill was reasonably soft, and he was not hurt when he landed twenty feet away.

"What in the name of Denwarf did you do that for, Fain Flinn?" the dwarf bellowed as he stomped back to Flinn, who remained sitting with his back turned. Braddoc reached up, cupped a hand over his blind eye, and added, "I've a good mind to—"

"A good mind to what?" Flinn asked. Braddoc spun around, his hand still over his eye. Flinn's voice was strangely cold when he spoke again. "I know few things of this world, but I know the power of that ocular, Braddoc Briarblood. It is an immortal artifact. What did you intend to do?"

Braddoc breathed slow and hard to calm himself. Gritting his teeth, he let his hand down from his eye.

"I was only trying to help you to your feet," he hissed. He clenched and unclenched his hands.

With a nod Flinn stated, "I think that when we were friends, you always had a temper."

"When we were friends, we both had tempers," Braddoc said under his breath. He looked down at himself and groaned; his once-clean clothes were covered with dirt. He began brushing himself off with his hands.

"What did you intend to do with that ocular?" Flinn inquired flatly.

"I—was rash. I apologize," Braddoc muttered. "These are unusual times."

Flinn tried to smile, but his mouth twisted into something unrecognizable. He motioned to himself and said, "As I well—know?"

Braddoc laughed. "Was that a question or a statement?"

"Both."

Braddoc laughed even louder and turned to go down the slope into the forest. He waved for Flinn to follow.

Flinn held up Braddoc's pipe. "This is yours," he said.

ɘɘ ɘɘ ɘɘ ɘɘ ɘɘ

The forest was colder than the hill, and Braddoc closed the buttons on his shirt and jacket. His pipe was filled with resins, and he was feeling especially good.

Braddoc watched with fascination as Flinn touched every bush they passed, seeking to remember, to understand. The dwarf tried to get glimpses of Flinn's expressions

and the looks in his eyes, but the man seemed too awk-
ward with his new, perfect body to give any indication of
his feelings.

"This was the forest in which you lived," Braddoc said,
motioning broadly with his pipe. "Do you recall any of
this?"

The dwarf glanced back over his shoulder, and his
mouth hung open with surprise. Flinn stood on top of an
old tree stump surrounded by a host of forest animals of
every description. They all seemed rooted in place, and
stared up at him in apparent supplication.

"What," Braddoc began, almost speechless. "What are
you doing?"

"They are frightened and they came to me," Flinn
responded without taking his eyes from the animals.
"They say that something poisons the world."

"What did you tell them?"

"That I would protect them all."

Flinn stepped down from the stump and gently put his
hand on a deer's soft head, petting her between the ears.
She bent her head down as Flinn walked back toward
Braddoc.

Flinn gave a natural-looking shrug and motioned for
Braddoc to follow, much as he had seen Braddoc motion
earlier. "Continue your story," Flinn said in a nearly
casual tone.

The dwarf turned to watch the forest animals slowly
walk and hop away from the stump. He decided he would
no longer act astounded when Flinn did something
astounding. Braddoc pulled deeply on his pipe, releasing
the smoke slowly through his nose to alleviate the snap of

the cold. He said, "There was a land called Blackmoor, a land of great technology and magic. But because the people of Blackmoor were foolish, they destroyed themselves in a cataclysmic explosion that changed the face of the world forever."

"Poison was released into the world," Flinn said slowly.

"Yes, strange winds blew, killing everything they touched," Braddoc replied, guessing that Flinn's mind held a great deal of knowledge waiting to be unlocked. "And that is when Kagyar the Artisan gave the dwarves much of the culture we have today."

Braddoc looked up to the sky and saw that the sun, though still behind the gray wall of clouds, would be setting soon. He hoped to reach his destination before dark. Picking up his pace, he said, "Kagyar made sure that the dwarves never forgot how to live below the ground so that if there was another catastrophe, the dwarves would be able to survive."

"I know a little of the immortals. Kagyar also gave the dwarves another gift, something that made them— resistant to such winds," Flinn added. "What was this thing?"

"There is no name for it. It is a resistance to such poisons—"

"As well as resistance to magic," Flinn interjected.

Braddoc nodded. "Kagyar also created Denwarf, a creature who was not a dwarf, but a being made of stone. Denwarf was created after the dwarves were taken to Rockhome, which is part of the original tale not known to most of the world. Kagyar instructed Denwarf in the ways that the dwarven race should be raised from its infancy. When his time was through, Denwarf disappeared into the lowest reaches of Rockhome."

Flinn stopped and turned to face his companion. Braddoc grudgingly halted his march, knowing the next question. He held up his hand before Flinn could speak and said, "As a dwarf gains knowledge and experience, the potential to be resistant to those strange winds increases, as does a dwarf's connection with the world."

Flinn continued to stare down, his eyes penetrating. Braddoc knew he could hide nothing from this man. Braddoc shifted uncomfortably.

"What is the matter?" Flinn inquired.

"I've never had to tell this tale before."

"Do you desire to stop?"

Braddoc raised his heavy eyebrows. "You would let me?"

Flinn said nothing for a moment, then slowly nodded. "Yes. It would be—right."

The dwarf smiled broadly, saying, "Now that's the Flinn I remember!" With another pull on his pipe, Braddoc spoke, letting the smoke escape with every word: "Most dwarves live to be two hundred years old. Some live to be a little older than that. And others—well, others realize that after about five hundred years they have a lot more life to look forward to."

"You are saying you are over five hundred years old?"

"No, I'm *telling* you I am over five hundred years old," Braddoc snapped. "There have been others older than me."

Flinn nodded. "And this is because of your connection with the world?"

"Yes. We, that is I, also became a keeper of dwarven knowledge. I am able to—commune with dwarven ancestors and ask them for advice on how to best guide my people of Rockhome. It was these ancestors who told me of your arrival, and that you must go to Rockhome. They also said I must help you in your mission."

"When did they tell you of me?"

Braddoc turned away, suddenly ashamed. He did not think he had ever been ashamed in his entire, long life. "I cannot lie to you, Flinn. They told me long before you lost your title and your love. The night we met, I knew you were going to be at that inn looking for a fight. I befriended you because I had to, but I never regretted it for a moment!" Braddoc added.

Flinn said nothing, continuing to stare at the dwarf. His mouth turned up at the corner into a half smile. "It's all right, Braddoc," he said, putting a gentle hand on Braddoc's shoulder. "I—I understand."

Braddoc lifted his head and returned the smile. Quietly, he said, "Thank you."

The dwarf sobered himself, grinding his teeth on the stem of his pipe. He let out a deep breath, then said, "This eye is, as you already know, not real. It was a gift from Kagyar, one of his artifacts."

Surprise crossed Flinn's features. "I did not know where you gained the ocular. You once attempted the path to immortality?"

"I did once, but not for too long," Braddoc replied, edging in the direction of their destination. "I decided that my duty was to my people and not to Kagyar himself."

"That must have been a difficult choice."

Braddoc nodded solemnly. "It was."

The two were within sight of a clearing in the forest. Braddoc glanced over his shoulder to see if Flinn recognized the area. The man seemed lost in thought.

"This is where you once lived," Braddoc said as he cleared the edge of the forest. "This is where you lived after you lost your knighthood."

Flinn peered around the clearing. "It seems that a house was burned to the ground. Was it mine?"

The dwarf nodded. "You built it with your own hands, alone."

"You say I lost my knighthood because of treachery. Does that mean that I was shunned by the people?" Flinn inquired.

Braddoc thought he heard a trace of unhappiness, or perhaps pain, in Flinn's voice. "Do you remember anything about this place? Or anything else?"

Flinn stepped over a burnt log.

"Why do you feel it so important to bring back my mortal memory?" Flinn demanded suddenly.

Braddoc almost fell on his back as waves of power battered against him, the charismatic charm of the immortal. The dwarf swallowed hard as he regained his balance. "You cannot force me to tell you the answer to that question, and I'm not going to tell you," Braddoc answered. He braced himself for any attack and was afraid that he would have to summon the full might of the ocular to resist Flinn.

Flinn took a step back, bringing his hands together behind his back. "I'm sorry," he said, his face downcast.

"I've heard Odin the All Father say that it is sometimes too easy to be an immortal."

"Of that I've no doubt," Braddoc mumbled. "But I do doubt that most immortals would have bothered to apologize to a mere mortal, even one like myself. Not even Kagyar apologized to me when—well, that doesn't matter," the dwarf hastily added.

Braddoc pulled his pipe from his pocket and lit it with the tinderbox. After the bowl glowed with heat, he said, "Let me tell you something of the decision you just made. When I said most immortals wouldn't apologize, I was not being trite. The fact that you did sets you apart already."

"I need to know more of the mortal world than that of the immortal," Flinn said, maintaining his pose. "It will help me in the fight to come."

"Well, you didn't force me to tell you why I want you to remember your past. And since you didn't force me, I will tell you. My ancestors told me that if you could not remember anything of your past, you might use your power for—undesirable purposes," Braddoc volunteered. He let the smoke clear his nose before he continued in a more somber tone. "I was told to accompany you on your mission—"

"To monitor my actions?" Flinn asked in a small voice.

Braddoc nodded, saying, "I was also told that I might have to destroy you if you worked against the betterment of Mystara."

Flinn turned on his heel and picked his way among the ruin of his mortal home. His face was expressionless.

Turning to face Braddoc, Flinn said, "I remember none

of this. I don't remember you, my honor, or my love. To me, none of that matters. I must close the gate between the worlds, and that is all. You will have to make your own decisions about the results of my actions, but I *will* allow you to accompany me on my journeys."

Braddoc bowed solemnly. There would be no easy way for him to stay with Flinn if the immortal did not desire it.

Flinn paced about the clearing, occasionally stepped over a fallen plank, or something that could have been furniture, saying, "I must travel to the lands of the ancient races of Mystara and unlock their—*mysteries*. Each race has a word for its own mystery. I believe the dwarves call theirs *Denwail*."

"Denwail is that which gives the dwarves their mastery over things mechanical and the elements of the earth," Braddoc replied, speaking the words mostly for his own benefit; the term was so old he barely recalled its meaning. "It is what gives dwarves the power to create beautiful pieces of jewelry and perform fine craft-work. I guess you could call it inspiration."

"That is what I must find. I must find the inspiration of each race," Flinn confirmed, crossing his arms over his chest. "When I have gained the last, my final course of action will be revealed."

"When will you begin this search?"

"Now."

Flinn broke his stance and waved his right arm, walking toward Braddoc. The dwarf stepped back, then realized he was standing in a different place—a dark, subterranean place. The protective powers of the ocular helped him quickly recover his senses. He shuddered to think of what happened to him in the past when he used the ocular's other abilities.

"We are in Rockhome," Flinn said. "Show me the way to Denwarf."

Chapter VI

"Explain to us once again why we must travel to Armstead with all speed?" Melios asked.

The Penhaligon council had convened in the council chamber several days after the blessing of Peace. Jo sat in the center of the half circle formed by the great council table. Her hand slowly caressed the abelaat stones mounted in the bastard sword's hilt.

"The gate leading to the abelaat world is open, letting them step through," Jo replied heatedly. "The sooner we attack, the fewer troops they will have to combat us."

"Are you saying that we will have to post a permanent garrison near the city of Armstead to attack these—things, as they come through this—gate?" Madam Astwood inquired.

Jo shot the noblewoman a hateful glance. Instead of

giving a belligerent reply as she truly wanted, Jo said, "Unless you have another plan, I see no alternative."

Sir Graybow stood and began to pace behind Baroness Arteris's chair. The baroness turned with a questioning look to face him. Sir Graybow stopped several times and seemed as if he were about to speak, but he always cut himself short with a shake of his head. Jo thought she heard him mumbling to himself.

"Sir Graybow?" the baroness asked.

"What?" the old man said under his breath. The expression on his downcast face changed to sudden realization. He turned to the baroness and said, "Please forgive me, milady. I was just thinking."

"Would you care to share these thoughts, Castellan?"

Graybow said nothing for a moment, as if considering his choices. With a self-deprecating shake of his head, he answered, "We cannot handle these problems on our own. According to what Squire Menhir has told us—"

"Why are we to believe what this *squire* has to say?" Councilman Melios demanded. "We still have only her word and the hasty message of a tiny outpost in Threshold—not enough evidence for me that these abelaats have invaded, or that the abaton, as it is supposedly called, is truly doing what she claims."

All the other council members turned to face Melios. Jo could easily see the man's point if he were not making it to cast aspersion on her for the sole reason that she had been Flinn's squire.

"I believe that Councilman Melios has an excellent point," Madam Astwood said. She turned from Melios to look directly at Jo. "I am sorry, young lady, but your claim is almost too fantastic to believe."

Jo grabbed the hilt of Peace and stood, holding the blade point down. She returned the accusing woman's stare and answered, "*Almost* too fantastic? I have seen the effects of the abaton firsthand. You still cannot raise the light from your lanterns, and your sorcerers cower in their chambers. Why do you continue arguing?"

Baroness Arteris stood and glared at everyone at the council table. "This has gone far enough. It is obvious that many of you have some personal score to settle with Squire Menhir due to her past affiliations. If that is so, then I suggest you either leave now or I will be forced to strip you of your titles—"

"How dare you!" Councilman Melios spat. "How dare you threaten my family, which has been loyal to the Penhaligons and faithful to the noble house of Karameikos since the kingdom was founded. You have no right and no power to carry out your threat!"

"I never accused you directly, Councilman," the baroness replied coldly. "It is you who have just identified yourself as the chief spoiler. If you insist on being counted as one of those whom I have just named, then I have already given you your options." The baroness gestured to Jo and continued: "These are desperate times. I believe Squire Menhir's veracity, and I believe in the judgment of Fain Flinn. A knight's word is her honor, and Squire Menhir's honor is more of a knight's than your own."

Councilman Melios slammed his fists on the table, his mouth twisting into a curse. Jo stepped back a pace and got a better grip on her sword, afraid that the man might suddenly leap over the table and attack. Melios slowly turned to face the baroness, who stood calmly, well out of arm's reach.

"If you have something to say, Councilman, I suggest you say it now before I have you removed from these proceedings," Sir Graybow intoned threateningly. He motioned for the glaive-armed guards at the door to come forward.

"You have no right," Melios muttered under his breath, each word slow and measured. "You have—"

"On the contrary, Councilman," Baroness Arteris said. "I have every right. I have already called for a Grand Marshaling of Forces. I have the right to give and relieve commands, the right to seize property, and the power to levy armies. If I decide that your estates would best be served as a headquarters, then you may rest assured that my commanders will be there by morning."

Melios strained against his chair as he heard the words of the baroness. He shook with such tension that Jo thought the man's blood was going to pour from his nose and mouth. She did not relax her stance.

The guards came forward and stood behind Melios, reaching out to take him by the arms. The councilman spun around and struck the first guard, breaking the man's nose in a shower of blood.

"Don't touch me!" Melios shrieked, his eyes darting madly. Melios kicked his chair backward and stalked around the table, ignoring the guards and everyone else in the room. "I'll bring this to the king personally!" he screamed as he approached the door. "Personally!"

The man departed without another word, leaving a heavy silence in his wake. The second guard helped his companion out the door, holding a handkerchief up to catch the blood.

"Do you think he'll honestly go to the king?" Madam Astwood inquired calmly.

"It makes little difference," Sir Graybow replied, taking his seat. Baroness Arteris did the same. "The Grand Marshaling of Forces will discredit any story he might compose. After all, our messenger has a three-day lead, and it seems that most magic either works erratically or not at all, so he probably won't be able to send a message that way."

"Which is why we must act quickly!" Jo implored. She stepped forward to address the baroness. "You already have reports of the abelaats attacking villages and taking people prisoner. *Your* people. If—"

"Squire Menhir," Baroness Arteris said, "do not presume to sway me with arguments about *my* people. It is because of my people that I have decided to raise an army to defend the cities not yet besieged, rather than attack Armstead directly."

"What? You already know the abelaats are crossing over! If they aren't stopped at the gate, they'll overrun the duchy!"

"It is precisely for that reason that we shall fight a defensive action," the baroness replied evenly to Jo's heated statement. "You have told us that the abaton destroys any who come near it except you, because you wield Peace. And you have told us that the abelaats are powerful creatures of unknown ability. Our troops stand a better chance fighting a defensive action in familiar terrain than meeting an enemy of indeterminate strength in the open field."

"What do you propose to do against them if they are able to wield magic?" Madam Astwood inquired, folding her hands on the table.

Jo was amazed at everyone's calm. "The most important matter is to kill Teryl Auroch and destroy the abaton. We can't waste time with mages," Jo said. "If you will excuse me, milady, I wish to be on my way to fulfill the mission I accepted when I was given this sword."

"Squire Menhir," the baroness said sternly, "you may have been Fain Flinn's squire, but you are still just that. A squire. You have no right to leave this chamber or this castle without our permission. You will accompany one of the knights into the field of battle, wielding Peace against the enemy until the enemy is defeated."

Jo reddened and said, "I was given this sword to defeat Teryl Auroch!"

Baroness Arteris stood angrily. "You are a squire of the court of Penhaligon and you will act accordingly! We give you freedom enough to say and act how you please because you have become something of a symbol of hope to the people, but that does not mean you may demand anything of this court. If you wish to stay a squire, you *will* do as commanded!"

Jo ground her teeth and clenched the hilt of Peace so tightly she could feel the abelaat stones marking her flesh. With a great sigh, she backed away from the baroness and resumed her seat.

"Very well," the baroness said, also taking her seat. She swept her gaze over the silent councilors. "Sir Graybow and I have already discussed the plans for the levy of our forces. Each of you will come forward and receive your orders."

Jo watched through the haze of her anger as each of the nobles rose from his or her seat and took a parchment envelope from Sir Graybow. The parade of nervous nobles and flapping envelopes only strengthened Jo's conviction of the futility of their plans. She lost track of the time and what was said to each as she thought about the dreadful ramifications of letting Teryl Auroch live a moment longer.

❧ ❧ ❧ ❧ ❧

Peace cut a vicious arc through the air and struck the wood-pegged practice dummy. The top of the post fell to the ground, and Jo quickly recovered her balance from the swing.

She relaxed her stance and wiped the sweat from her brow with the back of her hand. The light tunic she wore was soaking, and she was warm despite the cold weather. The more she thought about the decree of the council the greater her anger became, and the more vivid the memories of blasted Armstead grew.

The practice dummy lay in pieces. The pegs that had once jutted out at right angles to the edges of the tall block of wood were scarred with sword marks, and most had been shorn off. There were three huge gashes in the wood where Jo had nearly severed the block with a single stroke. She checked the bastard sword's edge. The silvered rim was still as sharp as when she began.

Jo still did not know which of the knights she would

accompany. She supposed that she was still Sir Graybow's squire, but he would obviously be too busy with the duties of the castle to actually take to the field. Furthermore, as a squire, she would not be allowed to fight.

The red silver of the blessed sword reflected Jo's eyes. She truly did look like the immortal Diulanna as Donar had said in the Hall of Heroes. Jo had never given much thought to revering any of those great beings; she wondered if it was time to choose a patron from among them. She figured she more strongly believed in perseverance and dominance of will, the sphere of Diulanna, than in the warrior aspect of Thor.

The idea of reverence to greater powers was strange to Jo. While she had lived on the street of Specularum, Jo had never called on anyone's strengths but her own. Others on the streets had implored the immortals for favors, most without seeing any reward for their trouble.

Jo sighed loudly, the sweat pouring off of her arms. Her elven armor lay nearby, covered with splinters and wood chips. She had been loath to take it off but she also did not want to chance ruining it before reaching the battlefield.

"What's this, then?" a gruff voice asked from behind.

Jo turned and saw a man in trainer's armor carrying a sword and shield. He was shorter and stockier than she. His beard and mustache were neatly trimmed. Jo wasn't sure she had ever seen this man before during her training sessions with Braddoc.

"What do you mean?" she asked hoarsely.

With a gesture toward the practice target, he replied, "Fighting against wood when there's plenty of good flesh around, waiting to spar with a pretty girl."

Jo frowned at the unnecessary remark. Without saying another word, she turned to retrieve her gear. As she leaned over to gather up the tabard and greaves, the man tapped her shoulder with the flat of his sword, saying, "Why don't you try practicing on something that fights back?"

Jo spun on her heel and brought Peace up in a short arc, knocking the other's blade away.

"Who are you and what do you want?" she demanded, backing off a pace and assuming a loose stance. "I've never seen you before."

"I was brought here to help squires like you while their masters are in the field," the stranger replied.

Jo matched the other man's stance and held Peace in a two-handed grip. Her training with Wyrmblight had shown her the strengths of fighting with a two-handed weapon, one of which was the ability to quickly over-come a shield-bearing opponent through sheer force.

"And where did they find you, sir—?"

"Brewster. *Sergeant* Brewster. They found me at the estates of Councilman Melios."

With his last word, Brewster stepped inside Jo's guard and thrust the hilt of his sword into her chin. Jo staggered back into the post of the practice dummy, hitting her head. Before she recovered, the man swung his shield hard against her body, knocking her senseless. Jo fell to the ground, and her vision dimmed.

Through the roar in her ears, Jo heard, "You'll never survive a fight against a *real* knight, let alone one of your imaginary monsters."

Sergeant Brewster stepped back from Jo, outside the reach of her bastard sword. Jo's vision cleared, and she forced herself to stand, rising first to her knees, then to her feet. She was outraged and wanted the man's blood. Peace was still light in her hands.

"If you are going to stand against an armed opponent, don't give him time to gain advantage over you," the sergeant said with apparent disappointment. Brewster stepped forward again, and Jo brought the tip of Peace up into the man's stomach. The moment it touched his cloth armor, he knocked the blade down with his own sword and kicked her in the midriff with his knee. Jo sprawled breathless onto the grass.

"You know," the sergeant said, "it's one of those classic things. You make too many people angry and they do something about you."

Brewster did not wait for Jo to recover. He slapped the side of her head with the sword's flat, pushing her backward with his foot.

"I was not told to kill you, Squire Menhir. Merely teach you a lesson." The sergeant kneeled down in the soft grass and whispered in Jo's blood-soaked ear. "But there is one who would like to see you dead, and I may just oblige him."

Jo's sight blurred again, and for a moment she was not sure what she was seeing. She doubled her legs beneath her. Kicking out, she caught the sergeant in the chest and hurled him back before he could react. He quickly recovered, but not before Jo rolled herself behind the practice dummy. She had just enough time to clear her head and assume a fighting pose.

Brewster's practice sword stabbed forward at her throat, and Jo dodged her head to the side, the dull blade whistling near her ear. The man tried another stab toward her leg, but missed. Jo used her left hand for power and her right for balance as she swung Peace in a wide arc, releasing her left hand's grip to give her more reach around the post. The sergeant ducked low of the stroke, letting the shining blade bite deep into the block of wood.

More sweat poured from Jo's limbs as she held on to the heavy hilt. She pulled hard on the sword and leaped back. The silvered edge levered through the hard wood, knocking off the top of the post at head-level.

The heated look in the sergeant's eyes told her that he would not give her another chance to recover.

With a great cry, Jo swung the sword. Sergeant Brewster maneuvered his embossed shield before him just as Peace arced around, the tip of the blade puncturing the boss and shattered the shield. Brewster staggered backward, holding the strap and remainder of his shield in his left hand. A new look was in his eyes, a look of fear and doubt.

Jo gripped the hilt with both hands and brought her wrists back to her right side. She straightened her arms and lunged. The sharp tip of the bastard sword pierced her opponent's side, drawing a line of blood.

Jo's body exploded with fire and pain. She felt as if she were caught in an inferno. All she saw was the silver line of Peace razing the flesh of the sergeant, who slowly collapsed to his knees. Blood.

Jo's vision suddenly shifted.

She saw inside a huge cavern. A conflagration raged within a sphere of power. Something died, reborn within a ball of flame. She was frightened but strangely comforted.

The sergeant's last breath left his lips. Jo withdrew the blade and staggered backward, letting the body fall. Her head reeled, and she could not imagine the reason for the vision of the cavern. The experience was almost like a memory from her own spiritual reforging at the hand of Vulcan, except that she was not the one being purged by the fire. Whatever the vision meant, it had something to do with Teryl Auroch and the abaton.

All the strength left Jo's body. She leaned against the castle wall, sliding down without letting go of Peace. She sat on the ground, and breathed hard, sweat continuing to stream over her skin. She had just killed an assassin. She hoped there would not be another attempt.

She had killed her first opponent. She felt sick.

Jo felt a burning in her palm and opened it wide. Wyrmblight's hilt was no longer gold, but the same silver as the rest of the blade. The three abelaat stones glowed deepest black.

❧ ❧ ❧ ❧ ❧

"He said there is one who would like to see me dead."

Graybow stood over the body of Sergeant Brewster. The trainer's blood stained the ground and the cold in the air had made it dry with unnatural speed. The castellan rummaged through the man's clothes, saying, "Melios is the obvious answer."

Jo shrugged, brushing her hair back out of her eyes.

"But irritation with me isn't really motivation for murder, is it? Of course, he did say he was from Melios's estate."

"You'd be surprised at what great evils come from minor motivations," Sir Graybow mumbled. "The fact that you were Flinn's annoying squire could be enough."

Graybow's expression changed to a grim smile as he reached inside the sergeant's tunic. The castellan pulled a dagger from a sheath in his own belt and tore open the rough cloth of the dead man's clothes, revealing a hidden pocket. Inside he found a parchment letter with a wax seal, already broken.

Jo did not recognize the seal. It was an eagle with two heads facing away from each other—not the symbol of councilman Melios, whose emblem was something like a salamander.

Graybow scanned the letter and held it up for Jo to see. She had never seen such strange writing before. It seemed to be a combination of many languages.

"What is it?" she asked, furrowing her brow.

"It's a note, written in the thieves' argot," Sir Graybow answered. "It says, 'The pawn sends his regards to the new blade.'"

Jo shook her head in confusion. "I don't understand."

Graybow glanced around him, and Jo became immediately cautious. The old man motioned for several yeoman to come forward and stand watch over the body, then led her aside.

"You are the new blade, Jo," he said, gesturing to Peace, still clutched in her hand. "And that man back there was 'his regards.' The only real question is, who is the pawn?"

Jo took the note from Graybow's hand and stared at the writing. After a moment, she turned the letter over and stared at the seal, asking, "Where does the letter come from?"

Graybow glanced behind him again and drew his face close to Jo's. "That is the confusing part. It comes from the Black Eagle Barony."

"I don't know anything about that place."

"Well, you'll get your chance for some personal observation soon enough," Graybow answered. He pointed behind Jo to the main entrance gate. "Here is their contingent."

Jo turned and watched as the first regiments assigned to stand against the abelaats rode through. They were heavy cavalrymen, equipped with lances and shields, and carrying broadswords as their secondary weapons. Jo marveled at the sight of these men. They were clad completely in black, riding great black horses that snorted loudly against the cold in the air. Fearsome and menacing.

However, the number of riders was unreasonably few. "There's only sixty! What good is that—?"

Graybow roughly pulled Jo farther aside, though they were at least a hundred yards from the gate. "Don't give yourself away like that! Your voice is easily heard!"

"Sixty men against the abelaats isn't enough," Jo replied quietly. "One abelaat almost killed Flinn! The only thing our armies have in their favor is terrain advantage," Jo explained.

Graybow released Jo's arm and stood back, glancing over her shoulder at the arriving forces. He said, "The Lord of the Black Eagle Barony wants control of Karameikos. He won't be sending his entire force in case an opportunity arises to take the throne."

Jo turned around and crossed her arms in derision, saying, "If he wants the throne, he'd better have more troops than this."

Sir Graybow stared down at the note in his hand, then brought it up to eye level. The image in the wax seal matched that of the banners flown by the cavalrymen.

"I assure you that Ludwig von Hendriks's overall forces, though smaller than that of Stefan Karameikos, are much larger than this," the castellan said. He folded the letter and placed it in his belt.

The two stared at the arriving units, a total of one regiment commanded by two captains, four sergeants, and one senior captain. More than half the troops were armed with nothing more than spears and shields. The remaining forces had crossbows, and most of them had shield-wall pavises slung on their backs.

The squires from the castle ran out to greet the horsemen.

"Leave Peace with me and go help the others," the castellan said, holding out his hands.

"No," Jo answered.

Graybow held out his hands farther.

"I'm sorry," she said slowly. "I can't part with Peace."

Graybow shook his head tersely. With a deprecating wave of his hand, he said, "Very well. But keep it under your tabard." He took Jo by the arm again and led her back to her armor, still waiting near the body of the assassin.

The yeomen let the two pass, smiling at Jo oddly. She

remembered with fondness that she had smiled at Flinn in much the same way when they had first met.

Jo quickly donned her armor and threw her tabard over her head. She put the sword through her belt, lifting the tabard to cover it, then ran out after the other squires.

The men from the Black Eagle Barony were not as stolid as Jo had first thought. After entering the castle and being attended by Penhaligon's squires, they became more boisterous, laughing and making jibes.

"Look at this one!" someone said from atop his horse as Jo passed by. "Thinks she can handle a man's sword!"

The knight's companions laughed. One of them added, "From the looks of her, she can handle my sword anytime!"

Jo could not stop herself from shooting the man an angry glance.

"I'd be careful if I were you," the first knight said, turning to his friend. "She might try to take you down."

The second knight laughed and said, "Anytime. Anytime."

Jo ground her teeth and kept moving. The other squires had taken care of most of the horses, and the knights were loosening the straps of their armor. She tried to help one of the nobles who could not get the buckle from his shoulder guard open, but he waved her away with an impatient hand.

"Get away from me, girl," he ordered. "I've been in the field longer than you've been out of swaddling clothes."

"Maybe," Jo answered, "but—" She cut herself short, unwilling to provoke a more hostile reaction. The knight removed his helmet, revealing a heavy-set man with a huge black beard. His eyes were dark and hard.

"But what?" he asked. He stopped trying to remove his armor.

Regretting that she had even approached the knight, Jo gave the man a tight-lipped smile and replied, "Nothing, sir. I'm just a squire."

The knight regarded Jo as she stepped forward and undid his buckle with a single hand. She kept her other hand behind her back to steady the bastard sword.

Grunting, the knight said, "Just a squire, eh? Looks like there's more to you than you want to show."

Jo stepped back quickly as the man tapped her elven shoulder armor. "I'm sure I don't know what you mean, sir," she muttered, hoping a show of humility would save her.

The knight grunted again, saying, "You're a bad liar, girl. Where's your knight?"

"My knight?" Jo stammered. She became immediately suspicious. These men were likely as treacherous as their baron. They may have escorted the assassin. She wondered if they might also be after Peace.

"You're a stupid girl and a worse squire," the knight said, removing his shoulder mail. "Now. Where is the man called Sir Domerikos?"

"Sir Domerikos has not yet returned from his estates, but he's expected back shortly," Jo said, glad for the change in conversation. Domerikos was one of the knights she had seen riding away from the castle.

The knight left Jo without a word of thanks. She pretended to take care of the man's fine war-horse as she listened to him talk to his comrades. She wanted to find out why he might be interested in one of Penhaligon's knights.

The knight said very little to his companions, merely pointing back toward the castle. The others shook their heads, placing their hands on their swords. Jo thought about leading the horse forward, but saw that the other squires were guiding them back to the stables. With a disappointed sigh, Jo led the mount away, looking back toward the practice area.

Sir Graybow was giving instructions to three yeomen standing guard over the assassin's body. Jo was anxious to hear what else Graybow had discovered. As she fell into line with the others heading back to the stables, she caught the attention of one of the other squires.

"Would you please take this horse back with you?" Jo began, hoping to come up with an excuse of why she should be allowed to dodge her responsibilities. "I've got to—"

The young man blinked as if he had been slapped. "Of course. Anything you want," he replied, taking the reins from Jo and glancing up at the gray sky. "I was there at the blessing. It—it meant a lot to me. Thank you."

Jo thought the man was going to kiss her, but he turned shyly and walked away, leading the horses. She stood in a daze, unsure what to feel, then shook her head as she dashed back across the field.

The assassin's body had already been put into a long box normally used for weapons. Sir Graybow motioned for the yeomen to take it away.

"Did you find anything else?" Jo asked, catching her breath.

"Nothing of any significance," the castellan replied. "What did you discover?"

Jo shrugged. "Nothing, as well, except that it seems that all the men of the barony are unpleasant."

"To say the least."

Sir Graybow sat down on a nearby bench and removed the assassin's note from his tunic. He looked intently at the seal. "Did they say anything, or want anything?"

"The knight I tried to help wanted to know where one of Penhaligon's knights could be found."

"Which knight?"

"Domerikos."

The castellan frowned and replaced the letter. "I do not recall any significant feud between Domerikos and anyone at the Black Eagle Barony. You must be careful when around them, Jo."

Jo nodded her agreement. "So I've seen."

"You must be *very* careful. Never let down your guard for an instant!" With a sweep of his hand toward the barony's troops, he added, "Each of these men is a cut-throat, and all have terrorized the countryside in which they live. They have constant battles with the Five Shires and are known to send raids into other parts of the country. They have many personal grudges that they want to avenge."

The castellan stood and faced away from Jo, folding his hands behind him. "You are to be sent out with a contingent of knights from Penhaligon into the field of battle. Sir Domerikos is to be your knight."

Jo peered angrily into the gray sky. In the back of her mind, she had thought that the chance of her leaving on her own was better the longer her assignment was delayed. She was about to speak when the old man suddenly turned and stared down at Jo. He said, "You are all to accompany the regiment of the Black Eagle Barony."

Chapter VII

phosphorescent glow from the walls lit many of the passages Braddoc and Flinn walked. The dwarf was well accustomed to the dusklike lighting created by the soft fungus carefully cultivated by workers from the underground city. A sense of longing and reminiscence filled Braddoc as he smelled the water-and-stone fragrance of the caves. He would have liked to stop at one of his homes, for he had several residences within the city, but Flinn's quest was too pressing.

The passages they walked were known as the Tunnels to Beyond, the undercroft of the city where no civilized races lived. Braddoc knew that Denwarf had traveled these tunnels generations ago in his legendary descent. Braddoc had never been able to speak with the spirit of the vanished dwarven ruler.

"How did you know to bring us here?" Braddoc asked, his voice's echo absorbed by the illuminating fungus.

"I can feel the source of the power, but do not know specifically where it can be found," Flinn replied. He shrugged his shoulders and added, "This was the closest point I could find."

"It's all right. It'll just be a bit of a hike."

The caverns became increasingly dark. Braddoc had no problem seeing in the dark, but he did not know if Flinn would have the same ability.

"Can you see anything?" the dwarf asked.

"I'm not sure," Flinn said. "I think I can see you, I—I don't know."

Braddoc nodded to himself. He guessed that the immortal ability of true seeing required time or the accumulation of power to manifest itself. Taking a deep breath, Braddoc raised his left hand to his eye. He turned his mind inward and delved deep into his spirit until he could see a vision of the shining orb that had been his companion for so many years. In his mind, he walked around the orb, still connected by fibers of light into the ether, finding their way through the planes to Kagyar himself.

The dwarf did not like to use the ocular for any reason, but its ability to create light would not drain his essence, like some of the other powers. He reached out gently with both his hands, bringing the light of his spirit into the physical world.

Braddoc's blind eye flared with illumination, as white and pure as the sun. It threw stark shadows against the walls of the cavern, grotesque, long, and unnatural.

"That is a most wondrous thing, Braddoc," Flinn said with a hint of amazement. "I can feel its power coursing through you."

Instead of giving a reply, Braddoc clasped his hands before him and closed his good eye. He let himself fall to his knees, momentarily throwing the light of the ocular around the cavern. He ground his teeth together to keep himself from cursing.

"Oh, great lord Kagyar, Kagyar the Artisan, Kagyar Flash-eyes, I, Braddoc Briarblood, your *humble* servant, thank you for blessing us with this, your light. May it shine for-ever in the dark to guide our path," Braddoc said without relish. He paused and unclenched his jaw. Before he did anything else, he had to pay his hated debt to Kagyar.

Flinn looked up to the ceiling and reached out with his hand, as if trying to grab something.

The dwarf continued to mumble to himself in the name of the immortal patron who had created the ocular. His words were soft and contained gentle ministrations and thanks, but he knew that somewhere, Kagyar was laughing at the dwarf who dared to leave the path to immortality. Humiliation was his penance, as it had always been.

A shimmering thread appeared in Flinn's hand, one of the strands of light connecting the ocular to Kagyar.

Before Braddoc realized what was happening, he fell over and gasped with unbearable pain. The harder Flinn pulled, the greater the agony. Even so, Braddoc did not give Kagyar the satisfaction of stopping the prayer. The strand disappeared. The pain immediately fled Braddoc's head and he stood, grabbing his forehead with his hands as if he had just been clubbed.

"What was that?" Flinn inquired, still staring at his hand.

"The—" Braddoc had to stop. He wiped at something running from his nose and found blood on his hand. He clenched his teeth to steady himself against the last of the pain and wiped his hand on a kerchief he drew from his leather jerkin. After a few moments of silence, he continued: "That was Kagyar's will connected to the ocular. Don't do that again."

"I'm very sorry," Flinn said, dropping his hand. "Is there anything I can do?"

Braddoc gave a short laugh that he immediately regretted as a red haze filled his vision. "Yeah, you can give Kagyar a kick for me."

"You do not get along with your patron?"

"*Ex*patron," Braddoc corrected, breathing in deeply through his nose. "I found this artifact in my quest of the polymath, the quest for immortality in the Sphere of Matter. Every time I use the ocular, I have to pray to Kagyar and thank him for his wonderful gift." Braddoc snorted. "Ha! Wonderful gift. I'd rather have my eye back."

Flinn crossed his arms over his chest, as though he was settling in for a conversation.

Braddoc held up his hand, throwing a gigantic shadow against the wall and over Flinn's angular face. He said, "Before you start asking a lot of questions I don't want to answer, I think we should get moving. There really is no time to lose."

Flinn nodded twice and lowered his arms. "Thank you for making this—sacrifice for me, Braddoc. I do not understand you, but I am growing to appreciate you."

Braddoc turned and resumed his walk down the now-lighted tunnel. He smiled broadly, thinking that Flinn might be more alive than he had hoped.

The two had walked for many hours, following winding cavern pathways and going down hidden tunnels familiar only to Braddoc and the spirits of his dwarven ancestors. Every once in a while they passed the bodies of dwarven adventuring parties, skeletons fallen to dust. The caverns beneath Rockhome were the dwellings of many horrible creatures, some mortal, some not.

Braddoc felt the air growing thinner. In the city above, the ventilation from its marvelously engineered vanes and ducts provided sufficient air for all of Lower Dengar and many of the adjoining caverns and tunnels. Where Braddoc and Flinn now traveled, though, there was no way for the air to flow.

"Flinn, I may be ancient, but I'm still mortal. I might have trouble breathing soon," Braddoc said without turning.

A great gust of wind from behind blew the dwarf's hair about his face and threatened to pull his braided beard out of its place in his belt. He turned and directed the full light of the ocular behind him, expecting to confront some strange denizen, but he saw nothing but Flinn. The air smelled fresh and pleasant.

"Is that better?" Flinn inquired, stopping.

Braddoc nodded. "Much. I didn't want to have to use the ocular for something as silly as breathing."

Flinn nodded and continued his pace, saying, "I understand."

The companions resumed their journey, but within a few minutes they came upon a cavern so large that the light from the ocular was lost in the darkness. The cavern was shaped like an inverted bowl for fish. The floor of the cavern was completely flat, and the walls curved away into impenetrable blackness. The walls of the cavern were covered with strange rock outcroppings that could have been stalagmites were they not pointing toward the center of the floor. Even the outcroppings near the entrance floor were pointing inward. All the rock visible in the chamber, floor and walls, appeared to have been sanded smooth by a crew of dwarven engineers. Braddoc shook his head in wonderment.

"You have never been here before?" Flinn asked, moving behind the dwarf.

Braddoc shook his head again. "No. I only know of it because of my ancestors."

The dwarf peered around the cavern, letting the ocular's light penetrate the cracks it could reach, but he saw no signs of any nests or dens.

"Do you feel it?" Flinn intoned as he clenched his fists and raised them to his chest. His muscles flexed with impossible strength. "Do you feel it, Braddoc? The power, the age, the incredible mastery?"

"I'm sorry, Flinn. I feel nothing."

Without warning, Flinn stepped forward into the field of outcroppings. Braddoc watched as the man slowly picked his way toward the flattened surface in the middle of the cavern. Braddoc was unsure if he should follow, was not sure if this were a path to be tread by mortals. Instead, he kept a lookout; there were many races of underground beings who had no respect for so obviously sacred a place.

Flinn walked about two hundred feet from the entrance, but then suddenly stopped. Braddoc saw that his friend had assumed a cautious stance, as if ready for combat. In fact, the dwarf recognized the pose from the first time he had met Flinn in the mortal world. It was the same unarmed combat position that Flinn the man had taken in the bar to brawl with Braddoc's mercenaries. Braddoc's mouth twisted at the memory.

Flinn continued to stand in place, completely still, and Braddoc wondered if he had been frozen by some dire enchantment. "Flinn, what is the matter?" he called out. His voice's echo was lost among the pointing fingers of the rocks.

Flinn did not move or answer. Braddoc furrowed his brow in concern. The dwarf felt his pulse quicken, sure something had gone wrong. His frustration grew as he considered his options.

"Damn you, Kagyar!" he hissed under his breath. Kneeling down, Braddoc twisted his hands together in supplication and lowered his head. "Oh, great lord Kagyar, Kagyar the Artisan, Kagyar Flasheyes, I, Braddoc Briarblood, your humble servant, ask for your blessing. Show me that by which my friend is enthralled." Braddoc paused, tightly shutting his good eye and cupping his left hand over the ocular.

Braddoc drew his hand back from the ocular, hoping that the artifact would be able to illuminate whatever had frozen Flinn in his place. He could not imagine what could possibly harm an immortal, except, of course, another immortal.

Nothing new was revealed by the eye. Flinn stood without moving. When the dwarf had asked for spells to be revealed before, he had seen the enchanted person glow like a will-o'-the-wisp, but no halo appeared around Flinn's body.

"Why didn't you heed my call, Kagyar?" Braddoc cursed. "Why do you pick now to turn a deaf ear when so much is at stake?"

Braddoc turned and struck the wall with his bare hand and cursed again the name of his former patron. He inwardly vowed that someday he would rip the ocular from his head and smash it to pieces just to thwart the immortal's power. There was only one course of action. He took a deep breath and stepped out into the field of outcroppings.

Braddoc had difficulty moving among the rocks. Unlike his immortal friend, Braddoc kept getting his feet caught between fingerlike projections. He glanced back when he was about twenty paces from the entrance. He suddenly felt like he had walked a thousand miles, fatigued beyond endurance, his limbs were too heavy to move. The entrance was lost behind a gray mist that filled the air behind him, but not in front of him or around the flattened disc in the cavern floor. He realized through his lethargy that Flinn must have been caught in the same magical trap.

Braddoc lifted his right foot and placed it before him. The effort nearly drained him of the remainder of his failing strength. He lifted his left foot and thought he might fall over from fatigue. Flinn was still hundreds of feet away. Only then did Braddoc realize that the power Flinn had felt emanating from the cave—its very life—was what had snared them, not the spell of a wizard.

With his final strength, Braddoc raised his left hand to the ocular and prayed for what he sought. The words tumbled slowly from his mouth. His spirit began to detach from his body. In time, he was watching himself from what seemed to be a great distance.

The negating power that Braddoc summoned to counteract the force of the place turned the ocular dark. The light from the artifact churned away from Braddoc's face, turning the thick air into shades of orange, then transmuting into reds and browns. Flinn turned his head, and Braddoc saw with relief that his companion was freed of the spell.

The dwarf screamed out loud, pain breaking him free of the grasp of the cavern for a moment. A great cracking sound split the air as the flesh of his feet slowly turned to stone. His vision blurred together with a haze of agony filling his normal eye, warping the power of the ocular.

"You must help me!" Braddoc screamed to Flinn. Another crack exploded from his leg as more flesh transformed into granite. "Pull me free! Bring us back to the entrance!"

Flinn backed away from the dwarf, finally turning and walking to the flat cavern floor. He stood in the middle and turned, seeming confused.

"Flinn, save me! I cannot keep this—!"

From the knees down, Braddoc's legs were heavy and numb. He felt the cursed effects of the artifact travel up his legs fraction by fraction. The only thing that could

stop the transformation was for him to stop using the
ocular. He could not stop or Flinn would become
trapped a second time.

"Flinn! What are you doing?"

Flinn was heedless of the dwarf's calls. He raised his
arms straight to his sides and craned his head back. The
floor of the cavern began turning, raising itself up. A
cylinder slowly appeared out of the floor, made of coarse
iron, welded and bolted together. The grates mounted
into the cylinder's hull revealed the flames of a great forge
within.

Braddoc legs were completely immobile, and he could
barely keep himself conscious. He watched with awe as
Flinn bent down and struck the top of the forge, shatter-
ing the stone covering. The immortal reached down and
grabbed a metal ring, straining his perfect muscles. A
hatch slowly opened, ancient hinges screeching. When he
had pulled back the hatch, he jumped inside the cylinder
without hesitation.

The grates and doors of the forge exploded outward,
leaving the iron cylinder filled with flames. Within,
Flinn's body was completely consumed by the inferno.

Braddoc attempted to peer down at himself, but he
could not bend at the waist. He could no longer find air
to bellow his suffering, but the power of the ocular would
not let him perish until his flesh was completely gone.

Exploding once again, the forge shattered, leaving a
huge ball of fire floating in the center of the cavern.
Braddoc wanted to shield his face, but he could no longer
move his arms. The flames singed his hair and blistered
his remaining skin.

Flinn stepped out from the flames, standing in the air. His body was whole, and his clothes billowed in the hot wind. Braddoc felt his soul quaver at the sight of his friend. He had never seen anything so frightening and inspiring. Behind him, the flames quickly died, leaving nothing but ash and the dead forge.

Flinn walked on the air toward Braddoc, sparks snapping around him. Flinn reached out with his right hand and covered the ocular, blocking its brown light. Too late. The flesh had given way to stone to the crown of his head.

Braddoc was glad to finally die.

Chapter VIII

o marched out behind Sir Domerikos and led a packhorse laden with his equipment. She had inspected each piece of his armor herself and found only one or two links that needed repairing. When she had pointed this out, the knight had fixed the mail himself, mumbling something about not wanting to waste time with the armorer.

Sir Domerikos was the commander of the forces leaving the confines of the castle. His contingent was taking the long journey to Threshold, which brightened Jo's spirits. Glancing over her shoulder, she saw another unit heading northeast, toward the Duke's Road Keep. The units marching toward Verge had left the day before.

The ground beneath Jo's feet was cold and hard, and the horses were obviously unhappy to be forced out into

the inclement air. Jo had to constantly pull at the horse's
lead to keep the animal moving. Her shoulder was
becoming increasingly sore despite her strength.

The horse stopped again, and Jo jerked to a halt as well.
She angrily pushed aside the hair in her face and stared
deep into the horse's eyes. She wondered if the animal
knew it was being difficult. A quick glance over her shoulder told her she was quickly losing ground to her knight.

"Let's go!" she muttered under her breath, taking the
lead rein in both hands. She had plenty of experience
with animals, but this one was being especially difficult.
The horse bobbed its head and snorted, taking a step
backward. Jo pulled as hard as she dared. She did not
want to hurt the beast just get it moving again.

"Are you having problems, Squire?" someone asked
from behind.

Jo turned angrily, expecting to see one of the Black
Eagle soldiers. Instead, she found herself staring into Sir
Domerikos's featureless helm from where he sat atop his
gray charger.

"No, sir," Jo said with an ingenuous smile.

"Then what seems to be the trouble?"

"No trouble, sir," Jo lied again. "This horse must be
tired."

The knight held out his hand and said, "Give me the
lead."

With a terse sigh, Jo complied. Domerikos wrapped the
rein around the horn of his saddle and wheeled his mount
around. The packhorse grudgingly started forward.

"I don't understand," she said under her breath as several more knights and squires passed by her.

"Squire Menhir?" Sir Domerikos said from within his helm. "If you wouldn't mind?"

Jo started at the voice, frustrated at herself for not paying attention to her task. She ran up to take her place by the horse, which still seemed to be ignoring her.

The knight looked down at Jo; she guessed she looked like an idiot. She could not quite force the thought of her quest from her mind or keep it at bay long enough to concentrate on the job at hand.

Jo tried to imagine what had happened to the boy Dayin and shuddered beneath her elven mail, making the links lightly ring. He and she had both fallen victim to an abelaat's poison bite, and in that common terror she felt a certain kinship.

"Squire Menhir?" Sir Domerikos said again. Jo looked up sharply, her brooding thoughts interrupted. The knight removed his winged helm and shook out his long, dark hair. His face was thin, with high cheekbones, and his eyes were dark beneath the ridge of his brow. He sported a neatly trimmed mustache that gave his face a kindly character over his stern features.

"Yes, sir?" she asked politely, staring into his eyes.

"Sir Graybow told me a great deal of your—experiences, of late," the knight said. "But I am still curious. Where did you get that fine armor and that tabard?"

Jo turned her head to keep herself from saying something rash. The man's voice was neither ingratiating nor demanding, but his distinctly aristocratic air annoyed her. She thought back to her hard times in the Specularum streets, when she had been forced to clean boots, carriages, even chimneys, to keep from starving. The people who had thrown a few coppers to her had been of the same cut as Sir Domerikos, though he was apparently respectful enough not to call her "girl."

"How much did he tell you of me?" she asked shrewdly, averting her gaze.

"Very little. Except that you had some remarkable companions."

"Remarkable companions have not made me a squire."

"I'm terribly sorry if I have offended you," Sir Domerikos said politely. "I meant nothing of it."

Jo peered up into the man's face and saw that he was not making fun of her; he was being open and honest. She felt guilty for thinking he would be deprecating because of his noble birth.

"There's no need to apologize to me, sir. I'm just a squire," she replied.

"So I have heard, from Sir Barethmor of the Black Eagle Lancers."

"You have spoken with him?"

Domerikos smiled and glanced back over his shoulder at the contingent of black-armored riders. Sir Barethmor was the senior captain of the lancers. Sir Domerikos said, "He and I have had words before."

"He asked after you," Jo said with concern. "I think he wants to—bring you harm."

Domerikos nodded and replied, "No doubt. He and I had a dispute once over a certain lady who—you don't need to hear this."

Jo was interested, and the longer she could keep Sir Domerikos speaking, the longer she could forestall answering any more questions. "No, please tell me," she prompted.

Domerikos craned his neck back and ran his gauntleted hands through his hair. His breath misted in the cold as he said, "The details are not important, but I once took from Barethmor that with which he was most obsessed."

"And that was?"

The knight turned with a slight expression of surprise to face Jo. "Why, his wife, of course."

Jo laughed at the sheer audacity of the statement. Sir Domerikos laughed as well, adding, "I heard the brute was beating her, and having ridden out from the Castle of the Three Suns to face him in mortal combat, discovered that she was already riding out to meet me with a plan of escape."

"Flinn never had a story like that," Jo said through her laughter. She regretted the statement, but figured that everybody knew she had once been the squire of Flinn the Mighty.

"Really?" Sir Domerikos said again with surprise. "What kind of stories did he have?"

Jo pursed her lips reluctantly. "I—" she began, trying to be as polite as possible. "He always had stories that were— illuminating."

Sir Domerikos nodded and said, "You mean the kind that tell of knighthood as it is, not how everyone wants it to be?"

"Yes," Jo returned, glad the knight was so astute.

"Then I think I understand something of the kind of man Flinn was. I've always wondered, and being with you is my greatest chance to pursue my scholarly endeavors."

"Your what?"

Sir Domerikos leaned down off his saddle and murmured, "Didn't Sir Graybow tell you? I'm going to write a book on Flinn the Mighty. I purposefully withheld any study of the man until I could meet you."

Jo arched her eyebrow and stopped walking. The knight halted his horse and turned to face her. Jo had the sneaking suspicion that he was going to tell her something she did not want to hear.

"I can tell by the expression on your face that you've already guessed, Squire Menhir," Domerikos said. "I knew of your affiliation with Flinn, and asked specifically for you to be my squire."

"What?" Jo cried, outraged. "I am here as your squire because you asked for me? What of my mission, what of— ?"

"I would not speak so loudly if I were you, Squire Menhir. There are some here who seem to take an even greater interest in you than I."

Jo turned and saw that a handful of men in the Black Eagle Lancers were obviously regarding her from a distance, pointing to her and each other, Barethmor among them.

Sir Domerikos turned his horse back, and Jo pivoted as well. She removed Peace from the sheath that had once held Wyrmblight. The blade was almost weightless in her hands. The minute ridges in her palms from the abelaat stones in the weapon's hilt had mostly disappeared.

"That is a beautiful blade, Squire," Sir Domerikos said, holding out his hand. "May I see it?"

"No, sir. I cannot let anyone handle Peace but me," Jo answered stolidly.

"I could order you to hand over the weapon, Squire Menhir."

"Yes, sir, you could. You could order me into battle, you could order me to my death, and I would carry out those orders to the best of my ability. But I will not hand over my sword."

The knight nodded without looking down at Jo. He said, "That is the blade blessed by the people of Penhaligon?"

"Yes, it is."

"And that is Wyrmblight's hilt, is it not?"

"Yes."

Sir Domerikos bent down off his saddle to get a closer view of the blade. He sat in thoughtful silence a moment.

"Fascinating," he said. "Someday, Squire, you must tell me your story."

The two went on in silence. Jo was thinking that if she had not been Flinn's squire, she would have willingly learned under Sir Domerikos.

Resting Peace on her shoulder, Jo observed the marching of the other troops. There were three regiments from the Black Eagle Barony, of which one was cavalry. Penhaligon had added three more units of horse, along with two more units of longbow archers and two units of infantry. The infantry's main weapon was the long spear, and they all had shields painted with the heraldry of their respective lords.

Jo tried to imagine commanding a body of men, but knew at the same time she would not enjoy it. In Specularum, life on the streets meant everyone for himself; acts of kindness were rare and often false. Jo had learned then

to rely on her own wits rather than anyone else's. She
learned of the bravery and resourcefulness that commanding forces on the field of battle would require, but
she lacked knowledge of the principles of morale and the
workings of men's hearts. Glancing back up at Sir Domerikos, Jo's respect for him increased.

Penhaligon was surrounded by hills and easy grades.
The contingent made its way northward through the
rolling hills until it reached a few scattered and unnamed
forests. Beside one such wood, one of the Black Eagle
Lancers cried out and pointed into the trees. Jo turned in
surprise to see a large buck standing at the edge of the
forest.

The lancer lowered his visor and knocked one of his
companions aside, goading his mount forward with a kick
of his prick-spurs. The horse whinnied loudly and set off
at a charge. The man's companion quickly recovered,
spurring his horse and chasing after the other knight. The
other lancers laughed and jeered, but Jo could not quite
make out what they said.

Sir Domerikos craned his head to see what was happening. He turned his mount and started heading toward
the forest, loosening the strap that held his broadsword to
his saddle. The moment he moved, Jo saw that Sir
Barethmor also turned his mount. He withdrew his long
warhammer from its stirrup.

"That's an odd weapon to hunt stag with," Jo said, gesturing toward the senior captain.

Domerikos arched an eyebrow as he glanced back toward
the Black Eagle Lancers. He smiled to himself and gave a
short laugh, returning to his place among the other knights.

"It's true, then," he said to Jo without looking down.

Jo shrugged. "I guess so. What are you going to do?"

"Command my troops and stay out of his way. I'll make sure that wherever I put him will be far away from me. And you," he added.

"What do you mean?" Jo asked.

"Sir Graybow told me of the—trainer, sent to you from Councilman Melios's estate," the knight replied, continuing to peer ahead into the distance. "Are you not the new blade?"

Jo changed her grip on the hilt of her sword, feeling the abelaat stones slide into the grooves on her palms, impressed there during the assassination attempt.

"Don't let that man get to you, Squire," Sir Domerikos murmured. "He has tried to get me to fight him on many occasions, but I would never give in."

Jo swung Peace forward in a one-handed grip. She brought her arm back behind her head for an exaggerated blow, then forward again. Her muscles warmed with the exercise.

"Weren't you going to challenge him when you took his wife?" she asked, beginning to breathe heavily.

"Yes, but that was different. I'm glad I did not."

"Why?"

Domerikos made sure that the strap on his blade was secure. He said, "Because I later learned that the man has a number of items, sorcerous in nature, that he would not hesitate to employ."

Jo stopped swinging and felt the cold return. The majority of the magic she had encountered had been malign, with the exception of the spells of transport cast by Karleah and the blink-dog's tail given to her by her father. With fear, Jo thought again of the power of Teryl Auroch and wondered how she was going to get past the wizard's magical defenses.

A cry rang out from the woods, and Jo and Domerikos turned. One of the lancers was either in trouble or hollering for joy. Many of the squires left their knights and also ran into the woods.

"Why don't you go with them, Squire Menhir?" the knight asked with a nod of his head.

Confused, Jo answered, "What are they doing?"

"Hunting the stag, of course."

Jo pursed her lips as she watched the squires run off into the darkness of the forest, carrying their own swords and short spears. Jo had never truly been one of them, and she felt uncomfortable. Shaking her head, Jo decided not to leave.

"Why don't you go, Squire? Give yourself some distraction from your charges."

"I don't think that's a good idea, sir, but thank you," Jo replied. "I'm probably not too popular with the other squires, considering my background."

Sir Domerikos appeared surprised. "On the contrary, Squire. You are the most popular figure in the castle."

"I think that's the entirety of my problem. I've gone from being reviled to being adored in a few short days."

"All right, then. If that is your decision, I command you to join the other squires. Seek out the stag, take its antlers, and bring us both fame and honor."

Jo stared up at the knight, who looked back down at her with a wide smile. Jo could not help smiling back.

She glanced over her shoulder and saw Sir Barethmor. Her smile melted to a frown.

"If Sir Graybow has implied to you that Sir Barethmor desires my blade," Jo said, holding up the silvered weapon for emphasis, "then I probably should not leave your side."

"If Sir Barethmor desires your blade, he'll have to fight me to get it," Sir Domerikos said flatly.

Jo lowered her head, flattered by the man's statement.

"Now, if we are done exchanging platitudes, I suggest you get moving," Sir Domerikos said with a slight smile. "I want you to get the stag, but most of all I want you to get it before those moronic lancers."

With an involuntary laugh, Jo stepped away from the line, cautious of Barethmor. The man's face was hidden by his full helm, but he did not seem particularly interested in her.

Without another thought, Jo rushed forward with the wave of other squires, holding Peace in both hands and listening to the light clatter of her elven chain. It felt good to stretch her legs and run rather than continue with the plodding pace of the column.

The woods were much colder than she expected, but Jo did not let the chill slow her down. A few paths ran through the forest, and Jo chose the one with the most animal tracks. In Specularum, there had been few opportunities to hunt for anything more than wharf rats or the untended lunches of over-fat merchants. Everything she knew she had learned from her short time with Flinn and on a few unofficial journeys into the royal Karameikos hunting grounds.

Running amidst the trees, Jo couldn't see any squirrels or other animals, nor could she hear any birds or insects. She moved deeper into the forest and purposefully sought for tracks or spoor but found nothing. She stopped to rest after a while and peered up through the leaves. The gray sky continued to block the sun's light, reminding her that the abaton was still draining the life from the world. She clutched Peace in both hands, anxious to resume her quest.

Jo suddenly heard the neigh of a horse directly ahead of her and caught a glimpse of the stag. It was much larger than she had expected, at least as tall as she, and its fur was a rich light brown, like a field of grain. She watched as the beast dodged around a series of trees, then turned toward the black rider. The knight was taken by surprise and his horse reared and stepped awkwardly back on its hind legs; the stag lowered its head to bring its antlers to bear.

"A beast possessed!" the lancer cried, grabbing madly for the reins. His huge horse continued to step back, pawing at the air and ground, its eyes rolling with fear.

Jo rushed forward, carrying her blade in a two-handed grip down and to her right side. She kept a healthy distance between herself and the berserk horse. When she was within ten paces of the stag, it spun and faced her, keeping its head lowered to the ground.

Jo rushed the stag, choking off a yell so she alone could gain the prize. The beast bolted forward and stopped, confounding Jo's swing. Peace struck flat against the stag's antlers, and her right hand slipped, gouging itself on the bone. Jo jumped back and resumed her stance, her sword in both hands.

Her vision faded and shifted, and she could not move. She forced herself to remain standing though her legs threatened to buckle. The stag snorted loudly and pawed the ground, stepping back. Jo stared into the beast's black eyes, her sight growing strangely dim. She twisted her grip on the wire-wound hilt of Peace, and she felt blood from the gouge wash against the edges of the abelaat stones.

Standing in the middle of a forest, Jo peered down at the ring of animals. In supplication they begged for help, their savior who had returned from the dead to save the living.

The yell of the squires startled Jo, and she fell forward, losing her grip on Peace. She scrambled for the weapon in panic, but saw that the stag and the horseman were gone. Ten squires ran past her, yelling and smiling with the sport. Jo stood, staggered, and pressed up against a tree, glad for the support. The animals in the forest had begged for help, and she had understood them, each and every voice, from mouse to rabbit, from bird to deer. She lifted her hand and saw the blood drip from her arm onto the forest floor, creating droplets of steaming crimson.

Jo suddenly understood what had triggered this newest vision, along with the vision of the furnace below the world. She could divine events—perhaps the past or present or future—when the abelaat stones made from her blood came into contact with living blood, whether hers or someone else's.

"But what are these events?" she asked herself in frustration. Jo tried not to let her blood stain the hilt or the

blade of Peace, but she discovered that the red-silver
metal seemed to drink it before it pooled. Her blood
darkened the blade slightly, giving it a glow of health.
Beneath her grip, the three abelaat stones shimmered
darkly, as they had at the Castle of the Three Suns.

The horns from the contingent outside the forest blew
loudly, startling Jo. She saw that she was now alone in the
forest, and that all the other squires were heading back
toward their knights. Gathering herself together, she held
Peace in both her hands and ran out of the wood.

The lancers and Sir Domerikos's regiment of knights
were at opposite sides of the field. The warriors had
drawn themselves up on a ridge that overlooked an open
plain. The plain was very wide, and it ended in another
series of hills. Messengers and squires ran between the
two units, occasionally making stops to speak with the
captains and sergeants of the infantry.

"Squire Menhir!" a voice called out from behind the
lines.

Jo saw a young man waving to her near the Black Eagle
Lancer's formation. She took a deep breath to steady herself and ran toward him, suspiciously watching the men
from the barony. Within a few minutes she was behind
their formation.

The young man waved Jo on, matching her pace. He
said, "Sir Domerikos wants you to attend him now!"

"Where is he?" Jo asked, chagrinned for being slow to
leave the forest.

The squire pointed up a slight rise overlooking the soldiers. Sir Domerikos and the other leaders waited there,
their banners snapping in the wind.

Jo heard the call to arms. The run from the forest to the top of the slope had worn on her endurance, and she breathed heavily as she fought against her fatigue. The moments seemed like minutes later when she reached the top of the rise.

"Please forgive me, Sir Domerikos," she said around gasping breaths, hugging Peace to keep the blade from dropping. "I didn't—"

"Enough time for that later, Squire," the knight said without looking at her. His eyes were fixed on a point far in front of the lines of men-at-arms and cavalry. Jo strained to see the threat.

The gray sky made the horizon blend with the land, but after a few moments Jo made out ragged lines of men scrambling for safety. As they drew closer, she saw that many of them ran on all fours, as if they were animals. Next moment, Jo lost sight of the approaching force, as they dropped into a valley in the rolling terrain.

Sir Domerikos signaled for the trumpeter to give a final call. At the end of the last note, the spearmen lowered their weapons into a deadly wall. The crossbowmen braced themselves against their black shield-wall pavices.

The howl that erupted over the hill made Jo step back with fear, bumping into Sir Domerikos's tethered horse. The approaching men now moved on two legs, but their faces were like those of wild animals. They snarled and spat as they advanced, and Jo clutched Peace, quickly regaining her composure.

"What are they?" she murmured to herself.

"Beastmen," Sir Domerikos replied evenly. "They do not take prisoners."

Chapter IX

he beastmen were more akin to animals than they were to humans. Whenever one would halt for a moment to sniff the air, it stood on hind legs, but often would hunch down on all fours to dodge or run. The beastmen's heads and shoulders were like those of animals—bears, boars, wolves, wildcats, snakes. . . . In all their fierce variety, they vastly outnumbered the human forces. The rushing tide of them roared terribly as they closed on the ranks of humans. Jo trembled, and the impulse to run shot through her like lightning. Her shaking stilled, however, when she saw Sir Domerikos's stolid stance.

Sir Domerikos signaled for the archers to release their first volley. The air was filled with the twang of strings and whirl of shafts, which descended into the onrushing forces and cut down many of them.

The first wave of beastmen to hit the infantry impaled themselves on the wall of spears. Their inhuman howls and snarls of pain and anger made Jo wince.

"How can they do that?" she muttered, shocked.

Sir Domerikos did not break his gaze from his army. "Do what?" he inquired.

"Throw themselves against the spears." She gave a confused gesture. "I've never actually seen beastmen before, but I thought they had some intelligence."

Domerikos did not answer at first. He motioned for one of the heralds to come forward and gave the young man a parchment note. The herald read the name on the note and nodded, rushing down the hillock toward the units assembled below. Domerikos turned his eyes back to the boiling battle at the front line and distractedly commented to Jo, "Their tactics are sound for unarmed, ferocious, and fanatical troops."

Jo thought about that statement, then said, "They're trying to overwhelm us through sheer strength of numbers?"

"Exactly," Sir Domerikos answered. He gave Jo a quick appraisal, then added, "You have a good grasp of warfare."

Jo's smile was tight. She shrugged, embarrassed. "Thank you, sir."

Jo wondered why the cavalry was being held back from the attack. The bowmen continued to rain arrows down from their place behind the lines, arching their shots over the heads of the infantry. The beastmen in the back ranks were thrown into confusion.

Crossbowmen from the Black Eagle Barony, closer to the fighting than the longbowmen, fired from behind their wall of black-painted pavices into the rushing waves of the enemy. The rain of missiles thrashed the ranks of beastmen and many fell, but the surviving majority trampled them underfoot in their charge. Jo was going to point this out to Sir Domerikos but saw that he was busy giving an order to another herald.

Despite the onslaught, the other commanders around Domerikos seemed confident. One of them, a middle-aged man with short dark hair and olive-hued skin removed a silver drinking flask from his belt, unscrewed the cap, and saluted to the others.

"To your health, Commander Montesey."

Domerikos knocked the flask to the ground and slapped the commander in the face, bringing up a red welt on the man's cheek. "Never do that in my presence again!" Domerikos bellowed. Jo stepped back in surprise at the knight's unprecedented change in demeanor. "Are you fool enough to think that a battle against beastmen is so easily won?"

"What are you talking about, Domerikos?" the commander demanded, bringing his hand to his face. "You're still scared from your last defeat to these—things."

Domerikos stepped close to the commander. Jo worried Domerikos was going to take the commander by the throat. Domerikos's heated reply was so quiet that she did not hear.

Jo advanced a few paces down the side of the hillock to observe the battle. The lines of the Penhaligon troops were no longer even and ranked. The men were obviously hard pressed by the onslaught, and the noise from both the throats of animals and the throats of the men was nearly deafening. Jo could not imagine how these troops would be able to stand against the forces of the abelaats. She clutched Peace tightly in both hands.

The crossbowmen's squires and support troops took their positions in front of the pavices, drawing their short swords and removing their bucklers. The bolts continued to strike hard into the enemy lines, but the creatures continued to pour in from over the hills. The general path of the charging beastmen was straight away from the line of hills directly to the north.

Jo thought back to a time in Specularum when a visiting merchant had driven cattle through the streets, only to have them all panic when a building caught fire. The conflagration spread because of the wind, and the animals had moved in a direct line away from the danger, crushing everything in their path, including the abandoned warehouse where Jo and her companions had made their home.

"All right," she said to herself, straining her sight into the gray distance. "What is forcing them to come in this direction?"

Before she could divine an answer, Sir Domerikos came up from behind her and thrust his shield into her hands. "Come with me," he commanded, marching down the slope at a quick pace.

Dumbfounded, Jo obeyed. She saw that the other commanders were not following, and that the commander who had accused Domerikos of cowardice seemed to have vanished.

"We are going to face the enemy directly and turn this battle into a decisive victory," the knight said to Jo as he picked up his pace. He drew the sword from his sheath and held his hand out for his shield. Jo handed it to him while trying to determine the best way to express her observations about the beastmen's charge.

The infantry from the Black Eagle Barony was beginning to buckle beneath the fanatical assault of the beastmen. As the spearmen withdrew their weapons from the bodies of their foes, the remaining beastmen had time to close against the defenseless soldiers. The sword- and shield-armed soldiers could deal more easily with the onrush, but the sheer force of numbers was beginning to wear them down.

The most horrible aspect of this battle to Jo was the demoralizing screaming and howling of the beastmen. Only half an hour ago, she had been sure she had the courage to lead a regiment; now she found herself wavering.

Domerikos grabbed Jo by the arm and pulled her to his side. He put his face up against her ear and shouted, "Stay close! Let nothing take me by surprise."

"I have to tell you about the beastmen!" Jo implored.

"No time! Fight!"

Sir Domerikos waved his sword above his head, and before Jo could reply, she heard the herald's horn from the hillock. The Black Eagle Lancers gave a great shout that matched the ferocity of the beastmen's howling and set off into the field as a single mass of black steel and horses. Jo saw that at least a hundred of the enemy were instantly killed by the first charge of the lancers. Lances broken, the cavalry drew their secondary weapons and maneuvered through the beastmen, attacking with swords and maces.

The charge of the Black Eagle cavalry threw the beastmen into confusion, allowing Sir Domerikos to rally the failing troops. Jo was so preoccupied with her duty to the knight that she did not hear his words of inspiration. She only heard the clash of steel and the hideous snarls of the beastmen.

The barony spearmen regrouped behind the crossbowmen's line of sword and buckler defenders. The crossbowmen had already abandoned their pavices and were attempting to run back behind the Penhaligon archers. Though many of the beastmen were cut off from the rest of their forces by the horses and men of the lancers, they continued to fight to the last.

"They're fanatical!" Jo shouted to Sir Domerikos.

"Naturally! They are animals!"

Jo attempted to shout a reply of her own, but her words were cut off as a number of swordsmen were torn apart by a gang of lion-headed beastmen. They leaped over the bodies, ignoring spear thrust and shield bash, and headed straight toward Sir Domerikos.

The knight brandished his sword and braced himself behind his large shield. The first beastman threw itself forward, striking the shield and bowling the knight over. Jo moved to help him, but she was forced aside as four more of the creatures followed in the path of the first.

Jo swung Peace in a double-handed arc, cutting off a beastman's head. The blade came back for a return stroke that hacked off the arm of another as it came barreling forward. Jo staggered but thought with satisfaction that she would never have been able to strike such blows with Wyrmblight.

None of the spearmen could offer aid against the lion-headed beastmen because the spearmen were busy battling wolf-heads. Jo lunged forward and stabbed another beastman through the chest.

Sir Domerikos hid beneath his shield and turned his face away from the fanged jaws of the creature that had knocked him down. Jo withdrew her shining blade from the chest of the beastman and jumped to Domerikos's aid as he rolled out from under his shield and leaped to his feet.

A lion-head roared, and Jo prepared another side swing. With a final swipe of its paws, it dodged to the side and raced off across the hillock. Jo started to give chase.

"Wait!" Domerikos yelled with confusion, grabbing her by the arm. "It's obviously not going to attack the command."

The knight was correct. The lion-head rushed off around the side of the hillock, ignoring the plight of the other beastmen.

Domerikos faced Jo and said, "I don't understand. I've fought these creatures before. Why didn't it stay and fight?"

"That's what I've been trying to tell you!" Jo replied, looking around to make sure that another gang of beastmen didn't suddenly break through the lines. "They're moving in a straight line away from something, like they're frightened."

"What could possibly frighten a beastman?"

The remaining beastmen rushed forward as a single body, howling and screaming, pawing to get over each other and over the lines of the Penhaligon soldiers. The creatures no longer attempted to fight the men, but allowed themselves to be cut and stabbed, creating a rampart of bodies among the human troops. Jo backed away from the carnage. Her heart beat hard, and her blood ran cold. She mechanically raised Peace to defend herself and began the drills that Braddoc had taught her with Wyrmblight, applying them against the hapless beastmen. She killed three within one minute, then ten more, finding an odd solace in putting these creatures out of their fear-fed misery.

The Black Eagle Lancers were finally able to attack the flanks and rear of the beastman force. They struck hard and fast, causing and taking huge casualties. While catching her breath, Jo saw Sir Barethmor crush a beastman's head with his black warhammer, moving on to the next target with the efficiency of a butcher.

Jo lost track of time. Peace was a silver bolt in her hand, lightning to strike down the enemy no matter how fast they came. She was not harmed by a single blow; no claw or tooth came near her flesh. Blood from the beastmen covered her hands and spattered her face, but her tabard and armor were clean as the day she took them from the wooden chest. Peace was not nicked by a single parried attack.

As the bodies mounded up around her, Jo slowly realized what had to be causing the beastmen's panic. She felt a great despair and dread, not for herself, but for the men and women around her. It was the same evil Peace had been forged to fight, the same evil for which Jo herself had been reforged in Vulcan's fires.

The last of the beastmen died, screaming on the end of a broken lance. Sir Domerikos was covered in blood and wounds, and his shield was so scored with claw marks that the beautiful heraldry was ruined. He breathed heavily and wiped the back of his hand across his face, wincing as he accidentally touched his broken nose.

"We've won," he said, trying to catch his breath.

Jo shook her head. She was tired and full of despair; she wanted to cry. She clutched Peace in both her hands and choked back a sob.

"No," she replied leadenly, pointing in the beastmen's original direction. "We have lost."

The sky was as gray as a stormy ocean, and a strong wind pushed the air in odd directions. Jo smelled something like spices, pungent and intrusive, on the wind. Sir Domerikos's eyes followed her gesture, then he staggered backward.

Black figures marched over the ridge line. Shaped like humans, the creatures were limned by a dark, shimmering halo and seemed to steal the light around them. Their rigid ranks and the discipline of their advance made the forces of Penhaligon seem like boys playing as soldiers. The abelaats were ranked in regiments like the forces of Penhaligon, though their formations were tighter and their numbers smaller. They carried armaments like those of the knights—lances, swords, hammers, flails—except that the weapons all seemed to be extensions of the bodies of the warriors themselves. Shimmering halos surrounded the depthless blackness of the blades.

"Are these the creatures of which you spoke?" Sir Domerikos whispered.

Jo nodded and hugged Peace to herself. "Yes. Those are the abelaats, finally come to Mystara."

The abelaats maintained their position at the other end of the clearing; their force created a wall of darkness. An eerie and dread-filled silence gripped the ranks of humans.

Sir Domerikos quickly recovered his composure. "They're just another foe," he said flatly to Jo. Jo looked to the man and saw that his face was expressionless. She admired him all the more for his futile courage and nonchalance.

The soldiers around her muttered their doubt to each other. A few whispered of leaving the field and routing back to the Castle of the Three Suns, but the older soldiers were quick to silence any such talk. The slightest hint of unrest among the ranks could easily spread. Hearing the murmurs, Sir Domerikos summoned the regimental captain of the spearmen and commanded him to rally his men and reform ranks with the other regiments.

Jo straightened her shoulders and walked to his side.

"But, sir," the captain pleaded quietly, glancing around him to make sure that none of the other soldiers would hear. "Who knows what those things can do?"

"What does it matter, man?" Domerikos demanded. "When we took to the field, we knew we'd have to fight them sooner or later."

"But we were to be in a defensive position. Here we're out in the open."

Sir Domerikos pointed back over his shoulder and said, "Then we'll wait here until they attack. Take two men from every regiment and scout the terrain to make sure we're not being flanked. Have them report back to me within the hour."

The captain pursed his lips and wiped his hand across his face. He was about to give his reply when one of his sergeants came rushing forward.

"What is it?" Domerikos spat.

The sergeant's reply was terse. "We've got about half our men back in fighting form, sir. Everyone else is either dead or wounded."

"And the archers?"

"Expended most of their supply in the first three volleys."

"How many infantry are dead and how many are wounded?" Sir Domerikos asked.

"About forty dead, sixty wounded, sir."

Domerikos shifted his gaze between his two subordinates, then said, "Reform the wounded back into the ranks."

The sergeant's face was expressionless. "Yes, sir," he answered. Without another word, he turned on his heel and headed toward the back of the formation, shouting orders to regroup.

Jo looked back to the abelaats, who continued to wait on the hill. The scent of spice she had noticed earlier was much stronger now, and the wind continued its irregular shifting. The abelaat bite wound in her shoulder, long since healed, began to throb at the memory of her first encounter with these beasts.

The creatures on the hill were nothing like the one Jo had encountered, however. These monsters seemed to consist more of dark magic than of flesh and bone, and their black halos seemed to draw life out of the air around them. Jo wondered if the abelaats were draining the world's magic even as they stood there, the power making the air flicker and dance like a mirage in the desert.

Domerikos was saying something about bringing the cavalry together on the left flank as he handed a note to a breathless squire.

"Do I have to ask the lancers for scouts as well, sir?" the captain inquired. Jo could tell from the sound of his voice that the prospect of speaking with the cavalry from the Black Eagle Barony did not seem like a pleasant idea.

Domerikos shook his head and made a sweeping motion with his hand. "No. Pull the men back and give them as much time to rest as possible. And make sure the bodies of the beastmen are removed, or we'll be fighting for footing as well as for our lives."

"Sir," Jo said, stepping forward. "Should we send word back to the baroness that the abelaats have come this far?"

"An excellent idea, Squire Menhir," the knight replied. He pointed to the top of the hill and said to her, "Send Commander Chilatra. His wounds won't prevent him from riding."

Jo ran up the hill, passing numerous squires and heralds on their way up and down the slope. She noticed that some of them looked at her with adoration; she also saw that they all looked at Peace with a sense of hope.

The commanders on the hill were heatedly speaking of something, and Jo caught the name "Domerikos" as she approached. The moment she arrived, they all fell silent and began scanning the battlefield.

"Excuse me, sirs," Jo began, catching the eye of each

commander. "I am here to inform you that Commander Chilatra is to return to Penhaligon with word of the abelaats' penetration into this region."

The leaders all regarded her coldly, but Jo was not going to be intimidated.

"You may tell Sir Domerikos that Commander Chilatra has already taken it upon himself to inform the baroness of—certain matters pertaining to this conflict," Commander Montesey stated harshly.

"May I say how long ago he left?"

Montesey turned away from Jo and said, "No."

The other commanders turned as well. Jo felt the cold on the hillock increase. With a shrug, she made her way back to Sir Domerikos, seeing that the troops had already been formed back into their lines. The wounded filled the back ranks, while those still reasonably fresh were placed at the front. Those with minor wounds were doing their best to remove the corpses of the beastmen, an unpleasant task. She smelled the spice of the abelaats over the scent of the dead bodies.

Sir Domerikos turned from another of the regimental commanders and asked, "Did you dispatch Chilatra?"

"I'm afraid that he probably left some time ago," Jo replied.

The knight nodded and smiled grimly. "I've no doubt that the 'truth' of my reckless abandon on the field of battle will soon be told in the Penhaligon council."

Jo nodded in return. She looked over Sir Domerikos's armor and saw that some of the links needed minor repair. The shield he continued to clutch needed its strap reaffixed to the backside. Without asking, she took the shield from his hand and attempted to slide the strap back into its holding socket.

"There's no time for that, Squire," Domerikos said, taking back the shield. "I need you to do something important for me."

Jo was confused. "Yes, sir?"

"Walk among the soldiers. You don't have to say anything, just make sure they can see that sword," he said, pointing to Peace.

Nodding, she softly replied, "Yes, sir."

"And move! There's not much time! The scouts are already returning."

Jo straightened her shoulders and nodded again. The first of the scouts rushed up to Sir Domerikos and informed him that there was nothing to the east that he had seen. Jo left before she heard Domerikos's reply.

She decided not to walk among the commanders and troops at the front ranks, figuring she would be more a distraction than an inspiration to them. Instead, she circulated mostly among the wounded in the back of the formations. Their bandages—torn from clothes, packs, and banners—were soaked with blood. Jo remembered the excruciating pain from the mountain dog's fangs and felt sympathy for those who had been injured by the claws and teeth of the beastmen.

Jo held Peace lightly in the 'shoulder arms' position as she walked. With each step she took, the blade rang softly against the elven shoulder guard beneath it. The wounded looked up at her and her sword with the shine of hope in their eyes, the same look that Flinn and Wyrmblight had evinced many years before.

Jo had reached the end of the line, and she started to double back. Just then, the wind shifted strongly again. With dread, she turned to face the ridge line where the abelaats had stood. They were advancing now, silent and black. The heralds' horns blared the defense and the warriors picked up their weapons and assumed positions. Jo started to run back across the field to where she had left Sir Domerikos, noticing that the marching lines of the otherworldly creatures were tighter than the Penhaligon lines had been even when fresh.

A herald blew another horn, and the Black Eagle Lancers charged downfield beside the Penhaligon knights. The abelaats had crossed half the distance to the knights in an impossibly short time, but Jo still could not make out their appearance. She slowed her steps to watch the clash of arms and heard another horn sound, a horn that sent the remaining infantry forward.

Now Jo could clearly see that the weapons of the abelaats were extensions of their bodies, made of their dark flesh. The black halos along the shafts of spears and down the lengths of swords seemed hungry for life.

Jo watched with horror as the cavalry was cut down before it contacted the enemy, abelaat throwing darts penetrating armor with ease. Before the remaining knights could react, the abelaats' second line struck out with black halberds and short spears.

The heralds blew their trumpets again, and the infantry charged forward with a shout. The last vestiges of the cavalry disengaged moments before the infantry struck. Jo was astounded that the soldiers of Penhaligon had the fortitude to continue the attack when they saw what had happened to their heaviest troops. She yelled her anger and her inspiration, adding her voice to theirs. Picking up her pace, Jo ran to the front rank, forcing herself to ignore the overpowering scent of spice and the cold of the black halos. She struck downward with Peace in a two-handed attack, cutting the first abelaat in half. The creature disintegrated into a pool of darkness on the ground as she brought her sword up on the backswing, pivoting on her right leg for power and balance.

Jo removed the head of the next abelaat, seeing in her battle fury that these creatures looked in features and form much like the twisted abelaat that had bitten her shoulder, though these were more the size of a normal man. Wielding Peace in one hand, Jo hacked through the haft of a magical spear, which sparked and dissolved away into the body of its bearer. As she brought the blade of Peace up into the throat of the inhuman enemy, Jo forced all thoughts but hatred, vengeance, and fury aside. The scent of spice filled her lungs and nearly made her gag, the unnatural wind shifting directions. Peace struck out ceaselessly, killing with every blow. Not a single abelaat escaped with a mere wound; Jo wielded death.

Her enmity guided her deep into the ranks of the enemy, and her own shouts of rage and fear rang deafeningly in her ears. She consequently didn't notice that the retreat had been sounded until she was completely alone, swinging Peace in the midst of the abelaat hordes. They continued to die on all sides of her, taking no action to stop her.

Panting, Jo halted her berserker attack and stared at the

ground around her. The abelaats she had slain had fallen to black dust in an ashy circle. Beyond, the dead troops of Penhaligon littered the field, their blood flowing into the ground. Jo's emotions raged uncontrollably; her need to kill was matched by her sorrow for the dead Penhaligon troops. This regiment from the Castle of the Three Suns had been nearly wiped out.

The living abelaats formed black walls around Jo. She continued to breathe hard, wondering why they didn't attack her. The abelaats' true forms were almost completely hidden by their dark halos of magic, and Jo only caught occasional glimpses of a face—or something she took to be a face. They did not speak to one another, or signal, or gesture. Only those in the front ranks continued to battle, continued to press forward in their tight lines. The rest of the creatures stood over the wounded knights. Jo turned away before they sank their fangs into the bodies as they had once sunk their fangs into her, and into Dayin.

Peace still felt light in her hands. Jo heard herself cry, though she could not feel the tears on her face. She squeezed hard on the hilt and felt the blood flow from her hand again. The wound from the stag's antlers had reopened, torn in the heat of battle. Her vision slowly dimmed.

Jo stood inside a column of light, stood before a young man—handsome, pale, familiar—hovering asleep in the air. His arms were down at his side, palms out. His right leg was crossed over his left, bent at the knee. She could not reach out to touch him, to wake him.

He was incredibly beautiful.

The light flowed around her as if she stood in a waterfall, but the light raged upward and out to some unknown place. Jo felt a great presence nearby, directing the light, guiding the waterfall. The presence also kept the young man's eyes closed.

Jo was determined to wake him. She pushed forward against the strength of the light, against the power of the presence. She moved slowly, maintaining her motion through force of will.

Suddenly, Jo could not feel her body. She reached out with a numb hand.

The man's eyes opened. Jo stared into pale depths, as bright and cold and lovely as the light that surrounded them both. He had nothing in his eyes but the light, and Jo was afraid that he was dead. She could feel his power, and the power of the other presence, the one guiding the waterfall.

The young man opened his mouth to speak, but was forced back to silence. In fear she pulled back, withdrew into her own body and her own self. A single name rose in her thoughts.

Dayin.

Jo's vision cleared, and she heard a snuffling sound behind her. She barely rolled out of the way before an abelaat stumbled into the space where she had been. The air grew increasingly chill as the creature came near; Jo held her breath and tried not to move any farther.

The abelaat pivoted its head away from Jo, then turned back. Its shadowy eyes were humanlike, but large and pupilless, fixing Jo where she had fallen. She fought down her panic as the thing continued to stare directly into her face. She tensed, ready to strike with Peace.

Sniffing the air again, the abelaat turned away and shuffled back to its place among its reforming ranks. Some of the other abelaats ceased their feeding and moved to do the same. Jo rose to her feet and was forced to step out of the way several times to avoid detection.

She gritted her teeth and watched and waited. The impulse to flee shouted through her mind, but she remained still. "Diulanna," she murmured, more in way of comfort than of prayer. "Diulanna. Please, give me guidance."

Jo realized she had not relaxed her grip on Peace since the vision of Dayin. She found she could not relax her hands, her emotions locking her fingers and forcing more hot tears from her eyes. The sight of the abelaats all around her was paralyzing.

"Help me. Anything you ask, any task, I'll do it." Jo's need for comfort was quickly giving way to abject fear. "I choose you, Diulanna. I'll be your hero."

"I do not need the broken, Johauna Menhir," a woman's voice whispered in Jo's ear. "Heroes choose my way because they are heroes."

"What am I to do?" Jo murmured. She blinked hard to remove the tears. She knew she spoke with Diulanna, the Immortal Diulanna, Patroness of Will. And yet she felt no fear of her.

"You have been chosen to defend this world. Defend!"

Jo turned about, finding she was suddenly alone. She took a deep breath and wiped her hand across her eyes and face. Jo stared at the ground for a moment, thinking of the path she had chosen, wondering if Flinn had made

the same choice. She felt no need to show ritual reverence to Diulanna now; giving thanks through action
seemed best.

Jo quickly backed away, finding the trail of hoofprints
left by the retreating cavalry. Her only thought was to kill
Teryl Auroch and end the madness.

Chapter X

raybow stood on the cracked ridge of a mountain and looked sullenly at the blasted plain. His skin felt cold, and the oily air clung to his flesh and peeled the remaining heat away from his body. Not even the heavy riding cloak, worn with leagues of travel, nor his most comfortable boots and garments could ward off the chill.

The sky was nearly dark, clouds continuing to choke the light from the sun. Graybow vainly attempted to peer through the haze to find the star of the north.

The ground beneath Graybow's feet felt like pumice, as though the soil had suffered an irreversible shock. The rock, though it appeared solid, crumbled easily, giving way to yellowed sediment and little green stones. A strange odor accompanied the dirt, something like a cross between a butcher's shop and a smithy, blood and iron and sweat, and perhaps a little pain. The scents reminded Graybow of times when he was a young man, learning knighthood in Darokin, his homeland. But the scents did not bring back memories of pleasant things, only of hard times and unhappiness.

Graybow recalled a favorite poem by Marmerand. It described the mountains as "pure and taintless, rising from plains of strife, stairways to the sun and stars. Here do men and women come, here to converse with immortals, here to know themselves and learn of wisdom." As Graybow disdainfully crushed a rock with his foot and peered up at the dark sky, he realized that this region of Mystara was now rotted with evil: nothing could purge the land. That was the only wisdom left for this place.

Despite the lack of light, Graybow had been able to spot the castle in the distance. The black, silver-veined stones used to build the castle had been quarried from the earth long ago. The devastation there could be only worse than it was here.

Turning, the castellan looked back to his little entourage. He had brought four of his favorite knights with him, and they all seemed to be ignoring the cold admirably. He wondered if his age were making him soft.

Sir Nigelle, the youngest knight, waved. "I see nothing but desolation, sir," the man said in a strong voice. Graybow had brought Nigelle for his keen eyes. If the knight saw nothing, the castellan guessed there was little to see.

Graybow nodded, turning back to face the castle. Each tower of the castle had a gate house with a black portcullis, but only the front gate was raised. The high wall surrounding the inner courtyards was filled with arrow slits.

The entrances had murder-holes where incendiaries could be dropped onto anyone who managed to raise the heavy iron gates. Nothing had stopped the abelaats.

Graybow pulled out a small journal and a stylus from beneath his riding cape and began to write:

Councilman Melios and his family must be dead. There is no life in this forsaken place. The abelaats have destroyed it all. The monsters have reached our very doorstep and yet we still know nothing of their tactics, their powers, their strengths or weaknesses. Before this day is through, I intend to address this want.

Graybow's stomach tightened in anger, and bile burned his throat. Despite their long-standing differences, Graybow still would not have condemned Melios to this sort of end. Whether or not he was implicated in the attempt on Jo's life, the man had been a noble of Penhaligon, and the barony's armies should have been here to prevent this disaster.

Graybow blinked hard to remove the burning sensation from his eyes; the oily substance in the chill air was irritating. He considered taking a sample of the earth back to the Castle of the Three Suns so the incompetent magicians could see the damage of the abelaats and devise some plan of defense, but he shivered at the thought of touching the green and yellow dirt. Stinging tears rolled down his face and fell to the corrupted ground, sinking through the soil.

"Water," he murmured to himself, as he noted the conspicuous holes where his tears had fallen. He scribbled a marginal note in his book. If the corrupted ground was so affected by water, perhaps the abelaats would be likewise affected. "Or, perhaps salt water." He decided in that moment to double the siege kettles on the wall and add salt to the solution. It was only a hunch, a guess, and probably a futile one; but guesses and hunches were all they had against this foe.

Graybow placed the journal back under his belt, and the heat trapped under his cloak escaped.

The castellan clenched his fist tightly around the hilt of his heirloom sword, a golden weapon called Sage. The sword was said to inspire men to battle when wielded by a man of character. Graybow thought about the cold air and his age, sighing. Sage's inspiration had best work through him in the coming days, or Penhaligon would surely fall.

Graybow stared down across the ridge to the land below, then back down to the ground at his feet, where his tears had left holes in the earth. Despite his repulsion for the stuff, he scooped a bit of the ruined soil into a drawstring bag and fastened it to his belt. Stepping closer to the edge of the ridge, Graybow felt the rock give way beneath his feet. He scrambled backward.

"Are you all right, sir?" Oertropolis, the oldest knight, asked.

Graybow lifted a hand in confirmation, edging his way more cautiously to the edge of the ridge. He looked down over its edge to reassure himself that the slope would be gentle enough for him to scale. He could not see any tracks of animals or siege engines, and he hadn't found any on the trip from the castle. How the abelaats had destroyed Melios's estates was yet a mystery, as were the dark creatures of magic themselves.

He turned and said to the knights, "I'm going to the castle. Wait here for me."

"I'm sorry, sir, we can't let you do that," one of the knights replied. His twin said, "We're here to protect you. You don't know what danger—"

Graybow peered skeptically at the knights and said, "Thank you both, Byron and Lyraan. I'm sure your family would be proud, but I think there is little danger, as Nigelle has already made clear."

The twins glanced at each other and crossed their arms over their chests, determination on their hard faces. Graybow knew he was in for a fight if he were to argue with the two noble knights, both direct cousins of the noble Hyraksos family in Karameikos.

"The baroness wants a report as quickly as possible," Byron stated.

"The journey has already taken two days," Lyraan added. "We should be quick."

"Very well," Graybow sighed, waving them down the slope; he did not have the strength or desire to argue. The two knights smiled at one another and nodded in satisfaction as they mounted their horses. "Lead your horses," the castellan added. "The ground on this slope is soft. I want you other two to keep watch. I'll leave my mount with you; I don't want to be encumbered, and two horses will bear us out in a pinch."

"Are we expecting any assistance from this direction, sir?" Nigelle inquired, removing his helm. Its white plume whipped in the wind.

Graybow arched an eyebrow and gestured toward the field and castle. "In this matter, or from the other kingdoms in the war?"

"The other kingdoms, sir."

There were a number of kingdoms that lay beyond the land of Melios's estates that could respond to the Grand Marshaling, but Graybow doubted word would reach them in time. "There is a great deal of fighting among the nobles in this region, Sir Nigelle. Don't bother looking for them to come riding to our aid."

The young knight nodded and placed his helmet on the horn of his saddle. The horse attempted to back away, but Nigelle held tightly to its reins and forced it to keep still. He reached into his saddlebag and pulled out a carrot, but the horse was too frightened by the smell of the ground to eat.

"If you see anything, yell. We should be able to hear you in this silence, even if we're in the castle," Graybow said. He stepped over the edge without waiting for Nigelle or Oertropolis to reply. His feet slid on the loose dirt and rocks, sending up a shower of foul dust; he put his hand over his nose and mouth to block the stench. He fell faster down the slope, keeping his right leg bent and higher than his left to control his slide. He would have preferred to have one of the knights tie a rope to one of the horses, but he did not trust the animals to keep still.

After a few moments, Graybow gracefully reached the bottom of the slope, glancing behind him as the two knights led their uneasy mounts down. Sir Byron's mount stumbled and nearly fell over, but the horse quickly recovered.

Graybow saw that the slope was much longer than he had first imagined, and much higher. His passage had left a long, deep gouge in the loose earth. The dirt on the level ground was more firm than the ridge's, but the little green stones were everywhere, and the smell of sweat and blood was even more pervasive. The oily cold continued to cling to his flesh. He had hoped that the difference in elevation would have reduced the cold.

Once the others had joined him, Graybow started out over the empty fields leading to the black keep. They moved along without speaking, looking and listening for signs of life from the castle. At one point, they thought they heard something like a hammer against an anvil, like a sound Graybow remembered from a Darokin training ground. But the wind picked up and stole the sound from their ears, leaving nothing but an unpleasant howling that made them stiffen.

Graybow moved forward on foot, and the twins led their horses at a walk a short pace behind. The castellan knew they would keep two paces behind and a pace to either side, as was called for in the rules of knighthood. These disciplines, though sometimes an exacting annoyance, provided a certain comfort and familiarity as they crossed the ruined plain.

Graybow looked down at the deep impressions his feet left in the earth. He remembered from a previous journey that Melios's estates had had some of the most fertile land in all of Penhaligon. Not now. He shivered, glad that his heavy boots kept his bare feet well protected from the poisoned dirt.

Both horses whinnied loudly and Graybow stopped,

wondering if the twins were having too much trouble
with the mounts. He was about to send them back, but
they both smiled, assuring their leader they were fine.
Graybow nodded sternly and peered back up the slope
where the other two knights waited. They stood where
they had been left.

As they neared the castle, Graybow got a better look at
its defenses. Sections of the keep had apparently been
built at different times in its history, as if carpenters and
masons had been ordered to add makeshift constructions
to the original walls. At least one of the towers had been
reconstructed, using little more than dirt to fill a huge
breach in its wall.

The castle walls were so black that Graybow had difficulty telling where one stone ended and another began.
The silver veins lining the walls created a never-ending
tracery around the structure. The high walls were guarded
by five small turrets, evenly spaced across the veined surface. Within the walls rose the three towers of the inner
courtyard.

The castellan crossed his arms and stood in thought.
The councilman's castle had originally been constructed
of the same stone as the Castle of the Three Suns.

"What's made it so black?" Lyraan asked his brother.

"Quiet."

Graybow turned and regarded the twins. "It seems that
the abelaats are more a mystery than was described by
Squire Menhir," he said. "This is not what happened to
Armstead."

Sir Byron nodded and said, "It's like they drained all
the life from the place and left it rotting."

Graybow considered the man's words, then asked, "And you think that the abelaats have drained the 'life' from the castle walls as well?"

Byron's eyes grew wide with embarrassment, and he smartly bowed his head. "I'm sorry, sir. I realize what I said—"

"Was a brilliant piece of insight, Sir Byron," Graybow interrupted. "I don't doubt that you are correct."

The knight kept his face blank, but Graybow saw relief in the young man's eyes.

Graybow turned back to face the castle and walked through the open portcullis of the front gate house. He glanced critically toward the ceiling of the structure, finding the gate's murder-hole. It had clearly proven ineffective in this assault.

The road leading from the gate house went directly through the courtyard, merging with the roads from the other gate houses at a crossroad, which led to the entrance of the middle tower. The inner courtyard of the castle was dark and bare, dominated by the three inner towers. Fresh earth had been used to fill a breach in one of the tower walls, the only soil not ruined by the draining power of the beasts.

Graybow walked out onto the road, his boots drumming loudly against the hard stone. He was glad to step off the rotted earth and onto a more solid surface. With a vague gesture of his hand, Graybow motioned for the twins to follow.

The horses whinnied loudly, followed by the clatter of their hind hooves, shifting on the stones as they reared. Graybow ducked to the right, a reaction he had learned early in his training. Spinning about, he saw that the knights were struggling to keep the animals from breaking loose, and only just succeeding. The white-eyed fright in the beasts' eyes showed that they had no interest in entering the keep.

"You can't afford to tie them and leave them," the castellan said. "Take them back a few paces. I'll return in a short while."

"Sir," Lyraan began, his brother attempting to step closer. The horses continued to buck.

"Do as I say. There's no danger in this place." The knights bowed their heads and retreated, pulling their mounts with them. Graybow watched for a moment before he returned to the courtyard, thinking again about Sir Byron's observation about the life having been drained. The castellan found the thought even more chilling now because there was not a single body to be found.

Graybow moved toward the main tower. He approached with caution, putting his hand on the hilt of Sage. He did not like to draw weapons until necessary, and especially did not want to hold a magic weapon without direct cause. The great door to the tower stood ajar, as if something had once battered it open from the inside, trying to get out.

Edging his way inside, Graybow listened for any sounds of movement, either from survivors of the siege or from the shifting of loose stones and timbers. The entrance chamber was huge and black, unlit except by the gray light laboring in through small windows. All of the upper floors to the tower had fallen to the level where he stood, and not a single upward staircase had survived.

The cold made the broken tower feel even more inhospitable. Graybow raised his cloak's collar and leaned against the entrance's frame. The abelaats had decimated Melios's estate but, as of yet, had not left a trace of how they accomplished the task. The castellan peered into the gloom, but saw no sign of siege equipment, no footprints, not even a broken arrow.

Graybow sighed loudly, bending and sitting on the cracked tile floor. He had hoped to find evidence of some definitive weakness for the abelaats, but as of yet was armed only with guesses about water and salt, about tears. Running his hands through his long gray hair, he hoped that the Grand Marshaling of Forces and the Castle of the Three Suns's remaining sorcerous defenses would provide the strength needed to repel the invaders.

"Sir!"

Graybow pushed himself up and turned. Sir Lyraan was waving from the remains of the castle gate, pointing up to the crenelated curtain wall. His brother was a short distance away with the horses.

"What is it?" the castellan returned, walking back toward the knight.

"I think we've found something!"

"I'll be grateful for that," Graybow mumbled as he crossed the courtyard. He studied the remains of the castle again for some clue as to the strength of the abelaat army. He had the nagging feeling there was something he should remember about warfare, an early lesson from one of his studies that he had not considered for quite some time.

Just outside the gate, Lyraan continued to peer up at the wall, squinting his clear blue eyes. Graybow was slightly relieved to see that the young knight's eyes watered as well; he felt a little less old.

"What do you see?" the castellan asked, looking up to where the man stared.

Lyraan pointed to a spot near the top of the wall.

"There! Do you see them?"

"See what?"

The knight shook his finger at the spot and said, "There! Those marks! Those look like the marks of a siege ladder."

Graybow doubted that creatures of magic would use something as mundane as a siege ladder to scale a wall. He sighed loudly and crossed his arms over his chest in disappointment. He was about to voice his opinion when the nagging sensation returned. He peered up.

The strange black stone of the walls had two indents at the correct point for a ladder. Graybow blinked hard to remove the tears caused by the stink and the cold. He checked the spot again, shaking his head.

"I can't quite tell what that is," he said, squinting.

"But I could be correct," Lyraan said rhetorically.

Graybow shrugged and walked up next to the wall. He rapped the stones with his knuckles, purposefully avoiding the unnatural-looking silver veins. The stone was cold and hard, and despite its appearance, seemed to be nothing more than stone. If the wall had been made of some other substance, or had crumbled at his touch, Graybow thought he might have found another clue to help him defend the castle in the upcoming battle.

He breathed deeply, closing his eyes. The smell from the ground was powerful and continued to evoke the

images of smithies and slaughterhouses. There was no
smell of plant or dirt, or any of the other familiar castle
scents. The castellan shook his head in confusion and
pulled out his journal again. One of the first lessons of
investigation he had been taught was to list the information at hand and worry about conclusions later. He began
to scribble with his stylus.

"What do you think, sir?" Lyraan asked.

"I don't know what to think, Sir Lyraan," Graybow
replied as he finished his entry and put the journal back.
"Did you find any other marks like this one?"

The knight shook his head. "No, sir. I happened to be
looking at the sky when I found those."

"Should we bring Sirs Oertropolis and Nigelle down
for their opinion?" Sir Byron asked, hands tight on the
reins of both horses.

The other two knights were dutifully keeping their
vigil at the top of the slope.

After a moment's consideration, Graybow said, "I think
it would be best for them to maintain their position. We
need to be alerted of any approaching force, and deviating
from plans already in motion is rarely wise."

Sir Lyraan nodded once and returned to his mount,
taking the reins from his brother. Graybow heard the two
quietly confer, but could not hear what they said over the
whinnying of the horses. He glanced at the walls again
and had difficulty finding the scrape marks in the poor
light. He still could not understand what significance the
marks might hold, but the very fact that they existed, and
where they had been found, was enough to make him
interested.

"I'm going to the top of the wall," he said without turning. "I might be able to find out more there."

Sir Byron handed his twin the reins and pulled the footman's mace from his saddle. "Allow me to accompany you, sir." he began. "Perhaps the two of us can—"

Graybow held up his hand for silence and smiled to himself. "There is no need to convince me of the worth of two sets of eyes, Byron," he replied. To himself he thought that there were definitely times when those of noble blood acted like anxious children.

As he walked back through the gate, Graybow peered up into the mechanisms of the portcullis. There was not enough light to see any detail, but he guessed that the ropes and cables tied to the raising winch would be rotted like those of the catapults. He made a note to investigate to see if the gate had been lowered, then forced back up and jammed, as was sometimes the case during a siege.

Sir Byron coughed into his gauntlet and shifted his long-hafted mace from hand to hand. Graybow halted and, without turning, focused his attention on the young man. The knight stopped as well, his mail clattering as he shifted from foot to foot.

The castellan craned his head as if to look about the castle grounds, but was actually giving himself time to think. Graybow realized that Byron was nervous, though the nobleman was doing his best to suppress his fear. The desolation, darkness, and very smell of the place must be taking a toll on their fortitude. They had entered with a mission, but had little to keep their minds occupied.

"Sir Byron, tell Sir Lyraan to lash the horses's reins to something and join us," Graybow said without moving.

He added, "Tell him to bring the Book and the Banner."

The castellan waited for his young charges to return. They wasted no time, tying the horses to a hitching post outside the walls despite the animals' protests. They both ran back to their commander a few moments later. Lyraan held a short horseman's spear.

"We're ready, sir," Byron said. "I've brought rope and spikes as well."

"Good," Graybow returned in approval. He was now acutely aware of the need to bolster his men's confidence, both for the mission at hand and for the battle to come. If they were shaken by the appearance of the castle after the siege, they would certainly not react well to the sight of the abelaats. Graybow was not so sure that he himself would react well to his first vision of the abelaat legions. The castellan held tightly to the hilt of Sage and berated himself for his doubt, thinking of the other battles he had witnessed. Nobody, not even the baroness, knew of his time spent in the swamps of Karameikos fighting the undead. He had yet to see a foe more horrible than that; he still could not talk of it.

Graybow led the knights into the courtyard, attempting to find the way up to the battlements. The temporary stairs normally found near the walls were missing, and the permanent stairs had either crumbled or been smashed.

"We seem to have a problem," he said.

Sir Lyraan pointed toward the repaired tower. "Why don't we climb the dirt rampart on that side tower? It seems to be a short jump between the tower and the wall."

"Excellent idea," the castellan replied, heading for the tower. He watched for any clues he might have missed in his earlier walk through the courtyard, but there didn't seem to be anything to find. The knights were doing their best to help, but their nervousness distracted them.

The dirt slope rose to the center of the tower, which Graybow estimated was about fifty feet high. He had no idea where the defenders had found the dirt to fill the huge breach; there seemed to be no sign of excavation in any part of the castle. Attackers sometimes used ramparts of dirt to scale walls, but that tactic was more common among the less sophisticated nations far to the north of Penhaligon. Graybow doubted that the abelaats had used dirt to enter the tower, figuring that a siege engine missile had smashed the wall and Melios's sappers were given the order to shore the breach. If this were the case, the abelaats must have fired this missile long before the initial assault, since the sappers obviously had enough time to construct the slope.

"I suggest you let me investigate first," Sir Byron said, dropping his shoulder bag full of climbing spikes to the ground. He hefted his long mace in both hands and began scaling the slope.

"You have not been given the order to proceed," the castellan said curtly. He was not angry at the young man, but it was obvious that fear was creating false enthusiasm. "For the moment, control and discipline are more important than climbing the rampart. We must keep our heads."

The knight stepped down from the dirt and stood before Graybow, ready for an upbraiding. The castellan sighed and smiled, thinking that some knights were too ready to accept punishment for their often-minute infractions.

"I am curious about this rampart's creation, but I am even more curious about the origin of the dirt," Graybow said as he stepped around the immobile knight. He dropped to one knee and inspected the slope. He was struck by a realization.

"Do you see this dirt?" he asked, scooping out a handful. "At ease, and take a look!"

Sir Byron dropped his stance and turned, his shoulders dropping in relief as he inspected the dirt in Graybow's hand. The castellan motioned for the other knight to look as well.

"This dirt is not the same as this," Graybow added, pointing to the rotted ground. "It's fresh—alive."

Lyraan shook his head and stood up. "What does it mean?"

Graybow thought back to Jo's description of the abelaats. She said that they had returned to Mystara to regain the magic they had lost, which included the magic that resided in every living thing. "It seems," he said, slowly drawing his conclusion, "that your observation was a good one. The life's not only been drawn out of the people who defended the structure, but from the very stones and earth of it as well. Even so, we have a pile of dirt that escaped the draining effects—"

"Or the dirt was dug up after these abelaats 'killed' the land," Sir Lyraan offered. He added, "Sir."

Graybow stood and nodded, saying, "That seems a much more likely conclusion. And I'd wager that the dirt was either taken from within the tower or was dug up from beneath this ruined soil."

"So we have one of two conclusions. If the dirt came

from within the tower, the tower walls were able to stop the abelaats' power from destroying the dirt. If, on the other hand, the dirt came from beneath the ruined soil, the top soil itself had let the draining effect penetrate only so far," Byron noted.

It was Lyraan's turn: "So if we want to protect certain persons, such as the baroness, from the draining powers of the abelaats, we should house them in thick-walled structures or beneath the ground."

Graybow nodded again, already writing in his log.

Once finished, he studied the rim of the hole that the rampart was supposed to seal. There were no scorch marks or clean blasts through the stone, as might be found in a battle where sorcery was present. He said, "These abelaats are confounding. They are creatures of magic, yet seem to use mundane weapons." Dropping the dirt on the ground, he added the new information to his journal. He knew now that the findings of this expedition, mean though they were, would be worth a legion of men.

"Let's go," he said, replacing the book. "We've no more time to lose."

The castellan mounted the sloping rampart and motioned for the others to join him. Byron picked up his pack and slung it over his shoulder, maintaining his grip on the mace. Lyraan adjusted the coils of rope in his backpack and stepped onto the rampart, using his horseman's spear as a walking stick.

The slope's dirt was well packed, though Graybow could not see any footprints or marks that would suggest logs or other methods had been used to flatten the surface. If his guess had been correct, the floor of the tower would be torn up, the planking and stone used as support for the ramp. He imagined that the hole in the bottom of the tower would be vast; the amount of earth required to make a rampart so large would have gotten down to the foundation. The fear of the occupants must have been extreme to inspire them to dig up, set, and pack enough earth to fill the massive breach in the wall. And all during escalade.

Clearly, the occupants wanted to keep the creatures out of this particular tower at all costs. He was sure that the sappers could have been sent on a more useful task than repairing a tower whose breach faced the courtyard. The structure must have housed something or someone that was both very precious and very immobile.

The castellan stopped and turned. A breach facing the inside of the courtyard meant the siege missile was hurled from the front of the castle. Looking in the opposite direction of the breach, Graybow saw that the front gate was open immediately ahead.

"What is it, sir?" Lyraan asked, a few paces away.

Graybow glanced around the rest of the castle proper. "Nothing," he returned. "Nothing yet."

Graybow was short of breath when he finally reached the top of the slope. The knights moved to help him the last few feet, but the castellan impatiently motioned them away. He was not going to show signs of infirmity, though he wondered if he had ever been able to climb slopes dressed in full armor and pack—even when he had been the age of Byron and Lyraan.

Peering through the gap between the rampart and the

breach revealed little because of the dim light within. The rampart filled the majority of the breach, forcing Graybow to hunch down to pass through the opening. He had hoped that some light might have filtered through the windows at the top of the tower, but they had been wisely boarded up for the siege; tower windows were favorite targets for the burning arrows of enemy archers.

"I take it we have no torches," the castellan stated.

"Sorry, sir," Byron said from outside the tower. "Do you want my surcoat? We could wrap it around my mace and light it. And I've brought my tinderbox."

"No, that won't be necessary," Graybow answered, stepping out of the breach. "We don't know the architecture of this slope, and heading down into the darkness would be unnecessarily dangerous. Let's make for the wall."

The curtain wall was ten feet from the rampart; the drop was about twenty-five down from it. Graybow looked skeptically at the distance, deciding that it was finally time to admit that he was no longer a strong young man. Fortunately, he had two strong young men with him.

"Can you make that jump?" he asked Sir Byron.

The knight glanced down at himself, patting down his armor. After a moment's consideration, he said, "I'm wearing my padding as well as my chain and plate. I don't think I could get up the speed. Ask Lyraan. He's the jumper in the family."

The other knight gave his twin a heated glance, which Graybow did not understand, but guessed it had something to do with the young man's reputation with aborted romantic engagements. Lyraan dropped his pack and stuck his spear in the ground. He pulled out the rope and looped it into a lasso.

Without taking his eyes from his brother, the knight swung the lasso around above his head, letting go at the last moment. The loop caught on a crenelation and tightened.

"You're the climber," Lyraan said under his breath to his twin, walking past. He turned and held the rope taught.

Graybow looked candidly at the brothers and decided to ask no questions; whatever feuds and reputations they had were at least keeping their minds off their apprehension. The aging knight grabbed the rope a few feet ahead of Lyraan.

Byron awkwardly slung his mace through his belt and took the rope in both hands. He leaned out over the edge of the slope, then let his feet dangle from the precipice. Graybow took in a sharp breath at the young man's weight, feeling an old wound in his back give a twinge of pain. He was glad that Lyraan was strong enough to do the majority of the work.

The young knight slowly walked his hands across the rope. This motion made him bob, and Graybow was forced to lean back and dig his heels into the earth to maintain his hold. He heard Lyraan grunt once and do the same.

Rock crumbled away from the wall where the lasso was tied. Byron stopped midway, waiting for the rope to come to a rest. When he stopped bobbing, he continued more slowly. To Graybow, the sound of the cracking rock was more ominous than distant thunder.

Byron hesitantly reached out to the walkway but was still too far to climb up. Graybow's breathing was hard and shallow, and sweat drenched his brow. He thought with some amusement that Jo's comment about his eating too many scones was correct.

A few more hand-slides brought the knight to the edge of the walkway. He let go of the rope, grabbed onto the ledge, and swung his legs up and over. Without a word, he undid the lasso and tied it to another stone.

"Come over now, sir," he called, holding the rope.

Graybow released the rope and tried to shake life into his hands. He cursed himself for letting his body fall to such ruin. A sudden discomfort came over him, accompanied as he was by two charges who were more than a match for him in strength and battle prowess. Still, they were loyal.

"Is there something wrong, sir?" Lyraan asked from behind, still holding onto the rope.

"No, nothing," the castellan replied. He stepped out to the edge of the rampart and held the rope in the same manner as Byron. Taking a deep breath to steady himself, he let his feet leave the earth.

The twinge in his back became a line of pain, but Graybow did not allow himself to return. The wound, made by a cursed elven spear, had never healed properly; he hoped the gash would not open and bleed.

Byron held onto the rope and kept it taught. Graybow heard the sound of cracking stone again and wondered if the walls were poorly built or if their weakness was caused by the abelaats. He glanced down once at the drop and increased his pace, unwilling to find out the unpleasant way.

Graybow reached the ledge and was pulled up by Byron. The castellan nodded in thanks to the young man but could not find the breath to speak. He walked a few paces away, gritting his teeth against the pain in his back.

"Shall I stay here, sir?" Lyraan yelled from the rampart.

Graybow nodded and tried to speak, but failed. He took a few deep breaths and managed to say, "Yes. We'll need your help getting back." Lyraan waved and took up his spear. Graybow waved in return and headed off with Byron toward the main gate.

Graybow walked slowly along the parapet. He wanted to make sure that the integrity of the stone had not been weakened to the point where it would collapse under his weight. He still could not see any sign of broken weapons, though he had hoped something small like a sling-stone might have fallen into a crack. Such an item would contain invaluable stores of information. Graybow and the other knight would occasionally stop and search the outer wall for signs of siege or assault, but they did not find anything.

At the front gate, Graybow turned and took note of the castle's damage. He was disappointed that he did not see anything different from his new vantage point. He let out a long breath.

"I think I've found the original mark, sir," Byron said, leaning out over the curtain wall. Graybow walked over to the wall and leaned out as well. The knight pointed.

Graybow saw that Lyraan had been correct. The marks were definitely made by a siege ladder.

"Do you see any others?"

"No—yes, sir! There's more. All along the wall!"

Graybow also noticed the scrapes. He straightened and said, "It seems that whatever has made the passage of the abelaat so mysterious is not infallible."

Peering out over the field, Graybow noticed something unusual. There were shallow depressions in the ground that he had not noticed on the walk up. Some were obviously shaped by siege missiles, huge rocks or iron balls, and others he recognized as tracks from wheels. The furrows all came from one direction.

The castellan turned again and reviewed the damage to the castle. By his previous conclusion, he knew that the siege stone that had demolished the tower had been cast from the front of the keep. The scrape marks of the siege ladders were found at the front gate and there were none on the other walls they had inspected; he guessed that no others would be found. The only portcullis to be raised had been found at the front gate. Pulling out his journal and stylus, Graybow made another entry. He slowly smiled.

"What is it, sir? Have you found something?"

"No, Sir Byron, I have not found something," the castellan replied, finishing his note. He replaced the journal under his belt and added, "You have."

"Sir?"

"You and your brother discovered the scrape marks at the front gate," Graybow said. "It seems that the abelaats' tactics are simple. They attack from the front."

"Is that why none of the other gates have been raised?" the knight inquired.

Nodding, the castellan said, "That would be my guess. It's also the reason why there are only siege-ladder marks on the front wall, and none on the sides."

Sir Byron looked back at the castle proper and pursed his thin lips in thought. He shook his head, confused. "What does this knowledge buy us, sir?"

Graybow shrugged. "Perhaps our lives."

Chapter XI

he trail of the remaining troops led northward, far off into the hills. Jo doubted that the abelaats would bother to send a party after the soldiers. The only casualties they had taken had been from Peace; not a single sword or spear from Penhaligon, not a single lance from the Black Eagles, had felled an abelaat.

Jo's legs threatened to give way at every rise, but she forced herself to keep moving, inhaling deeply through her nose and exhaling through her mouth as she had been taught to do when she worked with a messenger between Specularum and Threshold. It allowed her to move farther and faster than if she had let herself pant like an animal.

Jo wondered how many troops had survived. She remembered Graybow's words of caution about the men of the Black Eagle Barony and hoped that if they had survived, they would not cause trouble.

As she made her way over another hill, keeping herself crouched to avoid enemy eyes, Jo considered going back to Penhaligon and telling her story of the massacre. She was sure that the baroness would want to know the real story of what happened and not the lies of Chilatra. Jo pursed her lips in consternation, remembering that her only real veracity came from her affiliation with Flinn, and from the fact that she had become a symbol of hope.

Clutching Peace, Jo felt a wave of anger that she could not save the soldiers from dying. She felt that each one of them had relied on her to lead them, inspire them, give them hope and strength and courage enough to fend off the enemy. She wondered if she would eventually find her place in the Hall of Heroes or the Corridor of the Fallen.

Jo halted on the top of a hill and stood upright, arching her back to remove the cramps and pain. The sky maintained its iron-gray cast, and she still couldn't see the sun; the lack of light was wearing on her. She peered in the direction she guessed was northwest, hoping to catch a glimpse of the abaton's white column of light.

Jo suddenly remembered the vision of Dayin. The boy had been transformed into a young man so beautiful that her heart raced at the memory. She clutched Peace to her body, feeling the coolness of the red silver against her cheek. She imagined that Dayin's flesh would feel just as cool. The attraction she had felt for him was physical, yes, but she knew she had also been seduced by the power, by the inspiration that engulfed him.

When Jo had first met Dayin, the boy had shown her a small measure of adoration, but she had not thought of it as anything more than a small boy's crush. She wondered if those feelings of adoration still existed, and if they were dangerous to the abaton. Jo also wondered if the presence she felt guiding the light had been Teryl Auroch. The conclusion made sense; he had created the abaton and had taken Dayin, his son, into the pillar of light.

In the vision, Dayin's eyes had been pupilless pools of white light, matching the brightness of the abaton's pillar. The feeling of the cascading light momentarily buffeted Jo's body, and she swayed, then quickly recovered her equilibrium. She knew now that there was a connection between the abaton's power and Dayin's new form, but she couldn't express the connection in words, and it frustrated her.

The powerful presence had attempted to keep Dayin's eyes closed, perhaps so he could not see her. She wondered if Dayin had to concentrate to maintain the abaton's power.

The air was cold. Jo shivered and braced herself for the walk. The horses' tracks continued into the hills, but she could not tell how far; the rolling terrain blocked her view. She bent down and checked the prints, guessing that there were at least ten cavalrymen on the run. Jo touched the ground and picked up a small clod of dirt, rubbing it between her fingers, as she had been taught by the messenger in Specularum. The ground was firm and cold; the horses had passed through that spot at least two hours before.

Jo knew she was not a skilled tracker. If the horsemen

had passed several hours before, her sense of time must have been disrupted by the fight. She dusted off her hands, then rubbed her face and finger-combed her hair in frustration.

In hopes of alleviating her fears, Jo decided to increase her pace. She broke into a slow jog, holding Peace at the hilt and the center of the blade for balance. The red silver had become an even deeper shade. The blood on her hand was dry again, and she wondered how much of her life the blade had drunk.

But the blade's draining of life was not like the abelaats'. Jo was strangely comforted by Peace, assured that she was nurturing the blade's life. She did not doubt that the blessed sword had a life of its own, in the same way that Wyrmblight had lived. Jo held the blade up and let her eyes wander the intricacies of the final rune engraved on its flat, the rune of peace. It combined the previous four symbols of the Quadrivial into one; she did not think she had ever seen anything as wonderful.

Jo maintained her pace as long as she could, plodding over the miles of rolling hills. There were no birds calling, no animals howling in the distance, no rustles in the underbrush. Even the insects were quiet. The terrain grew soft, and Jo wondered if she were entering a swampy region. The air slowly changed from cold and clear to damp and heavy. She was forced to slow her pace again when the ground became soft, clutching at her hard boots.

Jo continued to wander through the dampness until the tracks finally ended, heading off into a shallow marsh. In confusion, she studied the trail, unsure why the remaining cavalry would consider going into such an inhospitable area. She stared into the marsh, her sight obscured by the mists that rose from the water.

Jo shifted Peace to her right hand and turned a last time to ensure that she was not being followed by the abelaats. She sniffed the air for the scent of heavy spice but sensed none, so with a sigh of resignation, she stepped into the marsh's shallow waters. The water was as cold as she had guessed.

The marsh was silent except for the sound of Jo's boots sluggishly lifting from the water. Jo held Peace before her in a double-handed grip, right hand in front of the left. She had heard rumors of strange creatures that roamed the swamps—giant insects, lizardmen, even undead. A moment after thinking this, she laughed at her fear; there was not a single creature on Mystara more horrible than the abelaats.

Jo remembered when she had once been forced to flee the Specularum city guards into one of the nearby swamps. The swamp had been at least as cold as the one she stood in now, and there she had contracted the sickness that breeds in brackish water. It had taken her weeks to recover. She hoped that she would not catch ill again.

Without any signs of the horses' passing, Jo attempted to maintain a straight course away from the battlefield and in line with the tracks. The area became obscured by mists and gas, and Jo's nose wrinkled every once in a while as she passed through a particularly acrid patch. Her muscles were beginning to ache from her slow, cautious walk. She knew it would not be wise to run through the water, as that would make her even more tired. She had stepped over sunken trees and rotting stumps on the swamp bed; if she had been running, she could have broken her leg, or worse.

Jo listened again for sounds of life. She stopped, standing perfectly still, Peace held out in the same stance as when she had entered the marsh.

"Hello!" Jo yelled. She drew another breath and bellowed, "Hello!"

She waited and listened for a reply, but not even the wind answered. She hollered again, holding Peace above her head and splashing forward. The water and mud did not stain her tabard or breeches.

"Where are you!" she finally managed, her breath growing ragged as her muscles slowly wore down. "Sir Domerikos! Where are you!"

Jo stared at the swamp around her, feeling as if she had entered some kind of nether world. A noxious mist rose in front of her face, causing her to sneeze. Then she laughed. Jo sneezed again, her laugh growing steadily louder.

"What's so funny?"

Kicking up water as she spun around, Jo brought Peace up, maintaining her two-handed grip. She directed the tip toward the speaker's throat.

Sir Domerikos stood perfectly still, his dark eyes regarding the sharp point of the red-silver sword. His arms were extended in a defensive position, and his head was cocked to the side; Jo could tell that he had flinched.

Jo smiled and relaxed her stance, rubbing her nose with the back of her hand. Embarrassed, she said, "I'm terribly sorry, Sir Domerikos. I was beginning to think I was the only one left alive."

Domerikos furrowed his brow and looked away with what Jo could see was shame and anger. "There are a few of us off in that direction," he replied, pointing off into the depths of the marsh.

"Who?"

"Five of our knights from Penhaligon, Commander Lyrates, Sergeant Yeats—Sir Barethmor and a few of the Black Eagle Lancers," the knight added, turning back to face Jo.

"Are you injured?" she asked politely. She stepped forward to check his armor for gashes or dried blood.

Sir Domerikos waved his hand for her to stop. "I'm fine," he said, running his hands over his face and through his hair. "It's a good thing you yelled, or we might never have found each other."

"I don't know how long I've been walking through this water."

The knight shrugged and gestured for Jo to walk toward the rest of the party.

"How do you know which way to go—sir?" she asked, momentarily forgetting to show the respect due his station.

Domerikos did not reply. She saw he was grinding his teeth and staring off into the fog, preoccupied with the ruinous battle.

"How do you know which way to go, sir?" she inquired again, raising her voice.

"What?" the knight replied, blinking. "I've an excellent sense of direction. And Barethmor gave me this."

Holding out his hand, Domerikos revealed a tiny bubble of glass; a directional arrow floated within.

"What's that on the inside?" she asked, squinting her eyes to focus.

"It indicates direction, apparently toward north."

Jo straightened. "Apparently?"

Domerikos shrugged again. "It is an item of magic, and as such, I know nothing of its nature. I only know that it always points north, and there is another arrow inside that points toward another of these baubles. Don't worry about my safety, Squire Menhir," Sir Domerikos said flatly. "I know Sir Barethmor had a specific reason for giving me this—thing, other than finding you."

"Specific reason?" Jo replied. "What are you saying, sir?"

The knight appeared confused. "I'm saying that this is Barethmor's perfect opportunity to exact his revenge. The attempt on your life, the note from the Black Eagle Barony, and the appearance of Sir Barethmor aren't coincidences."

Sir Domerikos held the glass ball up to his eye and peered inside. He gestured in the direction of the camp and said, "Let us continue, but keep thinking about what I just said."

Jo nodded, resting Peace on her right shoulder. The air grew colder, clearing some of the mist. The vestiges of an ancient forest slowly appeared, jutting threateningly from the water.

Sir Domerikos pointed into the dead forest, and Jo saw a moderate fire flickering. The five knights from Penhaligon were standing opposite the three knights from the Black Eagle Barony, and they all huddled around a small, scorched cylinder from which grew a tiny fire. The horses were tethered to one of the many dead trees.

The men from Penhaligon were tired and ragged. Their livery had been shredded, revealing battered plate and punctured links. Of the five, only three had swords, and one of them was broken. The men of the Black Eagle Barony seemed well equipped. Their black armor was perfectly preserved, as if they had not entered combat. They each clutched unscarred weapons—a spear, a mace, and a bastard sword.

"Where is Sir Barethmor?" Sir Domerikos asked those gathered as he and Jo entered the clearing.

"I am here," said the gruff voice that Jo recognized as belonging to the lancer's commander. She watched as his black armor slowly appeared wraithlike from the mists. He held his helmet in his left hand, allowing his long hair and beard to limply drape his mail. "I see you have found our little hero."

Jo could not stop her mouth from twitching at the man's sarcasm, though she maintained her stance.

"Well," Barethmor asked Jo. "Where have you been?"

"Fighting the abelaats," Jo replied evenly. She remained in her place at Sir Domerikos's side.

"Admirable, I'm sure. Why weren't you killed, then? Like the rest of them?"

Jo kept her silence, clutching the hilt of Peace.

Sir Barethmor stepped forward, dropping his helmet onto a rotting stump. His dark eyes evilly reflected the magical fire. "What is your answer, girl?" he demanded.

Sir Domerikos stepped in front of Jo and said, "Keep your distance, Barethmor."

The lancer commander pursed his lips and peered up

into the knight's eyes. Jo watched as the two waged a
silent battle. She grew more worried with each passing
moment. Barethmor eventually nodded introspectively
and backed away. He stood next to his knights and said,
"Well, I'm glad you're both finally here."

"And why is that?" Domerikos asked, taking his place
near his own men. Jo sensed the danger growing and
moved to stand with the men from Penhaligon.

Barethmor nodded again and peered around the
swamp, then said, "You once did me a grievous injury, Sir
Domerikos. I haven't forgotten."

"And your old wife has not forgotten the days and
nights of beatings," Domerikos answered hotly.

Ignoring the man's statement, the lancer commander
turned to Jo. He said, "And you. The stupid squire.
Thinks she's a hero because she wields a magic sword.
Well, let me tell you, I've plenty of enchanted blades. But
my master wants that one, and he shall have it."

Jo suddenly understood: Ludwig von Hendriks, the
baron of the Black Eagle Barony, wanted Peace to use
against King Karameikos. Councilman Melios had been
the "pawn."

The Penhaligon knights brandished their weapons and
Jo brought Peace up in a two-handed grip. The Black
Eagle Lancers readied their arms as well, but Jo noticed
that they did not seem particularly worried.

"It's a good thing I had that tracking crystal to give
you," Sir Barethmor said evenly. He gestured with his
hand at the Penhaligon knights.

The fire from the cylinder exploded, engulfing the
knights in its flame. Jo heard their screams over the roar of

the fire. She stepped up beside Domerikos as the flames changed their direction, the conflagration filling the air with heat.

Sir Domerikos turned from Jo and started to run. She watched with horror as the flesh on his body was charred and flaked away. His armor melted off his body and fell in steaming heaps into the water.

The fire raged around Jo, forming a sphere of sound and heat. She maintained her stance, Peace held forward, ready for combat. The sword shielded her from the cylinder's magic.

Stepping with her right foot, Jo swung the shining blade above her head and down at an angle. The tip passed through the first lancer's head. The blade came back up on the return stroke and penetrated the shoulder guard and neck armor of the next.

The remaining lancer swung his mace down, striking the armor on Jo's shoulder. The plate did not buckle beneath the assault, but she was forced to her knee. The fire continued to rage around her, and its flickering light dazzled her eyes.

Jo was struck in the back by the mace, and she slid forward on the mud, just beneath the surface of the water. Her vision began to fade, but she shook her head to clear the pain and rolled to her left, bringing Peace up in a defensive posture.

The lancer stood over Jo, mace raised above his head, and she was not sure if she would be able to parry in time. As he lunged for his next blow, the cylinder belched out another gout of flame, striking the man in the back. Jo stood and backpedaled, watching as the lancer's body was reduced to ash.

"Damn you, girl!" Sir Barethmor said from behind.

Jo spun Peace in a wide arc, using its weight to bring her around. Barethmor jerked in surprise. His head fell from his neck.

The fire from the cylinder suddenly fizzled, and Jo was left in silence. She let her shoulders sag with fatigue and anguish. For a long while, she simply stared at the remains of the bodies. At last, she dug through Barethmor's possessions, looking for the other glass direction ball. It was gone.

Jo left the scene without looking back.

Chapter XII

raddoc was not dead.

The dwarf lifted his head from Flinn's leg and stared up into his friend's eyes. He saw the fire that had glowed within the dwarven forge now reflecting out Flinn's eyes, the fire that had inspired the dwarves for hundreds of generations—since they were taken from the city of Blackmoor.

Pain lit behind Braddoc's eyes, and he was forced to lie back down on the sandy forest floor.

"Lie still, Braddoc."

"Why—what happened?" the dwarf asked through clenched teeth.

"You were saved," Flinn replied.

Braddoc felt himself unpleased with the prospect of finding out how he was saved. "You did not save me?" he asked cautiously. Flinn shook his head. "Then who did?"

Flinn shrugged. "Kagyar?"

With the intention of ignoring the pain between his eyes, Braddoc propped himself up into a sitting position. He awoke a moment later, his face in the ground.

The dwarf groaned loudly and pushed himself back up. "I feel as if I've been on another of our drinking binges," he muttered. The inside of his mouth tasted like sand, which didn't exactly surprise him.

"Why don't you lie back down until you've recovered?" Flinn asked, standing.

Braddoc shook his head slowly. He coughed to clear his throat of its gritty feeling and scratched his nose. As slowly and gently as he could manage, he brought his hands together and knelt down.

"Oh, great lord Kagyar, Kagyar the Artisan, Kagyar Flasheyes, I, Braddoc Briarblood, your humble servant, thank you for blessing me with this, my life. May I use your gift wisely." Braddoc paused, forcing himself to stop swaying.

Braddoc rolled back and sat with his legs crossed. He rubbed his face with both hands, attempting to bring some feeling back into his flesh.

"How long have we been here?" he mumbled through his fingers.

"No more than an hour," Flinn replied. He crossed his arms and stared down at the dwarf. Braddoc guessed it was time to continue the journey. He started to stand, but with a mere gesture, Flinn invited him to sit; the dwarf did not see any way to decline. He did not feel like refusing simply for the sake of refusing, though he did not like the idea that the being who had once been his friend had the power to force him to do practically anything. And he had a running feud with immortals of any stripe.

"And where are we specifically?"

Flinn craned his head back and sniffed the clean air. "The realm of Alfheim."

The news made Braddoc feel slightly worse. He had no personal feud with the elves, but it was every dwarf's belief that the folk of the wood were somewhat silly and flighty; they crafted items of great beauty but not anything of any permanence, as did the dwarven craftsmen. He knew that the elves considered the dwarves to be stoic to the point of atrophy, and he could see their point. Even so, and even despite his hundred years of travel, Braddoc had never quite been able to overcome his personal prejudices against elves.

Braddoc peeked between his fingers and saw that the sky still held a gray cast, choking the light of the sun. The large leaves on the trees created an additional canopy that blocked out even more of the light.

"All right," he groaned, getting to his feet and wondering if he was going to be forced to remain seated for his own good. "There's no time to waste."

"Are you sure you are ready to travel?" Flinn inquired.

Braddoc arched his eyebrow in amazement. He thought he actually heard a note of concern in the immortal's powerful voice. "You're the one with the mission," he replied gruffly.

Flinn nodded, letting his arms fall to his sides and motioning for Braddoc to walk. With a great sigh, the dwarf lifted his right foot, feeling with unusually sharp perception the age of his boots and the softness of the ground. Only once before had he only been forced to use the ocular until he hovered on the brink of death; now, as then, normal sensations were greatly intensified, as if every nerve in his body had been rubbed raw. He wished he had something to drink.

"Would you prefer red or white?" Flinn asked.

"What? Oh, er, how about red, something from the Lost Valley region," Braddoc replied, distracted by the new pains he felt in his body.

Flinn walked up behind Braddoc and handed the dwarf a crystal goblet. Braddoc mumbled his thanks and took a small sip. The wine filled his mouth with pleasure, and he felt it clear his throat and stomach.

He held the goblet to his nose and breathed in deeply. "Moolon Wraithchilde?" he guessed. He closed his eyes and breathed in again. His nose was filled with the wine's lustrous scent.

"You have an excellent palate, Braddoc," Flinn said.

"Thank you, Flinn." Braddoc smiled to himself. He had always prided himself on his ability to know good wine; it was one of the skills he had purposely developed over the last few hundred years. He took another sip from the goblet, attempting to determine where the vessel had been made. It was beautifully clear, with diagonal crenelations set about its base and up to the rim. "Is this crystal from Ylaruam?"

"Actually, it's from Glantri."

"Really?" Braddoc replied with surprise. "I have not been there in a long time."

Braddoc continued to drink, the wine making him forget about the pounding sensations in his feet, legs, and back. He glanced around at the foliage, and for the first time, he didn't think that trees were depressing. He rubbed his fingers against the crenelations of the goblet and had a sudden thought.

"Flinn," he began cautiously. "May I ask you something?"

"Yes?"

"Where did you get this wine?"

Flinn did not reply, but Braddoc knew he should be patient, and he decided to wait. The two walked for a few minutes, moving deeper into the forest. The light from the sky became increasingly shrouded by the leaves and branches, but Braddoc noticed that the light in the forest remained constant. He wondered exactly where they were in Alfheim.

"It seems that I can—conjure things when needed," Flinn finally said. "You needed something to help you, so I—reached out."

"Reached out?"

Flinn shrugged in reply.

Braddoc held the goblet up in front of his eyes, and with a sigh of resignation, downed the last of the wine in a single swallow. He put the crystal drinking glass on top of a large, flat rock.

He asked, "How much farther do we need to travel?"

Flinn pressed his lips together in confusion. "I do not know. We are heading in the right direction," Flinn answered, pointing deeper into the woods. "I suppose that if we get lost, we could always ask for directions."

Braddoc stopped and turned in disbelief, staring his friend in the face. Flinn was completely expressionless.

"What's that supposed to mean?" the dwarf demanded.

"It was supposed to be a joke."

"A joke," Braddoc said rhetorically. He did not know whether to laugh or scream. "Your timing is bad."

Flinn dropped to the ground, folding his legs beneath him. He motioned for Braddoc to do the same. "There is something I need to tell you," the immortal said with sudden seriousness.

Braddoc ran his fingers through his hair and sighed loudly. "All right," he said, sitting in the path they were following. "Talk."

"Do you remember why we were in Rockhome?"

Braddoc was taken aback by the question. "Of course. So you could find Denwail."

"True," Flinn said, nodding. "And who were we seeking?"

"I don't understand," Braddoc answered gruffly.

"We were supposed to be seeking Denwarf."

"Denwarf! I don't know where he is. Nobody does."

Flinn cocked his head to one side and fixed Braddoc with a stare that made the dwarf uncomfortable. Braddoc was again reminded that he was in the presence of an immortal. He thought hard about Denwarf but could not recall anything.

"You were forced to forget about Denwarf by Denwarf," Flinn said. He straightened himself and placed the palms of his hands on his knees in the martial fashion Braddoc had seen the khans use. "That cavern we were in was Denwarf."

"Was Denwarf?" Braddoc replied with skepticism. "How could that be?"

Flinn lifted his shoulders and let them drop in an exaggerated shrug. "You told me yourself that Denwarf was a creature of stone brought to life by Kagyar. Denwarf had lived so long in the caves beneath Rockhome that his spirit was infused in the rock of the cavern where he made his home. He was Denwail."

"Then why would he make me forget?"

Flinn turned his head slightly and seemed to peer off into the distance. After a moment of pondering, he turned back and said, "Dwarves should not know how to find the source of their inspiration. They should just know it is there."

"Flinn," he began, searching for the most polite, though penetrating, words. "There are two things I must ask."

Flinn nodded for the dwarf to continue.

"How much of your memory has returned?"

"Enough to remember that our drinking binges always ended up with my pockets being empty," Flinn replied. He broke into a smile that quickly faded. "What else would you like to ask?"

"What have you done with Denwail?" Braddoc replied, knowing that he was probably overreacting. He could not help feeling that the dwarven lifecraft was threatened by this meddling immortal.

"I have—done nothing," Flinn answered slowly. He peered into the distance again before saying, "Denwail still lies within the heart of the dwarves."

"But I saw you—embody the fire of the forge!"

"And that fire is still within me," Flinn said, pointing to his heart. "As long as it is here, Denwail still lives. This is the start. I must not only find the inspirations of all the races, but I must embody them."

In thought, Braddoc rubbed his jaw with his hand. He stood and arched his back. He was not sure what to think about Flinn's answer and knew that he could neither confirm nor deny the claim. He stared back into the immortal's eyes and saw the fire from the forge again.

"How much of this did you know before?" Braddoc inquired. He walked over to Flinn and held out his hand.

Flinn took the offer and let Braddoc pull him up. Braddoc suddenly remembered what had happened last time he had offered his hand, but was too late to brace himself; he was pleased that he wasn't thrown into the trees.

With a gesture, Flinn walked off in their original direction. Braddoc followed, catching up with his companion. "Well?" he asked.

"Nothing, Braddoc. Before the forge, I knew nothing."

&a &a &a &a &a

Braddoc did not allow himself to feel the beauty of the grove. His dwarven blood was too old to let him notice anything but the fact that the plants and trees around him, despite their beauty, would die and fade hundreds of times while he lived. But if he had been anything other than himself—perhaps even a younger dwarf—he would have wept.

The two companions stopped at the edge of a circular clearing. A single tree stood in the center of the space. Its leaves were wider than Braddoc's broad hands, and its bark contained veins of silver that shimmered with the life of the tree. The tree's canopy covered the entire clearing. Beneath its silvery leaves, the green grass looked nearly white.

After a few moments of stunned amazement, Braddoc spoke. "What are we to do now?" he asked.

Flinn said nothing, staring at the tree. Braddoc's brow furrowed in concern, and he nudged his friend. "Flinn?"

The immortal continued to stare.

Braddoc stepped back away from the grove in an attempt to get a better perspective. Flinn seemed paralyzed again, as he had been in Rockhome, but this paralysis felt different. Braddoc could sense no magic holding Flinn in place.

The dwarf stepped back next to his friend and looked into the man's eyes. He still saw the fires of the dwarven forge.

"Flinn?" he asked again, though in a louder voice.

"Yes?" The reply was distant and soft. Braddoc could not help but hear something he had never heard in Flinn's voice before, either as an immortal or a hero: he heard fear.

"What are you afraid of?"

"Afraid? I'm not afraid of anything," Flinn replied, his voice distant. A moment later he whispered, "I'm afraid of dying."

Braddoc crossed his arms and snorted derisively. "That's ridiculous! Immortals can't die."

"You are wrong, Braddoc. Immortals can die, and each time I enter one of these places I will die again."

"But you'll return, as before!"

Flinn shook his head but did not take his eyes from the grove. "I still am forced to die."

Braddoc glanced into the clearing. The single tree represented the inspiration of the elves, the beauty and life of the forest. When Flinn stepped under the canopy of leaves, he would start to die.

Braddoc suddenly felt extreme sorrow for his friend. The immortal's mission had the most personal consequence imaginable. Worse yet, Flinn's dread and fear would only rise higher with each new inspiration he came to embody. Each inspiration would awaken in him more of the long-dormant memories and hopes and dreams that make death unbearable. In his mortal life, Flinn had been the most robust and vigorous man the dwarf had even met; if anyone fought hard for life, it had been he. The end of that life was more than the ultimate sacrifice.

However, Braddoc knew that Flinn must complete his task, or Mystara was doomed. He took several deep breaths to calm himself and tried to think of what to say.

"There is nothing to say, Braddoc," Flinn murmured. He finally turned his head and stared down at his friend. "I know what I must do."

Flinn stepped into the clearing. Braddoc saw his friend's hair slowly turn gray. Flinn took several more steps, and his hair became white. He was still ten paces from the tree.

Flinn's back bent with his next few steps and his skin shriveled and lost its vitality. Braddoc wanted to rush to Flinn and provide help and comfort—he did not know how. But Braddoc would never survive beyond the edge of the clearing. He gritted his teeth and waited. Three more steps and Flinn was forced to the ground, his emaciated flesh cut and torn by the stiff grass. The light from the leaves so utterly engulfed his frail body that Braddoc nearly lost sight of him.

The length of an arm separated Flinn from the elven tree now, and he reached out, his body slowly falling away to dust.

"Flinn!" Braddoc cried. "Flinn! You're almost there!"

The immortal attempted to stand, but his drying bones would no longer support their own meager weight. His flesh fell to the grass and began to feed the earth. Braddoc looked down at his feet, then into the lush clearing. It had seemed a silver garden when first they came upon it. Now it seemed to Braddoc nothing more than a field of death.

"Oh, great lord Kagyar, Kagyar the Artisan, Kagyar Flasheyes, I, Braddoc Briarblood, your humble servant, ask for your blessing so I might aid my friend," Braddoc said in a loud voice.

The dwarf jumped forward, steeling himself against the pain. He was grabbed from behind by a hand. He tried to turn, but the hand was too strong. He strained forward as, ahead of him, Flinn's withered fingers touch the silver-veined tree.

The light in the clearing faded, leaving a moody dusk. The boughs of the tree cracked and split, and the leaves withered, curled, falling to the ground and covering the yellowing grass. A silent wind kicked up behind Braddoc, and he thought that he would be blown into the clearing if not for the mysterious hand on his shoulder.

The dust of Flinn's body was lifted by the wind and mixed with the flakes of wood and leaves.

The clearing was suddenly engulfed by a huge ball of fire that destroyed the remaining dust and grass. Braddoc threw his arms up over his eyes. He remembered the image of the sphere of fire in the cavern at Rockhome. This fireball slowly collapsed in on itself, shrinking until it hung in the air at chest height, no larger than Braddoc's fist.

The dwarf watched in awe as the image of a tree rose up out of the dusk, encasing the ball of flame in its trunk. The tree continued to grow, and the fire slowly spread outward, like veins. Within moments, the outline of a man appeared in the trunk.

"Flinn!" Braddoc cried, straining angrily against the hand that continued to hold him. He tried to turn against the mysterious hand, but failed. "Flinn!"

Flinn stepped out from the tree, his flesh taking shape and color. Braddoc saw that his eyes glowed with life, and they held the fire of the dwarves behind them. The immortal was even more beautiful and astounding to behold than before; the silver of the elven tree rushed visibly in his veins.

The hand finally removed itself from Braddoc's shoulder, and he tried to turn around. "I am sent by Kagyar," a woman's soft voice whispered in his ear before he could move. "He still thinks of you."

The dwarf did not turn, knowing the immortal's messenger woman would be gone by now. Instead, he stepped into the clearing and charged toward Flinn.

Tears flowed from Flinn's eyes, and he hung his head.

"I remember much more now, Braddoc," the immortal murmured. "I remember living; I remember life. I remember love."

Chapter XIII

Jo was hungry. She guessed she had not eaten in two days. The excitement and anger she had felt from the treachery of the lancers had originally left her without an appetite. Now she felt near starvation.

Resting Peace on her left shoulder, Jo brought her right hand up to her eyes; the scabs had begun to heal with unusual speed. Jo pressed on them with her fingers, finding that they hurt like normal cuts. She had expected there to be little sensation since they seemed to be under the influence of some kind of magic.

The iron-gray sky continued to choke the light of the sun. Jo stood on top of a hillock, which looked the same as all the other hillocks she could see. She had lost her sense of direction and could not find the rising sun in the east or the setting in the west. Her lodestone and string

had been left on the packhorse she led to the battlefield.
Jo considered using the abelaat stones to help find her
way, but decided against it.

Jo looked halfheartedly for the abaton's pillar of light
in the distance, but was not able to see anything more
than hills and valleys. She had already tried to get a better perspective from higher hills, tiring herself out as she
went. Jo tried to remember the geography she had
learned while studying with a cartographer in Specularum. She saw in the north what might be a line of
mountains. Jo realized with frustration that she could be
almost anywhere on the southern side of the Black Peak
Mountains.

"What would you do, Flinn?" she asked herself. She
thought about the times they had spent together and the
way he would always take decisive action.

Jo turned and strained her eyes until they hurt, searching for forests or groves. She did not see anything more
than a few trees standing in isolated patches. According to
what the cartographer had said in one of his lessons, these
groves meant that she was east of the Radlebb Woods. Jo
felt suddenly heartened and turned back to face what she
hoped were the Black Peaks. She estimated that she was
south and east of Armstead, the abaton, and salvation for
Mystara. Behind her lay Penhaligon.

"Which do you want to be, Johauna Menhir?" she
mumbled to herself, taking Peace in her right hand and
resting it against her shoulder. "A hero or a knight?"

The image of the Hall of Heroes appeared in Jo's
thoughts, as did the council chamber of Penhaligon and the
memories of Flinn's reinstatement. She reminded herself

that she had not earned her glory as had Flinn, but had it handed to her. She also knew that she had been chosen by powerful forces she still did not understand. After a while, Jo sighed and turned away from the mountains. Her greatest ambition was to become a knight, and it was this ambition that had brought her to this place and time. The forces she had let reforge her and Wyrmblight had also carried her to these hills. She decided knighthood and hero status were not simply titles for her to accept. They would be awarded if she proved herself deserving.

≈ ≈ ≈ ≈ ≈

Jo stopped walking and sniffed the air. The scent of heavy spices was carried on the shifting wind to her place on the hill. She stiffened with anger and listened carefully for the sound of the abelaats. She could not locate the origin of the scent and heard only the wind.

However, after waiting a few moments, crouched perfectly still on top of a hillock, she heard something she had not expected. Human voices, carried oddly by the wind, called out. Their collective cries rose and fell, making Jo suddenly feel more lonely than she had been in the marsh. The shifting wind confused her ears.

Holding Peace in a double-handed grip and pointing the blade back behind her right side, Jo ran in a crouch down the side of the hillock and listened again. The cries seemed to be coming from her left. Her face set in lines of determination, she ran off in that direction, waiting when she reached the top of the next hill. The voices were louder.

Jo dashed down the slope. Her heart beat hard and her lungs labored for air. There were obviously people nearby, and judging from their cries, they were in trouble. Whether she would be a hero or a knight, her duty was to protect them from the abelaats. Her shoulder throbbed in time with her heartbeat as she remembered what Keeper Grainger had said about the feeding habits of the inhuman creatures.

Jo ran over three more hillocks. She made her way to the top of the rise, which stood before an open plain. Her eyes widened with terror as she finally saw the people whose voices had been carried by the chaotic wind. The town's citizens were huddled together in a corral. Jo saw that most of them were silent and staring, their faces covered with soot. Some of the children moaned their fear to their parents, who were too shocked to offer any comfort.

A portion of the small plain was covered by a razed town. The town had been destroyed in much the same way as Armstead, evil magics engulfing every home and building and leaving nothing but ash and black timbers. Jo felt a mixture of sadness and outrage.

The abelaats waited in silent formations surrounding the town. Their black halos continued to absorb the wan light that penetrated the clouds, and the scent of spices was heavier. There were more abelaats here than there had been on the battlefield where the Penhaligon forces were routed; the regiment that had engaged the knights of Penhaligon must have been little more than an advance force.

The abelaats appeared to move in units of at least four,

and there were five of these units standing outside the corral. As Jo stared down into the plain, some of the people were removed from the group and taken back into the town. Jo strained her eyes to get a better view, but the abelaat guards and the stumbling prisoners were hidden by the remains of buildings.

A scream cut through the air, rising from behind the ruined buildings. Jo brandished Peace, lifting the blade above her head. She bolted down the hillside.

Halfway down the hill, Jo stopped herself. The abelaats had moved several of their smaller units together to form a single, greater unit that was moving toward her. The moment she came to a complete halt, the abelaats halted as well. Their unit integrity seemed to break up slightly, as if they were confused. Then she remembered the difficulty the abelaats had in finding her when she had been among them on the field of battle. She stood still a little longer, the wind shifting around her.

Jo backed slowly up the hill. The chords in her neck tightened with anger. She did not know if she would be able to withstand the might of an entire formed unit, even with Peace and the masking effects of the abelaat blood in her veins. The formation loosened the farther she backed up the hillside.

Jo circled around the town, hoping to find another way in, or perhaps to discover a weakness in the abelaat lines. The terrain was the same she had just left, hilly and grassy. It took her several minutes to race around to the other side of the settlement. Once there, she noticed that there was a long avenue where the buildings and houses remained standing, though they were severely damaged.

She decided to enter the town through the avenue in the hope that she might be able to hide among the buildings. She moved slowly down the hillside, alert for the telltale shifting of the wind.

Jo arrived at the bottom of the hill and stalked toward the lane. She tried to keep her anger in check as she heard more screams from the townspeople.

The ashes in the air filled Jo's lungs, and she coughed softly into the back of her left hand, keeping Peace ready with her right. She still hadn't determined if the abelaats possessed a sense of hearing, or anything more than a sense of smell, but she did not want to take the chance of being discovered. Her eyes streamed tears, making clean tracks on her sooty face, much as they had done in Armstead. The smell of ash was so overpowering Jo could barely breath.

An abelaat was snuffling very near, and its scent was heavy on the shifting wind. Jo froze and listened. Apparently, a small unit of the creatures stood nearby, on the other side of the burned-out building where Jo stood. The wind tore at her tabard and long red hair. She dared not turn, realizing that entering the town had not been the best course of action.

The avenue of buildings prevented Jo from seeing out to the corral, and she hoped the buildings blocked her from the abelaats as well. The snuffling noise grew louder; the abelaats were rounding the side of the building. Jo slowly backed away, the links of her elven chain ringing with the beating of her heart.

Living shadows filled the avenue. Their features were hidden by their halos of darkness, but Jo imagined that she could still see their large eyes and the venomous fangs in their mouths. Black glaives grew out of their raised arms. In her fear, Jo lost all track of time, continuing her retreat even as the creatures moved forward.

Jo pressed her back against a wall, realizing that she had not been careful to ensure she had been heading down the center of the avenue. The abelaats were confused by her presence, unable to find her but clearly aware there was an intruder nearby. Jo clenched her teeth to stop herself from screaming as the creatures moved slowly forward, pressing her against the building.

"Keep still," a man's voice whispered from behind.

Jo wrenched her gaze away from the abelaats and peered through a building's doorway into an open room; the roof planks lay in a heap on the floor within. At first she saw nothing else in the room, but after a moment, she noticed the air in the doorway waver, like the heat rising from a fire. Glancing back toward the abelaats, Jo cautiously moved through the doorway.

Her foot struck something soft, and she heard someone curse. The air shimmered more violently and the image of a darkly dressed man appeared, vanishing an instant later. Jo jumped back in surprise.

The air wavered again, the image of the planks replaced by that of a group of people huddled around a strange figure clad in purple robes. They were all nursing wounds.

"Now you've done it!" the darkly dressed man hissed in a panic. The illusion that masked them reappeared after his last word.

The abelaats smashed through the side of the building, glaives splitting the remaining wood to dust and splinters.

Peace arched out and cut the first abelaat in half, the sword's hilt blocking the metal of a glaive. Jo ducked and rolled back into the street to give herself more fighting room and to keep the presence of the party secret; she would worry later about their reason for being in the town.

The abelaats turned and brandished their weapons, pressing forward, each step slow and deliberate. They were still having difficulty finding her because of her tainted blood. Jo shook with a fury she could barely contain, the tip of her red–silver sword unsteady in her trembling hands. She resumed her retreat, attempting to remain alert to the presence of more of the creatures despite the chaotically shifting wind.

Jo's left foot was blocked midstep by a fallen timber. She fell backward the same instant the abelaats rushed forward. Their polearms struck, and Jo barely blocked them, holding the length of Peace in both hands. The strength of the creatures was astounding, forcing Peace against her chest. They raised their glaives again for another series of blows.

In desperation, Jo sat up and swept out with Peace, using both hands for strength. The bastard sword cut through the abelaats' bodies as easily as it cut through the air, leaving them to fall to dust in the blackened street.

Tears flowed from Jo's eyes. The grim smell of panic and death was oppressive, and the scent of the abelaats on the shifting winds made Jo feel weak, emotionally drained. She wiped her eyes dry with the back of her hand and forced herself to stop crying, though she was not entirely successful. A glance back into the building where the party hid told her that their illusion still kept them from sight. Jo waved toward where she thought they might be sitting, motioning for them to follow her out of the town. Given their wounds and their fear and their spell, Jo had know way of knowing if they would follow.

Jo pushed herself up from the ground, barely maintaining her grip on the hilt of Peace. The tip of the blade dug a tiny furrow in the ash and dirt as she staggered away.

On the other side of the hills, Jo, exhausted, fell unconscious.

Chapter XIV

s she asleep or is she dead?" a man's voice muttered a few feet away from Jo. Though she had just become conscious again, she kept her eyes closed and her breath regular so that whoever was around her would not know she could hear them.

"Just take the sword," another man answered. Jo guessed the second man was standing a few feet behind the first, off to her right.

Jo heard the scuffle of boots across the grass and the clatter of armored plates. This sound was to her left. She realized with dread that she was surrounded.

"Ask her to rise."

The voice was a woman's, and Jo was sure that she had heard it before. She was having difficulty keeping her breathing down.

A third man's voice answered: "What do you mean?"

"She's neither dead nor sleeping," the woman replied. Jo heard the boots step closer and felt the ground beneath her head shake slightly at the approach. The armor also sounded familiar to Jo, much like the armor she herself wore.

"Then get up, foolish girl," a fourth voice said. Jo could not tell if it was a man or a woman speaking, but the voice was soft and clear, and well beyond the range of her sword.

"Yes," the woman added. "Rise, for we—"

Jo held tight to the hilt of Peace and rolled. She saw that she was surrounded by four men; the woman was somewhere to her right, out of sight. Her roll brought her just outside the circle and gave her enough space to bring her red-silver sword up to the nearest man's throat.

"Anybody moves, this one dies!" she hissed.

"Johauna Menhir I presume," the woman said rhetorically. Jo did not take her eyes from the group. The man she held was tall and thin, wearing black clothes in the fashion of Darokin, light and vented. His handsome face sported a neatly trimmed black beard and mustache. Two of the other men were dressed as foresters, wearing green and brown breeches, the hoods of their cloaks pulled down.

Jo saw that the last man was most certainly a sorcerer, the same that had cast the illusion in the town. His robes were red and purple, sewn together with golden thread that shimmered, even in the gray light of the day. His features were completely obscured by his gowns, and even his hands were hidden from view. He was completely

motionless, unlike his companions, who shifted from foot
to foot and clutched their weapons.

"Squire Menhir, perhaps if you would look at me, you
would remember who I am," the woman added.

Jo was instantly suspicious. "I'll do as you ask, but only
after you two drop your bows," Jo commanded, nodding
to the foresters, "and you in the robes turn your back."

Jo watched as the foresters looked to one another, then
to the woman at Jo's side. She guessed that the woman
must have nodded her approval because the look on the
men's faces was a combination of anger and resignation.
They dropped their weapons and stood with their arms
crossed over their chests.

The mage did not turn. "And you," Jo said.

"Please do as she says," the woman implored. The mage
did nothing for a moment, then nodded from the depths
of his robes and turned. The woman said, "Now, complete your end of the bargain."

Jo kept the edge of Peace against her captive's throat
and turned him around, using leverage to keep him under
guard.

"Don't try picking up your weapons," she said. "I'm
not going to allow my mission to be stopped, and I'll cut
this man's throat if I have to."

Jo peered into the woman's face and blinked without
recognition. The woman was an elf warrior with long
golden hair and violet eyes. Jo backed away, startled, drag-
ging her captive with her; elves were a rare and wondrous
sight outside of their forest home in Alfheim.

The warrior spread her hands out in a gesture of peace.
Her lovely face was open and honest. She said, "Do you

not recognize me, Johauna?"

"Recognize you? Where would I—?"

Johauna suddenly remembered. This was the same woman that she had seen in Bywater the first time she met Flinn. It was also the woman that had attended the squires' ceremony at the Castle of the Three Suns.

"It's you," she mumbled, lowering the edge of her blade. The woman stepped forward with a slight smile, but Jo brought her sword-point back up, suspicious again. "What are you doing here? Why have you been following me?"

The man from Darokin jerked, the back of his head striking Jo in the face. Jo staggered, feeling the blood drain from her nose. She spat as she stepped backward and swung Peace in a tight arc, striking the man in the side of the head with the flat of the blade. Jo was not done having her questions answered, but she was not going to kill one of this party before she knew everything.

The man in black looked surprised for a moment, then toppled over, landing in the grass. Jo knew that the foresters were going to retrieve their weapons so she continued her advance and placed her foot on top of the unconscious man's chest.

"Why are you following me!" she demanded of the elf warrior, the point of Peace held down at the man's throat. "Why—why?"

Jo grew nauseated. She had not felt this exhausted since traveling through the Black Peak Mountains and nearly dying both from the cold and the hunger of a mountain dog. She dug the heel of her hand into the wire wrapping of her sword. The pain cleared her vision and allowed her to continue standing.

The elf warrior stepped forward, hands stretched out in what Jo thought might be a gesture of aid. Jo was not going to let weakness stop her ability to defend herself. She bit her lip and tensed the muscles in her arms.

"Kill her and be done with it," the magician said from the muffled depths of his robes. Jo had the distinct impression that he was not human, though his accent was not like that of any race she knew.

"No! Our mission is clear, and we require her aid," the warrior said without turning to face the mage.

"She can barely stand!" said one of the foresters in the breathy accent of the Achelos Woods. The dialect told her that the man would be well-skilled with the bow, the long sword, and perhaps the sling. He added, "We haven't time to waste bringing her back to health."

"And I say that you all know the consequences of such an action," the elf warrior stated. "If she does not live, then Mystara dies."

"Nothing is written in the stones," the mage answered.

"No, but it is written in the sky!" the elf replied. "Johauna, in the name of Diulanna, please trust us. We are your friends."

"Diulanna?" Jo muttered wearily. "Diulanna needs heroes. We've got to go back and save that town." She lifted the point of Peace from the Darokin man's neck and staggered backward.

One of the foresters gave a deprecating wave. "You can barely walk, girl. You might as well stay with us."

"There's nothing for it," the other forester said, sitting

cross-legged on the grass.

The man in black moaned and stirred, raising a hand to the side of his head. When he felt the bruise he moaned even louder. "Ugh! What did you do to me you—"

The elf warrior kneeled next to the man and cradled his head in her arms, saying, "Be quiet, Malken. Johauna is going to help us."

"Help us!" Malken muttered, propping himself up on his elbows. "Look at her. She can barely stand!"

"You're one to talk!" The first forester laughed. His friend joined in.

Malken pointed a finger and said, "Don't start with me, you two!"

"I can stand," Jo said, unsteadily raising Peace up in her right hand. "And I'll make sure you stay down if you don't—"

 za za za za za

Jo awoke some time later to the smell of cooking food and strong wine. The foresters had set up their stew pots and found a game hare to roast. She felt as if she had drunk the dregs of the worst wine in Specularum and gone back for more.

"Feeling better?" one of the foresters asked.

Jo slowly shook her head, recalling that she actually had once drunk the dregs of the worst wine in Specularum.

The forester laughed and said, "Well, you'll feel better once you get something inside you. By the way, my name's Bolten."

"Johauna."

"We know that," the man replied. "You're one of the reasons we're here."

Jo reached to her side. Peace was missing.

Struggling to move, Jo groggily got to her feet and nearly pitched over. She groaned in anger.

"Where's m'sword?" she mumbled. Clearing her throat, she forced herself upright with a supreme effort of will. "Where's my sword?"

Bolten gestured, and Jo turned around. Across the camp, the sorcerer sat, Peace resting in the folds of his robes. Jo still could not see his hands or face. She slowly stalked forward, holding out her right hand.

"Peace. Give it to me," she demanded.

"I'm not done with it," the sorcerer hissed from deep inside his robes.

"What are you doing?"

The hood of the robe lifted a fraction of an inch. "Studying."

Jo took another step forward. She had earned Peace through the reforging of her soul, and she would not be denied. "There's nothing to study. The sword is mine."

The mage sat in silence, and Jo wondered if he were preparing a cantrip. She knew she was too tired and sickly to mount an effective attack, and would not be able to dodge a missile. She did not care.

"You are correct, Johauna Menhir," the sorcerer hissed again. "The sword is yours."

Jo took the sword from the mage, hoping to see some glimpse of his features, but he remained in the shadows of his cowl. He smelled of strong oils, like the ones she had

smelled when a caravan from the desert Emirates of
Ylaruam passed her in the streets of Specularum.

"We knew this already," the elf warrior said from
behind. Jo breathed in the oils of the magician one last
time to clear her head, and she turned. The elf was still
dressed in her full armor. "We knew that Peace was the
sword forged of your soul."

"How?" Jo asked, careful to remove all tones of anger
or distrust from her voice.

The warrior approached Jo and touched her long red
hair. "You do look much like Diulanna," she whispered.

"So I've heard," Jo replied, stepping to the side.

The elf warrior said nothing, gesturing for Jo to return
to Bolten's fire. The other forester had arrived and was
stirring the black pot. The smell of stew and vegetables
rose from the fire.

Jo nodded and walked away from the strange sorcerer,
who continued to sit motionless just outside the camp. Jo
found a comfortable place on the grassy hillock and
dropped down, folding her legs beneath her. She laid
Peace on the ground within easy reach.

"This is my brother, Firamen," Bolten said with a nod
toward the other forester. Firamen gave a polite smile and
continued stirring.

"And I am Malken d'Auberon," the man in black said
with a great flourish, coming up over the rise. He carried
a small wooden target with hundreds of knife cuts near
the center. He attempted to bow but held his hand up to
the bandage that covered the fresh wound on his head.
"Pardon me," he added apologetically. "It seems I'm having some difficulty this morning."

"I am—called Tesseria," the elf said. Jo guessed from the way the woman had stumbled over her words that Tesseria was probably not her true name. The warrior pointed toward the immobile sorcerer, saying, "That is Hastur."

"We've got to eat quickly," Bolten said, adding a pinch of seasoning to the stew. "Oh, and thanks for rescuing us."

Before Jo could reply, Malken arched his eyebrow and peered into the pot, saying, "That wasn't *ratart*, was it?"

"Yes."

"Appalling."

"D'Auberon," Firamen said without looking up from his work, "You wouldn't know appalling if it came up and bit you."

Jo saw that Malken was taken aback. He answered, "On the contrary. I was once bit by an appalling on one of my adventures in Ylaruam. Here," he continued, lifting up his shirt to expose his hip, "let me show you."

"If you would please cease your bickering," Tesseria said sternly. "We have a guest."

All three men pursed their lips and nodded shame-facedly. They each mumbled an apology, the foresters continuing with their cooking and the man from Darokin sitting down next to Jo. Without looking, she could tell he was staring at her.

"What lovely green eyes," she heard him murmur.

"We do not have much time for talk, Johauna," Tesseria said firmly.

"After we finish this meal, we must rescue the towns-people from the abelaats," Jo said.

"Pardon?" Malken said.

Jo answered without turning: "Those creatures are called abelaats."

"Oh, I don't think so, miss," Firamen said. "We've been around. Seen an abelaat once. They don't look like that."

"The one that you saw was not a true abelaat," Jo began, unsure if the story needed to be told. "You see, the abaton—"

"The what?" Malken asked. He was smiling absently and looking at her with a peculiar expression. Jo frowned and said, "The abaton. The gate that opened between the two worlds."

"They do not need to know this, Johauna Menhir," the sorcerer said. "As desired by your Sir Graybow and the Baroness of Penhaligon, the call to arms has been heard around the world, and many seek to stop the invaders."

"We are one of that group," Tesseria stated with a sweeping gesture toward the rest of the party. "We have been together for quite some time."

"And have a great deal of experience at our disposal," Bolten said.

"Not to mention magic," Firamen added.

Jo released a great sigh and rubbed her forehead. For a moment she had felt hope that this group might be able to combat the abelaats, and together they could all rescue the townspeople. She had thought that they might have been able to accompany her to the abaton. They obviously relied on magic, and that would be dangerous near the abaton.

"The abelaats feed on magic," she muttered. "Magic and blood."

"Magic is blood," Hastur said, his voice muffled. "And blood is magic. I know your concern, Johauna Menhir. I have a means to combat it."

"How?" Jo asked skeptically.

Tesseria held up her hand for silence. "The method does not matter, Johauna."

"Then what is your plan?"

"Our plan, Jo," Malken said, shuffling closer, "is to wait for the—abelaats, as you called them, to leave the town unguarded."

Jo shot the man from Darokin a heated look. "Why would they do that?"

"Because we have given them another target," Bolten said. He reached inside another cooking pouch and added a pinch of seasoning from it.

"The only thing they want is people," Jo stated.

"That's right," Malken said. "Their next target is a village not far from here."

"You're willing to use another town as bait to save the first?" she demanded. She started to rise when Tesseria grabbed her tabard and forced her back down.

"Do not fear for the safety of the village, Johauna," the elf said. "We have made sure that only enough villagers to lure the abelaat have stayed."

"And made sure they all have horses," Firamen said.

Nodding to herself, Jo thought about the plan. It sounded fair enough, though she was not wholly convinced that the abelaats would leave the entire town undefended. She said, "What do you propose to do about the abelaats that remain as guards?"

"Well it's a good thing you're here!" Malken replied,

patting her hand. "You've got just what it takes to—"

"A while ago you said she could barely stand," Bolten muttered.

Malken raised his eyebrow again in a disdaining look. "That was a while ago."

"All right! I understand!" Jo shouted. She could no longer take the constant banter. She thought about all the soldiers that had been killed fighting the abelaats on the field of battle and hoped that a small, elite party might succeed where the others failed. She was not heartened by the possibilities.

"I believe you," she whispered, holding her head in her hands. "Can we please just eat?"

🐌 🐌 🐌 🐌 🐌

"We're facing north. This is our location," Bolten said, holding up a parchment map for Jo. He pointed to a place that was near a line of mountains, not far from a huge forest. He indicated a castle to the south and west. "This is Penhaligon."

"Then this must be Armstead," Jo said, peering closer at the worn map. The parchment was ragged around the edges, though the rest of it was in good shape. From the patterns of water damage and regions of reinking, it was obvious that the map had been through as many adventures as its bearer.

Bolten nodded, scratching his nose. He shivered under his heavy cloak and said, "That's right. And that's where this 'abeetone' thing is?"

"Abaton," Jo answered, nodding. "It's the place I must

go after we rescue these people."

The forester looked down at his shoes. After a moment, he said, "Why don't you come with us? When you're done, that is. We're always on the lookout for—talent."

"You wouldn't want me!" Jo replied. She was almost too flattered to add, "I'm just a squire, not even a knight."

Bolten shrugged. "I'm no knight. Neither's Firamen. Malken's a fool—"

"You let him stay—"

"—but he's a talented fool," the forester answered. He nodded back over his shoulder and said, "Hastur's something else, and, well, Tesseria—she's just Tesseria." Bolten glanced around to make sure his words weren't being heard by the others preparing to break camp. He added, "In all honesty, miss, it'd be nice for a change to have someone to talk to."

Jo smiled and backed away from the forester. She had seen many adventurers when she had lived in Specularum, and like everyone else in the city, had wanted to be brave and bold enough to explore the dangers of the world. But she now had a quest of her own.

"I'm sorry, Bolten. Your offer's very kind, but I have a mission—"

"As we already know," Tesseria interrupted, slinging a light backpack of elven silk under her cloak. "I asked you not to confuse her, Bolten."

The forester gave the elf warrior a disdainful look and said, "I didn't say *now*, did I? Besides, that—mage, he isn't always right about everything, you know. Even his predictions can be wrong." Bolten finished by disdainfully wiggling his fingers in the air.

"Bolten, you know that Hastur hears everything," Tesseria said sternly.

"Then let him hear! He says what he thinks, and I'll—"

"Do what he says," Malken interrupted.

"Will you stop bickering!" Jo yelled. Breathing hard and deep, she stared at each of the party members in turn. Bolten and Firamen turned away with regret, Malken smiled with shame, and Tesseria lowered her head in respect.

"Nothing to say?" Jo demanded. "Fine!"

Tesseria sighed loudly and raised her head, fixing Jo with beautiful, violet eyes. Jo felt her frustration dissipating beneath the elf's gaze, but her emotions had been compounded by too many confusing and heartbreaking events in the past months to give in completely. She let her frown melt into a blank face.

The elf warrior turned to her companions and said, "Let us be moving. We'll talk on the way."

Jo watched as the group members completed their tasks. The equipment they carried was remarkably compact, and it fit into just two backpacks, which the foresters carried. This group was more efficient than any knights and squires Jo had ever seen.

"Are we ready?" Jo asked, turning to head back toward the town.

"Where are you going, squire?" Tesseria asked, gesturing for Jo to stop.

"Back to the town," Jo said, confused.

Malken walked up to her and rubbed his nose with a finger, smiling awkwardly. He mumbled, "We've, ah, quicker ways to travel."

Jo nodded. "And how's that?"

Hastur raised his robed arms above his head, crossed them once, then brought them down to his sides again. He stepped forward with his right foot, then his left, and bowed his head, bringing his hidden hands together.

"It is done," the mage stated in his thin voice.

Jo spun around.

A disk hung in the air like a doorway. It shimmered and pulsed, as if showing the heartbeat of the winds. The opening was about the same height as Jo, but its width seemed to vary at the edges. The disk curved, flattened, shifted—dancing hypnotically, soundlessly.

"We have not much time," Hastur added. "The workings of the abaton affect even my disciplines."

"Let us go!" Tesseria commanded, pointing to the disk. Bolten and Firamen were the first to enter the shimmering plane of light. Jo watched silently as their bodies were absorbed by the moire of colors. Though she had not noticed any fear in their eyes, she felt cautious about the idea of entering a portal.

"Where does it lead?" she asked Tesseria as the elf was guiding Malken through.

"Most likely near the avenue you discovered in the town," the man from Darokin said, stopping before Jo. "You see, our plan also used that same—"

Tesseria pointed to the portal and said, "Malken! Through!"

With a discontented sigh, the man in black gave Jo a half-smile and walked into the disk, absently ducking his head.

The elf warrior smiled warmly at Jo and said, "You're next." •

"The portal will not stay open long," the sorcerer hissed from deep inside his robes.

Jo turned and stared at the sorcerer. She became entranced by Hastur's robes. The purple and red pulsed, and the colors ran together. The shimmering threads had become as thick as veins, though they carried light instead of blood.

"Do not look," Tesseria said, stepping into Jo's view of the sorcerer. "That is not for human eyes."

"Enter," Hastur said, his voice weaker, more distant. Blinking her eyes to remove the afterimages of the mage's wondrous robes, Jo turned and ducked her head as Malken had done, holding her breath as if she were entering a cold pool of water. She clutched Peace to her chest.

Jo was startled by the sensation of cold. There was a distinct taste of honey in her mouth, but her nose picked up a scent like the orange blossom fruit that was sometimes imported to Specularum from the Ethengar Khanate. She saw nothing but blackness and thought for a moment that her eyes were closed; she shut her eyelids tight and opened them again, but found she remained in blackness.

Jo attempted to walk, but her feet hung in nothingness. She felt panic creep into the back of her mind as she thought that she actually might be underwater and drowning, though she did not feel anything pressing against her from the sides. She cautiously opened her mouth to taste the air.

The only sound Jo could hear was something she could not quite describe. She imagined it was the same sound she might hear if someone were yelling at her through a

thick wall, shouting very slowly. She attempted to find the
source of the sound but the darkness continued to block
her senses.

The strange sound grew louder, shifting in volume. Jo
suddenly had an impression of motion. Tucking her legs
up to her waist, Jo attempted to somersault in the darkness, as she had underwater while swimming in Specularum Bay.

Jo had the sudden fear that she had been betrayed and
was trapped in some dimension between the worlds, like
her father always said would happen if she used her blink-
dog's tail too often. Her fingers tightened angrily around
Peace's scabbard, and she edged it up until her hands were
around the hilt. Summoning her strength, she stabbed
upward, not knowing what she might strike.

"Make the portal wider!" Tesseria pointed directly at
Jo.

Jo stared out of a strange place, an ocean of smells and
textures and no sounds. She was now several feet away
from the disk of the portal, the only source of light in the
darkness.

"The blade blocks even my works," the sorcerer replied
thickly. Though she had been told not to look, Jo glanced
at the mage. His purple and red cloak no longer pulsed: it
had become his flesh. The sorcerer's hands ended in three
long tentacles, as did his face. His eyes seemed carved
from the coldest yellow stone. Jo had never heard of such
a creature in any legend, and its horrible appearance confirmed her fear that she had been cast adrift between the
worlds. Jo stabbed out again, betrayed, her fury giving her
arms strength.

The sorcerer opened his arms above his head and spread his strange fingers wide. Jo became suddenly nauseated and found herself drifting away from the portal. She attempted to move back to it but there was nothing for her to push against.

The portal vanished and Jo felt the sensation of crossing a great distance. Before she could react, she was dumped hard on the ground.

"What was the matter?" Malken asked politely, holding out his hand to Jo.

Jo glanced up in confusion at the procession that had gathered around. The brothers stared down at her in concern; Malken had donned his most charming smile—that of a fool. Jo breathed through her nose to calm herself and took the proffered hand.

Turning, she saw Tesseria step through the shimmering portal, quickly followed by the sorcerer. He once again wore the guise of his robes.

"We are truly sorry, Johauna," the elf warrior said, bowing low. "We did not understand the full power of your blade."

"You mean her sword stopped even Hastur's—whatever he calls them?" Malken exclaimed. "How rich!"

Jo nodded grimly and rested Peace on her shoulder. "Have the abelaats already gone to the other town?" she inquired, ignoring the admiring glances from the man from Darokin.

Bolten nodded. "The other town has just sent their first men out to lure those creatures away."

"Then there is no time to waste," Jo said. "We should head up through that avenue and kill the remaining abelaats."

Tesseria drew an ornately crafted sword from a sheath. She said, "Anyone free from fighting must release the prisoners."

Jo nodded and held Peace in a two-handed grip. She walked cautiously down the other side of the hill and discovered her own tracks leading into the town.

Chapter XV

he moment that Jo reached the edge of the avenue, the wind shifted, and she smelled the heavy spice scent of the abelaats. She glanced cautiously to either side to ensure that none of the creatures were in the immediate area, then stalked out between the buildings.

The first cross-street was twenty feet away, and only two of the four buildings that made up the original corner were still standing. She slowed to a stop, then tilted her head to listen carefully above the sound of the wind.

Malken poked his head out from the building to Jo's right, and she brought Peace down in a tight arc, halting the weapon's strike at the last moment.

"Are you insane?" she hissed.

The man from Darokin held his finger up to his mouth and made a silencing sound, rolling his eyes to the side.

Jo maintained her relative calm and listened again. The wind shifted, and she knew that there were several abelaats nearby.

"Hastur assures me that I will be able to kill those beasts with nothing more than my daggers," Malken whispered, placing his lips close to Jo's ear. She jerked her head back to increase the distance between them. "He says he's going to do something to help."

Jo gave the man in black a confused look and asked, "Like what?"

Malken shrugged in return.

The odor of heavy spice suddenly smothered Jo's senses, and she glanced around for somewhere to hide. Malken grabbed her by the arm and pulled her down into his hiding spot, which was little more than the remains of a closet that had been connected to the outer wall of the building.

Jo could not see out from where she was crouched, but the winds and smells told her that the abelaats were close.

The breeze calmed slightly. Jo began to rise, but Malken pushed her head down below the line of the building's remaining supports. She angrily batted his hand out of the way and pushed herself up again. Malken kept her back with a dagger near her face.

Jo stared at the point of the weapon and tried to control her breathing by clenching her fists. The flood of anger washed away the lingering fear in her heart. For whatever reason Malken was keeping her in place, he had her at the advantage. Peace would be useless in a fight in such close quarters. Jo was helpless.

The wind shifted and the beams of the building swayed and groaned. Jo ignored the dagger for a moment and peered up, wondering if the building might collapse. Malken meanwhile ignored everything but the abelaats on the street. His dark eyes were intent and darting, and his lips silently counted out their numbers.

Jo's discipline eroded, and she pushed the dagger out of the way with her finger, attempting to find a knothole or other opening in the charred wood so she could see what Malken was observing. She found a crack between two slats.

Twelve abelaats stood in the intersection, their black halos melding and shifting together into a pool of darkness. They were standing in three groups of four, all facing toward the center.

Jo heard a dripping sound near her shoe. She peered down in confusion. Only then did she realize that her finger was bleeding from where she had pushed away Malken's dagger.

As one, the abelaats turned their heads and began sniffing the air. Jo's heart froze. She attempted to stanch the wound by sucking away the excess blood. Malken meanwhile remained still. Even his dagger stayed in the same spot where Jo had moved it.

Two of the abelaats from the group nearest the building turned and left their ranks. They moved slowly, but not in caution. They snuffled like wild dogs around the lair of a rabbit. Jo held Peace tightly to her body.

Her sight dimmed.

The huge abelaat siege engines cast black stones into the cracked walls of the castle. Sir Graybow commanded the sappers

*to continue their repair work while drawing his heirloom
sword—a brilliant weapon of gold. It shone in the air as he
waved it above his head, inspiring the soldiers of Penhaligon to
repel the invaders.*

Jo was startled from the vision, brought back by the
noisome sniffing of the nearest abelaat. She clenched her
teeth hard against her anxiety, forcing herself to think
only of the people in the corral.

The blood from Jo's finger finally stopped flowing. For
the first time since they had crowded into the burned-
out shell, Jo heard Malken release a slight breath—
though she could not tell if it was from relief or fear. He
held his left fist for Jo to see, then pointed down with
two fingers, made a cutting motion, and closed the hand
into a fist again. Jo shook her head in confusion. The
man from Darokin repeated the gesture, then added a
point toward the two abelaats who were closest.

Jo slowly nodded. He was going to attack the two
abelaats closest to the building but was not going to step
out to do it; he was only going to attack if they came too
close. Jo held onto Peace with both hands, resting the
hilt on her hip and the blade against her right shoulder.
She searched for a place to maneuver if Malken's plan
failed.

The two abelaats approached the doorway where they
crouched. Jo held her breath, unable to see anything
more than the creatures' black halos through the crack in
the wood, unable to hear anything more than the quick
beating of her heart and the rush of the wind. Her skin
felt incredibly cold, though the temperature did not
change. It was the same empty sensation she had felt in

the place between worlds when she had used her blink-dog's tail.

The creatures continued walking the perimeter of the building, and soon all the abelaats were back in their original formation, facing each other in groups in the middle of the intersection. Malken dropped his fist again and held all his fingers flat and extended. He silently mouthed the word, "Wait."

Jo attempted to take a deep breath; there was no air. She panicked and tried to stand, but Malken held her head down with a hand. The man in black tilted her head back, and Jo tasted the air again. She forced herself not to gasp. When she tried to draw another breath, she couldn't until Malken pushed her head forward. Jo guessed that Hastur was using his magic. As long as she continued to move her head, she found more air.

The wind slowly died down, then stopped. As Jo took another slow breath, she had the impression that most of the air around her was frozen in place.

Malken let go of Jo's hair and brought three more daggers out from under his belt. Holding them in his left hand, he grabbed one with his right, flipped it over so he held the point, and released it with a flick of his wrist. While Jo blinked, Malken threw the other two daggers.

Four abelaats smashed through the side of the building, and Jo was thrown from the external closet into the ruined frame itself. She lifted herself up from the ash as an abelaat charged her. Its halberd tore a gash in her indigo tabard, glanced off the shoulder guard, and caught on the elven chain beneath. The halo surrounding the abelaat writhed snakelike along the shaft of the polearm and struck Jo's body, leaving her cold where the darkness had touched.

Jo buried Peace in the creature's chest; the abelaat fell to black dust before the cross-guard touched its halo. Jo followed through with the attack, driving the long sword in a tight arc. The next abelaat that rushed in deflected the swing with his halberd and locked the haft of his weapon with Peace. She pressed forward and attempted to drive the creature back. Locked in place by the struggle, she felt her breath betray her, and she lost her footing, falling backward and drawing Peace back with her.

The head of the halberd dropped to the ground and sent up a slow shower of dust and ash. Remembering to find new air to breath, Jo rolled out of the way as the abelaat drove the shattered haft down like a spear, snagging her long red hair and tearing some away. Jo was instantly on her feet again and was about to lash out in a wild swing when another of the abelaats appeared and shoved its weapon into her stomach.

The tip of the halberd did not penetrate the elven chain, but the strength of the creature's attack stunned Jo. Her red-silver blade fell to the ground and settled in the debris.

Three daggers struck the abelaat's flickering eyes and its nose. Another sank into its chest, and two more pierced the armor of its shoulders. Jo blinked hard against the pain in her head and abdomen, then searched for Peace in the black ash.

The daggers clattered off Jo's armor when the abelaat fell to dust. Her hand found the hilt of her sword, and she pushed herself up on her elbows, still trying to clear her head.

She could not seem to focus her vision. Something stood in front of her. Jo leaped to her feet and forced the tip of Peace into the abelaat, driving the blade hard and deep. She felt the sword penetrate through the armor in the creature's chest. When her hand touched the halo surrounding its body, Jo again felt the painful cold. The creature disintegrated before her, the halo vanishing.

Jo turned and looked for her companion. Malken clutched a huge gash in his side and leaned heavily against a charred support. Jo ran to him, scanning for any new abelaats. She rested Peace against the support and kneeled to check the man's wounds.

"You can talk now," he muttered, clenching his teeth. Jo no longer heard any charm or adoration in his voice.

Jo saw that the wound was deep, but not fatal. She patted at her clothing, wondering if she had brought anything to sew up the wound, but everything she had taken was with the packhorses of the Penhaligon forces.

"Do you have anything I can use for sewing?" Jo asked, slowly pulling the man's hand from his side. "I think I can—"

"Where in the name of the immortals were you?" Malken hissed. "You were the one supposed to save us, save everybody!"

Jo brought herself up to her full height, confused and resentful. "What are you talking about?"

Malken's lips curled back in a sneer. "Hastur said you were the one to save the world, with that sword—"

"What did you expect me to be?" Jo returned, careful to keep her voice low. "Some kind of hero to step in and—"

"That's exactly what I expected, but all I got was a girl who got lucky."

"Well," Jo began, unsure what to say. She knew that the man from Darokin had a valid point. "Well, I never claimed to be Flinn the Mighty," she said, stepping forward again to check the man's wound. "But it's lucky for you I'm here now."

"And why is that?"

"Because you could never do what I'm about to," Jo answered, tearing a strip of black cloth away from the man's impeccable garment. "Do you have any spirits?"

Malken closed his eyes and nodded, reaching inside his tunic with his right hand. He pulled out a small silver flask. Jo uncapped the flask and jerked her head back at the strong smell of alcohol. She poured a little onto the cloth and began cleaning the wound. Malken kept his eyes closed and clenched his jaw against the pain.

"Where are the other abelaats?" Jo asked as she wiped the blood from the edge of the wound.

"They were—they were killed by Hastur," Malken spat from between his teeth. "Sent away, or whatever he does."

"What did he do to the air?"

"Nothing to the air, and everything to—why should I know? He made sure those things could be killed with . . . mundane weapons," the man in black replied.

Malken breathed fast and shallow, keeping his eyes closed. Jo continued cleaning as quickly as possible. She was not a practiced chirugeon, though she had studied with one on a journey between Specularum and another city she could not remember. The man had taught her some things about wounds and healing.

"Find Tesseria," Malken said.

Jo glanced up from her cleaning, then peered around the building to make sure that they were not in any immediate danger. "What?"

"Find Tesseria and send her to me. She can—fix me," Malken returned, swallowing hard.

"I am here, Malken," the elf warrior said, stepping into the building from the door frame. She held a small crystal vial filled with some kind of liquid that had the sheen of pearls. "There's not much of this left."

"Then next time you take the lead," the man from Darokin replied. He pushed Jo away and put his hand back over the wound. Jo stood and looked at Malken. He was pale from loss of blood; she was surprised he was still conscious.

Tesseria held out the crystal vial to Malken, who took it with a shaking hand. She said, "The remaining abelaats have been destroyed, and the citizens of this town are prepared to leave."

"How many abelaats were left when the twelve came searching here?" Jo inquired.

Malken tilted the bottle to his lips and choked slightly as the liquid entered his mouth. The bleeding stopped immediately. The man in black took another sip and the wound slowly closed, healing as Jo watched. After a third sip, he handed the vial back to Tesseria.

"Stop hedging, Squire," Malken replied. "You were a decoy to lead the majority of the abelaats away. Just as you guessed."

"Malken!" the elf warrior said tersely.

"What?" the man returned, taking a forceful step in front of the woman. "What is it? She was supposed to be a great hero and isn't."

"Show respect. We already knew—"

"I don't care what we already knew!" With his last word, Malken bent down, picked up his daggers from the dust, and left the building. He was gone before Jo could respond.

"I think it would be best if I left," Jo muttered, disheartened. She rested Peace against her shoulder and tried to think of the best route to Armstead.

"There is no need, Johauna," Tesseria said, her beautiful face as open and honest as Jo had ever seen. "If you stay with us until these people are in safety, I assure you that we will give you every assistance."

Jo was dubious. "I don't think Malken would agree."

The elf warrior arched her eyebrow and said, "Malken does not lead this group."

"I'm still not too sure."

Tesseria nodded, her mouth dropping to a frown. "Very well," she said, replacing the crystal vial under her armor. "Then let us at least part friends and we can—"

"Tesseria!" Bolten yelled from the direction of the corral.

The elf walked out of the building. Jo followed. Bolten appeared from between two of the remaining buildings on the avenue, and he was frantic.

"What is it, Bolten?" Tesseria asked.

Jo felt the wind shift again. She glanced around her cautiously as the forester replied, "The scouts say the abelaats are returning."

❧ ❧ ❧ ❧ ❧

The people rushed out, channeled by the slope of the hills north and west of the town. Jo looked back over her shoulder as she directed the flood with waves of her red–silver sword.

The town's citizens rushed out in unorganized columns, kept from bottlenecking by the directions of the adventuring party members. Bolten and Firamen stood on either side of the remains of the corral's gates, which had long since been smashed by the people in their haste.

They were desperate, but Jo could see the hope in their eyes. These were not the dull-faced, cattlelike folk that she had seen standing in the corral when she first arrived. These people were alive and fiercely hopeful. It was hope that drove them onward, that gave their limbs the energy to push forward as the forces of the enemy returned behind them.

The wind continued to whip Jo's tabard, and she made sure it was tied securely to her waist. She stared at the indigo cloth and realized that despite all the dangers and trials she had been through, the cloth had little been soiled or damaged. She rubbed the fabric of the tabard between her fingers; it felt strangely ordinary.

A small group of people broke away from the main lines and started to trek out across the open plain. Jo ran after them, waving once to Firamen.

"Where are you going?" she demanded when she reached the group. They were all members of the same family. The oldest of the group, a burly man with jet black hair and beard, waved the others on when they hesitated. Turning back to Jo, he said, "We're leaving—going back to the old country."

Jo did not recognize the man's accent. She asked, "Where's that?"

The man replied by pointing vaguely to the south. "We have family there. You take the rest of them wherever they wish to go, but we are going home."

Jo was astounded by the man's words—he must have known the abelaats would be returning from the south. She could not deny, however, that the man might have a better place of retreat than what had apparently been proposed by Tesseria and the others. Maintaining her calm, Jo asked, "Should everyone go there?"

"It will not matter," the man replied, shaking his head. Without another word he turned and left, quickly catching up with his family. Jo stared after them a moment, seeing that the man's wife clutched a baby. They shuffled off with that same sad urgency she had seen in her own father and mother as the ship beneath her slid soundlessly backward, toward Specularum. She wondered if her parents were still alive and if they were happy.

Firamen ran up to where Jo stood. He stared after the family as well and asked, "What did he say?"

Jo shrugged. "Nothing. Nothing that matters."

The forester slung his quiver over his back and removed a map from inside his tunic. It was the same map Bolten had shown her earlier. The location where Jo had met the adventuring party was now circled in black. Another black line joined the circle to the end-point of Hastur's gate. Taking the map, Jo gauged that the distance between their location and Penhaligon was at least three days forced march, assuming full provisions. Clearly this rag-tag and impoverished army would take much longer than three days.

Pointing to the line of travel, Jo said, "We want to head them in this direction. There's a stream here that will give them fresh water and a forest nearby where some of them might be able to hunt for food." Jo folded the map and began to hand it to Firamen but he shook his head, indicating for Jo to take it. She put the parchment into the belt that held her tabard to her waist.

"Where's Tesseria?" she asked, stepping back near the line of people to ensure that they kept moving.

The forester shrugged. "With Hastur, I suppose. He seems weak after destroying those things."

Firamen looked Jo in the eye and smiled oddly, the same look of adoration she had noticed from the squire at the Castle of the Three Suns. The forester turned and walked away before she could say anything.

Jo peered out over the heads of the crowd and attempted to find the elf warrior at the head of the column. Despite the fact that she was taller than most, she still could not quite see over the heads of the people. Jo wanted to ask where all these people were ultimately going to stay. The Duke's Road Keep or the Castle of the Three Suns seemed to be the obvious choices. She knew that Sir Graybow would give them all food and shelter.

The thought of the castellan made Jo wonder whether he was doing well, or he was continuing to lose weight. Looking back toward Firamen, Jo hoped that she would be able to introduce her new friends to the others she knew, including Braddoc. She shook her head in dismay and raised herself up on her toes, looking out over the masses again.

"Where are we going to go?" a young boy asked his father. The man glanced at Jo and raised his eyebrows in question.

"You're going to a place of safety," Jo answered, momentarily stepping into the rush. She held Peace above her head to avoid accidentally hurting someone.

The boy's eyes locked onto the red-silver sword and grew wide with wonder. "I've heard of that sword," he murmured, absently reaching up to touch the blade. "It's called Peace."

Jo smiled warmly and let the boy see the sword more closely. His hand moved within a few inches of the runes carved into the flat of the weapon, but he pulled away before touching it, and he smiled at Jo.

"Thank you," he said, moving to keep up with everyone else. The father whispered his thanks as well.

Jo maintained her smile as the two walked away. When she spotted Tesseria, she let her smile slowly fade and started toward her. The elf warrior was busy directing the flow of people while maintaining her vigil, watching the hills for the enemy.

"Johauna," Tesseria began, her voice clear over the muted sound of the crowd. She kneeled down and helped a young girl retrieve a doll of rags, then stood back up. "What is it?"

"I wanted to say how—happy I am to have met you," Jo answered, stepping up close so she might be more easily heard.

The elf smiled and put her hands on Jo's shoulders. "Diulanna watches over you," she said. Tesseria pointed behind Jo and added, "Hastur would speak with you."

Jo was confused at the elf's words, but she turned in the indicated direction. The mage stood a short distance away, the ends of his sleeves tucked inside one another. As Jo moved in his direction, she wondered what he would have to say.

"Tesseria said you wished to speak with me," Jo said. She peered deeply into the sorcerer's robes to see his face, but she could not penetrate the disturbing darkness that lay within.

"I have foreseen the events that will happen within a few short minutes, Johauna Menhir," the mage replied. "Before that time, there are things I would have you know."

Jo turned back to the line of people and wondered if she could afford to spend any time away from them. Hastur interrupted her thought, saying, "You have seen my form true in the daylight and know I am not of your race, nor of any you have heard. As the elf woman said, there are many who are coming to the world's aid. My people thank you."

Before she could reply, the magician stepped forward, the scent of his oils overwhelming the spice of the approaching abelaats. He said, "We will all be killed within a few moments. Only you shall survive."

Jo blinked in confusion, then felt terror and anger take hold of her heart. She looked to the gentle-eyed elf woman and moaned, "We've got to tell Tesseria. We've got to tell the others."

"They know," the mage whispered.

Jo turned and started to run back toward Tesseria. The air suddenly shifted around them, and some of the people screamed. Jo looked up to the hills and saw that the abelaats had finally arrived.

The townspeople panicked, no longer guided and controlled by the adventuring band. Jo attempted to rally them by holding Peace high in the air and shouting, but her voice and the flash of her blessed sword were lost in the tumbled shouts and rustling tumult of the crowd. Bolten and Firamen called out futilely to the mob, but like a river that had overrun its embankment, the villagers rushed heedlessly away from the advancing abelaats.

The shadow monsters swept across the plain, razing the remaining buildings with vicious chops of the polearms and swords that emerged from their bodies. In moments, the advance units set upon the human stragglers.

Jo tried to block out the screams as she ran to the fighting, Peace shimmering above her head. With her free hand, she pushed her way through the rushing tide of people. Still the screams rang out, still the abelaats advanced. The creatures' black halos stole the light and heat from the air, and their feet trampled the bodies of the dead into the ground.

Pressing on, Jo wondered how Hastur—how Tesseria!—could so mislead these people into believing they could survive. Next moment Jo was struck to the ground by a yammering swarm of children, and in that instant, the answer to her question was clear. Even in those young, fierce, frightened faces, there was a light she had not seen before, a light that was missing when they were corralled for the slaughter.

And that light was hope.

Chapter XVI

raybow peered out of the baroness's waiting room in the high tower of the castle. He wore his leather-padded armor over a cloth undersuit, which he had darned himself upon returning from Melios's estate. In its gold scabbard, Sage leaned against the wall.

The Grand Marshaling of Forces had been heeded by every castle and keep within a weeks' ride of the Castle of the Three Suns. Many of the units were forced to maintain their position outside the castle proper, along the wide road leading up to the gates. Graybow had sent his most trusted knights into the field to act as liaisons between the troops. He sighed in disappointment; a majority of the leaders were more interested in personal glory and the spoils of war than successful cooperation with other forces.

The door leading to the hallway opened, and the

castle's oldest mage entered. Graybow contemptuously regarded the man before turning back to observe the troop movements.

"What have you to report, Aranth," the castellan inquired evenly.

"Nothing, milord," the mage replied, his long robes throwing dust into the air as he walked forward.

Graybow had expected the old man's answer. Since Teryl Auroch had arrived in the castle, all the mages had turned out to be either incompetent or turncoats. All the turncoats had been dealt with, leaving the castellan to deal with the rest.

"Is there any way to speed the word of the Marshaling?" he asked.

Aranth dipped his head, then squeezed his hands together nervously. "In what way do you suggest, milord?"

Graybow cursed. He thought about asking some of the landholders for the loan of their sorcerers. "The way we have always communicated across distances. Communication magics. Travel magics—"

"None of which are working since the opening of the abaton, milord," the magician replied, as if speaking to a forgetful child. "As you can see, the castle is still lit by torches and our—"

"Aranth," the castellan interrupted, "if you possessed an ounce of craft, I would listen to you." Graybow peered down into the courtyard toward the troops of Ludwig von Hendriks, the Black Eagle. A black-robed magician suddenly appeared amidst their ranks, his magic sending up a flash. "Aranth, leave me. Go back to your studies, or whatever you were doing." Graybow did not look up.

"Milord, I fail to see why—"

"Go!"

Aranth raised his eyes and shook his head in deprecation. He left without another word, for which Graybow was grateful. The sorcerers of a castle were not like other sorcerers; they had to be skilled both in their art and in courtly functions. It was their duty to understand the workings of the castle to ensure its safety, in much the same way as the castellan.

"Is there a problem, Castellan?" the baroness asked as she entered the room.

Graybow ran his hand through his long gray hair and said, "I have waited many years for the court of Karameikos to send a better class of magician, milady. It seems I wait in vain."

"There seems to be little use for magic now, Castellan," the baroness replied. "Your wait is over."

"No, milady, it still seems that—"

Graybow turned to face the baroness, but could not finish his sentence. The lady had donned her family surcoat and finely crafted armor. The metal had been lacquered in shades of blue, like the color Graybow had once seen reflecting from an elven lake. The plates themselves were edged with silver and held together by clasps shaped like the heads of lions. The shoulder guards extended a hand's length from the neck piece, giving the lady a more stately appearance than she already possessed. To Graybow, she seemed a vision—inspiration.

"What is the matter, Castellan?"

Graybow blinked once, at first embarrassed, then angry

with himself. He did not allow himself to turn away. "I apologize for staring, milady. I have never seen you in such—splendor."

"Let us hope that others agree," the baroness replied. "But I thank you for the compliment, Castellan."

"I have never seen such raiment before. Was it made by your father's master artisan?" Graybow asked.

The baroness checked the buckles between the neck piece and the shoulder guard. "I do not know who made this armor. I do not even know if it carries protective enchantments," she said.

"You could always ask one of your sorcerers."

Running her right hand along the smooth lacquer of her left vambrace, the baroness replied, "I, like you undoubtedly, would rather speak with the magicians of one of the other courts." The baroness shook her head in anger and sat down in a wide chair across from Graybow. "I fail to see why Stefan Karameikos sends us the worst from the magical colleges. We are fortunate we do not rely on magic for more than the most minor conveniences. And we can do without magical lighting."

Graybow removed the journal from his belt and opened to a very early page. With a certain trepidation, he glanced over the words and said, "There is one particular magical light we cannot do without, baroness."

The baroness pursed her lips and stared out the window at the assembling troops. Graybow waited for a reply, watching as the woman's austere expression slowly gave way to disappointment.

"You know, Graybow, I have no great love of sorcery," she finally replied. "I believe it has brought more harm to the world than good."

"Especially in this instance, milady."

The baroness sighed loudly and glanced across the vast room at her neat bookshelves. "If there were some other way to fight this battle, I would gladly accept it."

" 'In times of greatest need can the Three Suns be called upon to aid Penhaligon and her people,'" Graybow quoted solemnly from his journal. " 'It is given to the royalty of Penhaligon to use this power, with prejudice and with wisdom. To you, my daughter, I grant this power, and wish it may forever lie at rest.'" Graybow closed the journal and added, "Do you remember these words of your father, given to you on his deathbed?"

"Yes—it has my father's tone," the baroness stated. She stood and walked to the arched window, leaning against the white marble. "You would think that with the vast array of troops at our disposal we should be able to repel the invaders."

"If I thought that were the case, milady, I would have certainly said as much," Graybow said. He saw that the baroness had become introspective, a vast change from her normally stately pallor. "If you have found fault with my conclusions, I would be grateful if you would honor me with your own."

The baroness peered at Graybow out of the corner of her eye, and then she gave him a half smile. "There's no need for such formality, Lile. You are my castellan and my friend. And as always, your conclusions are sound."

Graybow pulled away from the window as the baroness turned back to regard the troops. He could not remember the lady ever openly stating their friendship. It made him feel slightly uncomfortable, and yet honored at the same time. It also reminded him of the gravity of the situation, as when comrades part for the last time.

"I do not think that Stefan Karameikos himself will make an appearance at this battle," the baroness said, standing away from the window and facing Graybow. "I hear that the noblemen of Specularum are worried about their holdings and demand that the royal garrison remain behind."

"We do not need the garrison, milady," the castellan said, glancing out the window. "We need the army for their cavalry and heavy infantry. The garrison is best suited for—less strenuous activities."

The baroness laughed at Graybow's joke and said, "I see those trips to the capitol have been enlightening. I will have to tell Madam Astwood to be less stringent with the expenditures of state."

Graybow nodded his agreement as he walked up to a large wooden chest that two of the servants had brought in before the baroness had arrived. He grunted as he opened the lid with both hands, then reached in and removed his mail shirt. It was rusting and worn, but still of the finest quality.

"I can tell you, milady," he said, lifting the heavy shirt over his head, "that the Grand Marshaling of Forces has reached the ends of the kingdom, and has gone as far as the Five Shires." After pulling his arms and head through the shirt, he straightened it out and checked for broken links, saying, "I'm not sure we can expect reinforcements from that quarter."

"When are the abelaats expected to arrive?" the

baroness asked, stepping closer.

Graybow untangled a piece of chain from its leather backing and said, "According to our scouts, their army will reach the Castle of the Three Suns within an hour, perhaps two."

"Then we have no time to waste," the baroness replied, reaching into the chest and pulling out the other pieces of Graybow's mail. "Which units have already arrived?"

"The two elite cavalry divisions from Specularum, which number eight heavy cavalry units, four longbow units, and four infantry units," Graybow answered, buckling his waist armor.

The baroness handed Graybow the guards for his neck and shoulders. She asked, "And the regular divisions?"

"Already deployed in the field," Graybow said. "The rise to the castle is difficult to navigate, and the heavy cavalry's shock of impact will be much greater when they ride from uphill."

"And the king's cousin?"

"Von Hendriks has brought another token force," the castellan replied with a grimace. He placed a greave over his right leg and ran the strap through the buckle connecting to his waist armor. He added, "Orcs with crossbows. But to assuage our suspicions of his intentions, he has accompanied the rest of the Black Eagle Lancers. They are all waiting outside the walls. I am not relying on them to fight."

With the baroness's help, Graybow quickly got into the rest of his armor. He checked the straps and buckles to ensure they were securely fastened. The baroness did the same again for her armor. "I am glad you advised me to take lessons in battle," she said.

"It was as much your father's request as my own."

"My father was a remarkable man, wasn't he?" the baroness asked rhetorically as she headed back toward her suite. "I hardly knew him."

Graybow had often wondered about the relationship between the Baron of Penhaligon and his daughter, and with the woman's words, he finally understood a great deal more about their family. He hoped that the baroness would one day take a husband, as there was currently no heir to the throne. He walked to the window and buckled Sage to his waist, thinking grimly that there might not be a need for an heir.

"I do not like last minute preparations, but it seems we have little choice," the baroness said, closing the door to the room. She carried a long spear and buckler, lacquered the same color as her armor; a silver sabre hung from her belt. "If we have only an hour, then we had better use it to our advantage."

The baroness motioned Graybow from the room. The castellan took one final glance through the window, his eyes lingering over the splendid castle and the stately troops. Had this been another war, he would never have doubted the outcome of the battle.

Graybow found the fervent activity within the castle walls astounding. The temporary markets and homes had been cleared away, and within minutes, smithies, arms makers, and fletchers were in their place. The captains and sergeants Graybow had put in charge of maintaining unit integrity and provisioning men and horses were performing their tasks admirably.

"You look very proud, Castellan," the baroness said, standing inside the doorway to the great hall. Graybow nodded his head in satisfaction.

"These are the finest men a leader could want. In a few hours, they are going to battle, without complaint or question," Graybow replied. He had been in many situations where troops would rebel against fighting when given insufficient warning to prepare. The nobility were notorious for this behavior. "They are ready for battle."

"Tell me what you see," the baroness commanded. "I do not take my public appearances lightly and will not show myself until necessary."

Graybow nodded his understanding. The baroness did not make more than a handful of appearances a month, and to appear prematurely in the window would unsettle the troops. "The soldiers are lined in columns, filling the courtyard. I have ordered the Penhaligon militia to man the walls and battlements, and they stand ready."

"There is only a token force at the sides and back of the castle?" the baroness asked, standing patiently.

"My findings at Councilman Melios's estate indicated that the abelaats only attack from one front—"

"Like a wave from the sea," the lady interrupted.

Graybow nodded. "Yes, much like a wave. We know they will be using siege engines of some type, so the sappers are standing ready to shore any breaches. They have worked since my arrival to ensure that there is enough raw material."

"Where have you placed our siege engines?"

The castellan hesitated before answering. When he had returned from Melios's estates, he had checked the few catapults and onagers in the castle's arsenal. They had not been kept in good repair, and he had been forced to have them hastily reworked. The task was yet unfinished.

"I'm afraid that the only engines at our disposal are those few brought by the Grand Marshaling. Our own ballistae are mounted on the walkways atop the curtain walls."

The baroness gave the castellan a skeptical look. "How many ballistae do we have?"

"Four—five, but one is not reliable," Graybow answered. "The commanders of the other forces insist on keeping their engines with them. They want to use them as rallying points." Before the baroness could say anything, Graybow added, "I told them that the castle was the rallying point, but they would not listen to reason."

"I could command them."

Graybow shook his head. "That will not be necessary. If the troops need to rally back to their siege engines, they will be moving too fast to stop." A sound of boots in the hall drew Graybow's attention. "There's commander Chilatra. I must speak with him."

Graybow left the doorway and ran to intercept the commander, who turned about with an annoyed look. He halted, rolling a piece of parchment and jamming it into a traveling bag at his side.

"Commander," the castellan began with a quick look back at the door, "have you heard any news from the others—Domerikos or Joline?"

"No, Castellan, I have not," Chilatra replied curtly, glancing at the formed troops. "Neither has survived."

"And what of Squire Menhir?"

Commander Chilatra shifted his darting gaze from the men to Graybow. The castellan was taken aback by the vehemence in the man's stare. "I do not know where she is. I must go now—"

"One more thing, Commander," Graybow said, grabbing the man's arm before he could push past. The castellan pulled the commander close and whispered, "I know of your feud with Domerikos. If I find out you had any part in his death, I'll have you tried and hanged."

Chilatra face contorted with rage, and he tore away from Graybow's grasp, stalking off without a word. The castellan watched as the man removed the parchment from his traveling bag. Graybow decided then that he must somehow obtain the scroll.

He heard a horn sound from afar, guessing it came from somewhere in the farmlands a few leagues away. The note was repeated a moment later. The activity in the castle came to an uneasy halt. Anyone in the castle would recognize the sound; it announced the approach of the invaders.

On the third note, everyone in the courtyard, castle proper, and outside the walls broke into action. The heralds atop the curtain wall sounded their horns in return. The song played by the trumpeters put Graybow on edge. Throughout the day, he had been awaiting the call to war, but he still felt unprepared. He doubted whether anyone felt differently.

Graybow heard a yell from the troops stationed farthest from the castle wall, the elite squadron of medium cavalry hired from Darokin. There was another yell from the same area, and the castellan saw twin clouds of dust rise up in the distance. He gritted his teeth; the duels of pride among the elite units had begun.

Graybow angrily turned to reenter the tower room, but stopped himself as the baroness stepped out of the doorway. She looked resplendent in her armor, and her sudden presence commanded the attention of those rushing now through the hall.

"It is time, Sir Graybow," she said. The castellan said nothing, gravely nodding.

The baroness reached under her armor and removed a golden key from a thong around her neck. Graybow saw that the key was engraved with three suns.

More trumpets sounded in the distance, but Graybow kept his attention on the baroness.

Together they approached the grand, high window of the tower. Arteris leaned her spear against a wall and handed Graybow her blue-lacquered helm, then faced the front of the castle and held the key above her head. Her hands slowly drew through the air in the rough shape of a doorway. Graybow watched in fascination as the key left gold traceries hanging in nothingness, slowly coalescing into solid form. A doorway.

The portal was taller than the baroness, partially filled with the golden light that now shone from the key, partially transparent, revealing the castle courtyard beyond. From his vantage, Graybow saw that the door perfectly matched the position of the doorway to the main hall. The baroness backed away a step as the sound of trumpets from outside the wall grew into a deafening cacophony. The wind had picked up, and it whisked dust from the field into the castle window. Graybow smelled spices.

The door's keyhole was a black void, and into it the baroness inserted the key, pushing forward with all her strength. The sound of scraping metal rang throughout the castle, as loud where Graybow stood as it was in the farthest corner of the courtyard.

Above the mountains to the east, the grayness in the air parted slightly.

The baroness tried to turn the key, but did not have the strength, even using both hands. Graybow placed her helm on the ground and added his strength to hers. The exertion brought pain from the wound in his back, and his clenched teeth ground together.

Outside, sunlight cracked the sky, traceries of gold raining down on the castle.

The sound of screaming metal continued to grow as Graybow and the baroness turned the key in the ethereal doorway.

"How much farther do we need to turn it?" the castellan asked between gasping breaths.

The baroness could not unlock her gritted teeth. "The entire way," she hissed.

Something heavy smashed into the stone outer wall of the castle, shaking the tower slightly and creating a patter of dust and stone chips. Muted shouts from men on the embankment filtered into the hallway, yelling as another siege missile struck.

The key was halfway turned when the sun finally broke through the choking clouds, appearing behind the peaks called the Craven Sisters. The twin spires split the light of the sun into three orbs, bathing the castle in its warmth.

The stones of the keep glowed with white power, and

yellow veins crept up from the ground like vines, covering and reinforcing the walls. Three horizontal shafts of sunlight danced around the towers of the castle, lighting and warming Graybow's face as he sweated to complete the key's rotation.

With a final scream, Graybow and the baroness forced the key to the block, and were thrown back. Graybow watched in amazement as the ethereal door slowly swung open, revealing a huge vault, a vault that held three suns.

The spheres shot out of the vault into the air, circled once around the castle, and sped away in the direction of the battle. Graybow and the baroness pushed themselves to their feet. The lady took up her weapon and donned her helm. Graybow drew Sage from its scabbard, the gold of the sword catching the light of the newly born sun.

"Fight, soldiers of Penhaligon!" he cried, rushing forward. "Fight, for we are the last hope of the world!"

Chapter XVII

linn sat on a rock in the middle of the forest, his chin propped up on his right fist. Braddoc stood a short distance away and waited impatiently for his friend to say something. The two had arrived in the forest some time ago, and the dwarf was beginning to grow uncomfortable with the silence and, especially, the lack of action.

The immortal's body now shone with even more vitality than when he had stepped from the fires of Armstead. Flinn's flesh had taken on the red glow of a sunset that Braddoc was particularly fond of remembering. The life from the place of the elves flowed silver in the man's veins, and his hair was wild and full. From the way the shadows fell across Flinn's face, Braddoc could still see the fire from the dwarven forge burning in his friend's eyes.

.

Peering around at the woods, Braddoc guessed that they were no longer in the forest of any elves. The trees here seemed friendlier to the dwarf, less presumptuous and solemn, and Braddoc was comforted by the earthy smells in the air. The sky was still gray, but the canopy of leaves did not completely block all sight of the clouds, as it had in Alfheim. He thought about smoking his pipe and started to reach into his vest, then decided against it.

"Go ahead. Smoke if you like," Flinn said. "It's expected."

Startled by the sudden statement, Braddoc turned to look at this friend. "Are you sure?"

Flinn fixed the dwarf with a brief stare that made Braddoc fall back a step. "That's a silly question," the immortal replied.

Braddoc snorted a short laugh, thinking that he shouldn't forget with whom he was truly dealing. Flinn's behavior and mannerisms were now more natural than ever. In this new place, however, Flinn had not been drawn toward one locus of power—one font that held the essence of the local people. So he had sat. And Braddoc had paced.

As Braddoc pulled out his long-stemmed pipe, he looked back at his friend, who stared into the woods, seemingly depressed. The dwarf tried to imagine what it would be like to feel love but not remember the people loved. He shook his head; it was too horrible for him to consider.

"What are you thinking, Braddoc?" Flinn asked darkly.

The dwarf was startled from his reverie. "What?"

"What is in your thoughts?"

Without answering, Braddoc reached inside his vest and produced a pouch of pipe-weed, taking an oversized pinch away from the rest of the moist clump. He thoughtfully filled the bowl and lit it with his tinderbox, letting the smoke fill his mouth and waft into his nose.

Flinn finally turned his head, but did not change his pose. "Well?"

"Don't you know what I'm thinking?" Braddoc inquired mildly, the blue smoke curling around his head. Perhaps this game would bring some levity to his friend's dark mood.

Flinn's eyes narrowed, and it seemed to the dwarf that the flames of inspiration burned hotter. "I am asking to be polite," he answered evenly.

"Thank you, Flinn," Braddoc replied, taking another long drag on his pipe. He made a note to remember that not only had he once been asked "please" by an immortal, but he was also being catered to out of civility; the thought amused him more than anything else he could recall. He held out the ceramic stem and asked, "Would you like to try?"

"I don't think it's a habit I want to begin," Flinn said, shaking his head and resuming his original posture. Braddoc thought about the answer for a moment, then could not stop himself from laughing. He laughed so hard that his sides began to hurt, forcing him to put the pipe down on a nearby tree stump so he wouldn't accidentally break it.

Flinn half-rose from his place and demanded, "What's so funny?"

"You!" Braddoc said, pointing. He wiped at the tears in

his eyes and added, "You don't think it's a habit you want to begin! What kind of thing is that for an immortal to say?"

Flinn stood to his full height and stepped forward, leveling an accusing finger at the dwarf.

Braddoc interrupted, "I've lived over five hundred years and never have I heard something so ridiculous. What a story!"

For a moment, Flinn said nothing, standing and pointing at the hysterical dwarf. He slowly relaxed his arm and covered his mouth with his hand. "It is a strange thing, isn't it?" he mumbled rhetorically.

"Strange? Strange!"

Braddoc could no longer stand. He fell to his knees and roared, holding his arms across his stomach, gasping for air. He thought about the austerity of their mission, the fact that the world was in danger of being laid lifeless by horrible creatures and their master, Teryl Auroch. He then thought about the fact that he was laughing harder than he could ever remember in the midst of all this danger, and that made him laugh even more.

Flinn began laughing around his hand, then lowered his arm and bellowed out loud. Braddoc was stunned by the richness of his friend's laughter and realized that it was Flinn's first laugh since being reborn to Mystara. The sound seemed to come from so deep within Flinn's heart that for a moment Braddoc felt his own monumental laughing was nothing.

Flinn's stance reminded Braddoc of some of their early travels together, when they had been nothing more than mercenaries. At the time, Flinn had told a particularly ribald joke, which had set them both off and had brought the two of them closer together. Braddoc laughed again, holding the memory fondly in his thoughts.

"What are we doing dawdling in this place?" the dwarf asked, chuckling as he tamped the embers in his pipe with a calloused finger. "We've got a world to save."

Flinn's laughter died down, though his smile did not fade. He sat back on his rock and said, "We are in the land of the halflings, and we are doing what we should be doing. We're remembering the old times."

Braddoc nodded to himself, finally understanding why he felt so much more comfortable in this forest than he had felt in the land of the elves. Halflings were like dwarves with a sense of humor. He asked, "How much of the old times do you remember?"

The expression on Flinn's face finally vanished, leaving him with a somber look. Braddoc quieted himself and sat on the stump, waiting patiently for an answer as he dug back into his pouch again. He engrossed himself in the task, too embarrassed to stare Flinn in the face as the man sought for an answer.

"I—I—"

Braddoc glanced up from his work and was completely taken aback by Flinn's reaction. The immortal sat with his head in his hands, tears running down his face and pouring over his fingers.

"Flinn!" the dwarf exclaimed, jumping to his feet in concern.

"Tell me about myself, Braddoc," Flinn said around his choked words. "I have feelings but no memories. I cannot bear this pain."

Braddoc moved awkwardly to comfort his friend, unsure how to do so. The dwarf reached out with his hand, but Flinn pushed it away and shook his head, murmuring his thanks. Braddoc's mouth jerked in a half smile, and he felt embarrassed again. He had seen Flinn in many states—raging mad and deliriously happy—but only once before, only at his reinstatement into the order, had he ever seen Flinn cry.

"What can I tell you, Flinn?" Braddoc said honestly. "I'm not much of a storyteller. . . . I could make the most interesting tale as dull as old iron. I guess the legends I know about you are the most interesting."

"Then tell me one of those tales. It does not matter in this place whether the teller is skilled or not—only that the story is told."

Braddoc peered around into the depths of the forest and wondered how old tales could imbue Flinn with the essence of this place. The dwarf looked back at his friend and upbraided himself. The greatest task Flinn had yet to bear was hearing of the life that had been robbed from him.

The first thought that came to the dwarf was to talk of Johauna. He hoped that she fared well among the trickeries and machinations of the Penhaligon court. Braddoc was sure that Sir Graybow would do his best to keep her from harm, though not even the castellan was capable of knowing every plot that was unfolding in the castle. Reconsidering, Braddoc did not think it best to describe the woman that Flinn had loved as a mortal; the pain of love lost would be only heightened if he could remember her face. Even so, by repeating Jo's words for describing

Flinn's last moments of life, Braddoc might bring her back to him in a less painful way.

"I will tell you of the most important event in your life," Braddoc began, taking up his pipe again. He pulled hard on the stem to ensure that the bowl would remain hot while he spoke. "I will tell you of your final days, as told by another chronicler.

"Let's see. We, that is, you, were on the field of battle somewhere near, uh—I'm afraid I'm not making a very good start of this," Braddoc mumbled, embarrassed.

"That's all right," Flinn said. "Please go on."

"Very well. In this life you were known as Fain Flinn, Flinn the Mighty, and you had a sword named Wyrmblight. Wyrmblight was a great sword blessed by the lord of the Castle of the Three Suns to slay the great green dragon, Verdilith. You and Verdilith had fought before, and he was your greatest foe, but another friend of yours, of *ours*—Karleah Kunzay—she told you of a prophecy that said you would perish when you next fought Verdilith."

"Apparently she was right," Flinn said softly.

Braddoc was glad for the interruption because he knew his words were rambling. He nodded. "Karleah wasn't popular like other sorcerers I'd seen, but she was well skilled in her art. Her dreams were never wrong."

Wiping the tears from his face, Flinn asked, "Were you friends?"

"Friends? Yes, I suppose you could say that. I often wondered if the old crone guessed who I truly was and if she knew that this eye wasn't an eye," Braddoc replied. He shrugged, adding, "She and I had our rivalries, but if she ever knew these things, she never mentioned it. Perhaps that alone proves our friendship."

Flinn nodded his understanding and shifted position. He sat with his knees drawn up to his chin and his arms enfolding his legs. He said, "I do not remember her name."

"She was destroyed in an attempt to discover the inner workings of the abaton. But that's not part of this story. This story begins with your final hunt of Verdilith at the glade where you had first fought. We had left the Castle of the Three Suns after your reinstatement into the knighthood—you, me, Karleah, and two others," Braddoc said quickly, hoping that Flinn would not ask about the others. Braddoc breathed out a long plume of smoke in relief. "You left our tents late at night without waking anyone. I have a feeling that Karleah might have known you were leaving, but she also knew she could do nothing to stop you. I suspected you might leave, but I didn't think you'd leave without me."

"Sorry."

"What?" Braddoc asked, unsure if he had heard his friend correctly.

"I said, sorry. I did not mean to cause you pain."

"Oh, well, that's all right," Braddoc muttered, staring down at the soft earth. The dwarf felt ashamed for bringing his friend obvious pain. He considered stopping the tale, but Flinn had asked to hear it, and the spirits of Braddoc's ancestors had urged him to provide the immortal as many of his memories as time allowed. Even that knowledge did not comfort Braddoc.

He continued, attempting to add a little levity to his voice, but the words sounded insincere. He said, "You were, after all, Flinn the Mighty. What did an old woman's prophecy mean to you, who were the hero of the land? You rode out on your griffon, Ariac, to the glade where you had fought before. According to this other chronicler, you struck Verdilith a mortal blow with Wyrmblight, cutting the dragon's wings so it could not fly, then driving it off in fear. But Verdilith had caught you in his teeth and . . . harried your flesh. You bled your life into the ground as you followed the dragon's trail."

Braddoc continued to stare down at the ground, unable to look his friend in the face. Braddoc realized that for the first time, he truly thought of the Immortal Flinn as the friend he had known in mortal life. It was no less painful now to remember Flinn's death than it had been to see the knight's tortured body. He regained his composure and said, "You died later that day, and we burned you four days later in the ceremony that befitted a knight . . . no, *the* knight of Penhaligon."

The light of the sun seemed to darken, and Braddoc glanced up through the leaves to see the sky above. Apparently the sunlight had been an illusion; roiling clouds still filled the sky.

The bowl in Braddoc's pipe had gone cold, but he did not feel like lighting it again. He shrugged despondently. The story he had told reminded him of things he thought he was old enough to let lie in legend. He had lived too long to allow the death of friends to cut him so deeply.

"What do you think of the story?" the dwarf asked, finally raising his head.

Flinn continued to hold his knees, but his tears had stopped. He did not reply.

Braddoc set his jaw in a tight line, determined to comfort his friend even if the man tried to push him away. He stepped forward, seeing that Flinn was so upset he barely breathed. Even the silver running through his veins and the golden sheen of his skin were muted.

"Flinn?" Braddoc murmured, reaching out with his calloused hand. "Is there anything I can—"

Braddoc jerked his hand away and jumped back. Flinn's body was cold and his flesh as hard as the stone upon which he sat. Steeling himself, Braddoc reached forward again and touched Flinn's shoulder, discovering that it *had* turned to stone. Flinn had become a statue, sitting in the woods of the halflings.

Not knowing what to do, Braddoc dropped to the ground and held his head in his hands. He could not guess if Flinn's transformation was part of the trial of this place of halfling *Denwail,* or was the end of the test.

Braddoc listened to the peaceful sounds of the woods, knowing now how memories of the old times could burn hotter than any dwarven forge, run colder than any elven stream of quicksilver. He wondered if he should get up and leave. He heard the rush of a stream nearby and the rustle of the leaves moved by a slight wind. He would never have admitted it, but he found he was actually comforted by the sounds, by the fragile pleasures of the moment; and he would always be able to return to this place in his memory.

Now Braddoc heard a different sound coming from deep within the heart of the woods. He looked to where he thought he heard footsteps walking over fallen twigs and leaves. Through the darkness, his eyes finally caught the motion.

In the flesh, Flinn slowly appeared, drawn from the very substance of the woods, becoming more corporeal the closer he walked to the clearing. Braddoc turned his head and saw that the statue of Flinn remained.

Flinn raised his hands in greeting as he stepped out of the darkness of the woods. The immortal's stature was more imposing and inspiring than before. "That is what has happened here," Flinn nodded, his voice clear and strong in the quiet of the trees. He motioned to his statue and added, "I have become a legend, and this is my monument."

Braddoc did nothing for a moment. He wanted to leap up and hug his friend, and he wanted to stare awestruck at the man who had risen from the dead to save the world.

"The inspiration of the halflings is that of tales and loves and journeys, told by friends and handed down to family," Flinn said. "The pleasures of time and all the times that come with such pleasures."

Braddoc ran his hands through his long braided hair. He did nothing for a moment more, then cradled his head in his hands and cried, for the first time in over four hundred years.

Chapter XVII

o sat in the middle of the abelaat forces, in the middle of the decimated village. She knew that precious time was passing, that each moment brought more abelaats through the abaton. And she knew she was almost beyond the point of caring.

The creatures shuffled about and sniffed the air around her, and many came close enough to touch her. Jo sat quietly, the tip of Peace jutting up from her huddled form like a red-silver banner. Her tears stained the indigo cloth of her tabard into darkness and wet the ground between her feet.

Despite her imminent danger, she thought only of Flinn, seeing him in the many places they had been together, exhibiting the strength that had made him Flinn the Mighty, had reforged Flinn the Fallen, Flinn the Fool.

Jo thought about the stories she told of his strength. She had heard others say that her ability to tell stories was like that of the elderly who sit by fires and smoke pipes and give the children their dreams.

Jo wondered if she could dream anything but nightmares now.

The dead covered the field outside of the town. Jo had fought the abelaats, slaying hundreds. She had continued killing them after the townspeople were dead, before her strength and her fury finally weakened. Even so, her killing spree had done nothing to save any of her friends.

Why the abelaats instinctually avoided Jo, she did not know. Tesseria could have told her, and Hastur would assuredly know, but they were dead. The sorcerer's body was buried now somewhere among the townspeople. Tesseria lay just outside Jo's reach. The elf's beautiful face had been pointed toward the sky when she had fallen. Jo raised her eyes and blinked her tears down.

The abaton waited to the north and west, but Jo's duty to Penhaligon lay south.

Jo watched with detachment as an abelaat turned from its companions and wandered near her, snuffling and glancing about with its dark, suspicious eyes. The ground shook near Jo as the creature stepped closer to her, but she could not bring herself to move. The abelaat's halo shifted, and Jo saw that the creature's plate armor was much like that of the heavy infantry Jo had seen parading through the streets of Specularum when the king had decided to make a show of force to some passing dignitaries. The abelaat's battle-axe, growing from his long arm, waved vaguely in the air before her. The creature stepped, then stopped, craning its neck and cocking its head to one side. Jo glanced up and could see the abelaat's long teeth, which were much like the ones that had bitten into her shoulder two winters past.

The abelaat turned on its heel and lumbered off into the ranks of the others. Jo's right hand was warm, and she thought that she might have broken the skin where the abelaat stones in the hilt of Peace are inlaid. She peered down at her hand and saw blood where she had been cut by Malken's dagger.

The stones had regained their deep red color, losing the black that suffused them when blood had been drawn from Jo's hand. Tainted with the poison of evil creatures, the stones worked no magic without a toll. Shuddering, Jo released her grip on the hilt of Peace and hugged the red-silver blade closer. The thought of the poison flowing in her veins made her want to cry out again.

The abelaats around her lifted their heads and turned; they had caught the scent of her blood. Jo's heart pounded with fear, and she stood, raising Peace in a defensive stance. To Jo, it seemed that the creatures were both confused and anxious, like animals stalking around freshly killed prey.

With the red-silver blade, Jo slashed off a piece of her indigo tunic. The sword cut easily and soundlessly through the cloth. Jo caught the swatch before it hit the ground. Propping the blade on the ground against her leg, she tied the cloth around her hand to stanch the bleeding.

The abelaats began to move in toward her. Jo was forced to step back as one of the creatures moved in front of her; its black halberd sliced quietly through the air. The

abelaats tightened the circle, forcing Jo to lift Peace verti-
cally so that the blade would not cut any of the creatures
until she was prepared to attack. The black halos created a
wall of darkness, blending the features of the abelaats into
strange, formless shapes.

Jo held Peace with a single hand and bit open the knot
she had tied in the cloth binding. A new flow of blood
started.

Jo squeezed the cloth into a ball and threw it far behind
her, hoping that she had chosen the right direction for
her escape. The abelaats turned at once, as if the blood-
soaked cloth was a lodestone, and raced away. Jo held
Peace in a steady grip and waited for the creatures to clear
away, but they all moved past her without stopping.

Jo turned and ran north toward the Black Peaks. She
kept her red-silver blade held above her head and to the
right in case she needed to defend herself. Her legs carried her through the ranks of the remaining abelaats, who
stood in their perfect lines and formations, perfect soldiers for the one whom Jo knew was the cause of the
world's pain.

Once she had fully escaped the abelaat camp, Jo
allowed herself only one thought.

Kill Teryl Auroch.

                         🙠 🙠 🙠 🙠 🙠

The light from the abaton pierced the curtain of clouds
that filled the sky with night. Jo looked out over blasted
Armstead, sitting on the final rise leading into the valley.
She recalled her first reaction to finding the town, every

building charred and every life taken to feed the power of the gateway. She had been angry and felt as devastated as the city. The abaton's powerful glare filled Jo's eyes, harshly carving her features with deep shadows.

Abelaats ringed Armstead as they had surrounded Jo on the field of battle. They formed thick shadows around the scintillating column of the abaton. Their numbers were so great that Jo imagined she looked down into a region of the night sky that had fallen from the heavens. The light from the abaton bathed the creatures in its pearlescent glow but did not repress their black halos. Their ranks were perfect and ordered. There was not a force on Mystara that could hope to defeat this army.

The journey from the south had not taken Jo long. Her body felt more lean and strong than it ever had before, despite the fact that she knew she had not eaten for a few days. She glanced down at her forearms and saw veins picked out by the abaton's glare. Her hands had the same lines of bones and sinew that Flinn's had when she had first met him in the town of Bywater.

"What would you say, Flinn, if you saw me now?" she whispered to herself. Jo had once been alone, abandoned by her family to live in the streets, where she had survived on little more than her wits and tenacity. She had struck out to find Flinn the Mighty and instead found Flinn the Fallen. Through him, she met others, Karleah and Braddoc—and Dayin, whom she knew from her vision waited patiently for her, archly suspended inside the shaft of light. She had met the court of Penhaligon, been surrounded by hundreds of people as her sword was blessed, ridden out among the ranks of the soldiery only to have them all killed.

Jo took another breath and sighed, thinking how she had gone from being alone to being with everyone, outcast to idol. Now she was alone again. Almost every person she had known was dead. Shaking her head in regret, she glanced down at Peace, whose metal had turned a darker shade of red. The four runes of the Quadrivial and the final rune of peace were dark, turned away from the abaton's power; she wondered about when she had last thought about the Quadrivial, or even about knighthood.

Jo shook her head again. Her limbs felt stronger than they had ever been, and she was a much more experienced fighter than most, having been taught by two great swordsmen as well as learning hard lessons on the field. Peace could cut through the creature's ranks as long as she could stand, and she would stand until Teryl Auroch was dead.

Unsure of what she would find on the other side of the abaton's gateway, Jo considered using the abelaat stones in the hilt of Peace in an attempt to scry the landscape of the abelaat world. She held Peace tightly in her right hand and began to squeeze hard against the stones, but then suddenly changed her mind. The abelaats could smell her blood at a distance, like a wild dog can smell fear and death. She had no doubt that the vast number of creatures waiting below in the valley could easily find her scent.

The entire region was perfectly quiet. Jo had not seen any animals or birds during her journey back to Armstead. Even the insects were hiding. Jo glanced at the abaton's light and remembered Dayin hanging in the waterfall of power. She decided it was time to act.

Jo checked her armor to ensure that the straps had not come undone without her noticing, but the shoulder guards were firmly in place, as were the greaves and vambraces. The only tear in the indigo tabard was the one created when she made a swatch to bind her wound. Even the light cotton undershirt seemed as good as if she had just purchased it new.

The abelaat formations surrounded the pillar of light in a pattern like a flower's petals, with gaps between the formations. Jo could not see any forces patrolling the area, as they had at the other town.

Jo lifted Peace and started down the mountain. Her feet picked out the same path she had taken the first time she had been to Armstead. She kept her concentration fixed on finding a clear route to the abaton through the ranks of the enemy. Glancing around and behind her, Jo almost wished that she were not alone among the enemy, imagining, just for a moment, that her friends were somewhere nearby. But they were not, and she pressed on.

The wind whipped Jo's tabard so hard it slapped against her skin and left welts on her arms and legs. The cloth that covered the shoulder guards struck her nose, and she winced but did not slow her steps. Eyes fixed on her objective—the pearlescent glow of the abaton—she became oblivious to the scuffle of her hard boots, oblivious to the howling wind in her ears.

The scent of the abelaats filled the shifting air. Jo swallowed hard to keep herself from vomiting, though she had nothing in her stomach. The thought of food made her swallow again, the acid and bile burning her throat. Only when she was within a few paces of the abelaat lines did the smell of ashes, the remains of Armstead, overpower the stink of the spices.

Jo allowed herself to stop. The abelaats around her stood motionless—silent and black. To her, they seemed to be little more than statues carved from the darkest stone. She had expected them to begin sniffing the air, but they remained still, perhaps because the cut on her left hand had mostly healed over.

Jo bit her lip to keep from laughing. She could not believe that she, once abandoned in the streets of Specularum, had, by her own hand, raised herself to this position. She wondered if this had all been an immortal plan. Everything she was and everyone she had known seemed to lead to this point as if it were all plotted out—a sponsorship most easily proven by the fit of her boots and the feel of the elven armor against her skin.

The wind shifted direction and struck Jo forcibly from behind and the sides as she stepped carefully through the units of black, immobile creatures. Despite the wind, which seemed to rush her toward the abaton, she maintained an even pace. Jo glanced behind her and saw that she had already covered a distance as long as the courtyard of the Castle of the Three Suns, but still the column stood ahead.

For a moment, Jo thought that she saw something dark moving within the column of light. She held her breath, expecting to see Dayin, but he did not appear. Even if he were there, he was not a willing part of Auroch's conspiracy. He had been a friend, and Jo hoped that the beautiful young man would receive her as such also.

Jo grew colder as she approached the pillar. She wondered if Karleah had felt the same chill when she had sat before the abaton with the last true abelaat stone in her hand. The abaton drew heat as well, an otherworldly hunger for power. Jo wondered if the old woman had prayed to any patron in her last hours.

"Diulanna, Patroness of Will," Jo began, slowly finding the words, "I ask for nothing more than strength and courage." Jo considered her prayer, then added, "I need nothing more."

Without further thought, she stepped, alone, into the power of the abaton.

Jo stood inside the column of light before a young man—handsome, pale, and familiar. He stood in the air, his arms down at his side, palms out. His right leg was crossed over his left, bent at the knee, and his eyes were closed in slumber or meditation. Jo could not reach out to touch him, to wake him. He was incredibly beautiful.

The light flowed around her as if she stood in a waterfall, though the illumination raged upward and out to some unknown place. Jo felt a great presence nearby, guiding the light and the flow of the power. The presence also kept the young man's eyes closed.

Jo was determined to wake him. She pushed forward against the strength of the light, against the power of the presence. She moved slowly, maintaining her motion through force of will alone. With numb fingers, she reached out.

The man's eyes opened. Jo stared into the pale depths, as bright and cold and lovely as the light that surrounded them both. His eyes were filled with the abaton's light.

She could feel his power, and suddenly the power of the other presence, the one guiding the waterfall.

The young man opened his mouth to speak but was forced back to silence. In fear Jo pulled back. A single name rose in her thoughts.

"Dayin."

The word was the key that opened the gateway.

Chapter XIX

raddoc sat upon a rocky crag, staring out into the chasm that stretched as far as his eye could see. The sun's light was still choked by the cover of clouds, choked and growing darker by the day. From this high vantage, they had seen armies of many different banners on the move, desperate villagers, galloping messenger steeds. And still they waited for the next inspiration.

Flinn stood with his arms crossed and his back to the dwarf. Braddoc glanced at his friend, who had not spoken for quite some time. The dwarf was beginning to worry that their mission was taking too long despite the fact that he had lost all sense of time since leaving the caves of Rockhome.

"Flinn?" he began.

"Yes?"

Braddoc said nothing for a moment, still attempting to formulate his inquiry. He decided to say the first thing that came into his mind: "How much longer before we go?"

Flinn glanced over his shoulder toward the dwarf. "What?"

"I think we've been here quite some time," Braddoc said, standing and brushing the dust from his brown pants. The joints in his knees cracked loudly, and he hoped that he was not going to start having problems after five hundred years of good health. "What are we waiting for?"

"You are unusually anxious, Braddoc," Flinn replied evenly, though he sounded amused. Turning, he added, "I am the one with the mission."

Flinn was now everything Braddoc remembered about his friend—everything and nothing. The man was strong and young and vital, powerful, terrible, and almost holy. His body was flesh, and it held otherworldly strength, and the fire in his eyes burned deeper than the dwarf had seen in any artist or king.

Gripped by sudden, irrational anger, Braddoc pointed an accusing finger at Flinn. "And *you're* lucky that I don't have to do anything to perform *my* mission."

"What is the matter, Braddoc? Why are you acting this way?"

"Because—because I can do nothing to help! I'm just here, tagging along after you like a dog does his master!" The dwarf paced, fiercely grinding his teeth.

"You are not a dog, Braddoc," Flinn answered, stepping toward his friend. The dwarf immediately stopped his pacing. Flinn added, "You should be ashamed of yourself for thinking that."

Braddoc glared at Flinn, taking out his pipe and lighting the resins in the bowl. His pouch had been empty for quite some time, and he did not want to ask Flinn to create more. "Fine," he mumbled around the stem of his pipe. "You're probably right. But that doesn't answer my question."

"No, I guess it doesn't," Flinn replied, turning back to face the chasm.

Braddoc waited for his friend to reply. They had both traveled to strange and mysterious lands, some of which Braddoc had been to before, some of which he had heard of, and others that he doubted were within the realms of sanity. Mystara had a great many races with inspirations wholly their own, and Flinn had died for each one of them, reborn greater than when he had begun. There was only one race left.

Instead of reiterating his question, Braddoc sat back down on his rock and smoked the resins from his pipe, pulling hard against the clog in the bowl. He had the strange impression that he would not smoke another fresh pipe again.

"I will tell you why we do not leave," Flinn finally said. He turned and sat on the ground, his legs crossed beneath him. He propped his chin in his hand and looked deep into the distance, an expression Braddoc had seen on his friend one night after the knight's expulsion from the ranks of Penhaligon. "We do not leave because I don't know where to go."

"What do you mean?" Braddoc inquired.

"I mean that I don't know where to go. We have been to the place of *Denwail* for every race but one, and that last race is not making itself known to me."

Braddoc bit hard on the end of his pipe and said, "What are you saying? We know that the last race is humanity."

"True. But I still do not know where to go."

"Can't you call your immortal friends?" the dwarf asked. "You said that they would provide whatever you needed to perform this mission."

Flinn shook his head in apparent frustration. "They cannot help me with this. Though they sponsored me upon this quest, they are not the only ones who have been part of my—rebirth."

The immortal scraped some earth into his left hand and let it cascade to the ground. Braddoc realized then that the world itself, Mystara, was also in some way one of Flinn's patrons. The dwarf had a sudden idea and raised his hand to his ocular.

"No, Braddoc," Flinn said, gesturing for his friend to stop. "Kagyar can't help us, either."

"Then what are we to do?" Braddoc demanded. "The world's peril grows with each passing moment!"

Flinn shrugged and put his right hand under his chin once more. "We wait."

🙚 🙚 🙚 🙚 🙚

When Jo was young and found herself in a strange place, the first thing she always did was grab onto the blink-dog's tail her father had given her, in case she needed to flee. Saddened, she found that she had reached down to her waist, but the tail, lost some time ago, was not there.

The rough corridor in which Jo stood was low, dark, and damp. Light emanated from things that looked like fireflies, buzzing about the hallway in one direction, without seeming purpose. The walls were not made of stone or earth or sand, but some spongy substance. Spongy and hot. Only the chill, magical winds that poured in through the abaton made standing there bearable.

Jo's eyes were slow to adjust, and her senses still reeled from the dizzying transport through the column of light. When eventually she could see how the corridors wound and stretched, Jo felt as if the ceilings and walls might collapse in on her, like the dripping walls of a mud cave. Her legs wanted to buckle beneath her, but she kept her breathing slow and steady to maintain balance, just as Braddoc had taught her to do.

"Living" was the first word that came into Jo's thoughts. Everything around her lived. The walls were alive, the ceiling, the floor, the buzzing will-o'-the-wisps of light. The air lived—the breath of this world, even the cold rush of Mystara's magic was part of the life.

With a settling sense of dread, Jo realized that the abelaats' once-slumbering world was, in fact, a once-slumbering being. A living world, for whom magic was life, and abelaats were organs of a sort. And, in the quiverings and pulses of the fleshy cave around her, she somehow knew that the being was aware of her presence.

Instinctively, Jo closed off those thoughts, knowing that she would otherwise fall to madness. Only thoughts about her mission would be admitted into her mind.

If this is a being, she conjectured, its lifeblood must be magic, because without magic, it slept. And blood flows always back to the heart. Her eyes studied the fireflies, being borne down the passage on the gusts of magical wind. And she knew where to find the heart.

Jo clutched Peace hard in her hand. The blade was her only connection to the life she had left on Mystara. She was not only a trespasser in this place, she was an outsider, a disease, the only one of her kind—the only human in this world. The simple irony of it made her smile grimly. The abelaat had once poisoned her blood, and now Jo herself had become poison in the abelaats' blood. Perhaps she would prove as fatal.

She wondered if she would encounter any of the abelaats themselves, wondered if the creatures had the same form on this world as they did on Mystara. With Peace in hand, she knew she could defeat typical abelaats, but Peace was all too small a weapon to slay a living, breathing world.

As she had hoped, the pulsing stream of magic guided her slowly, inevitably to the heart of the beast. Though she seemed to wander for many lifetimes in that hot and dark place, Jo found herself unprepared when at last she stood at the entrance to a vast chamber. The chamber was shaped like a rough teardrop, and Jo stood at its small end. The glowing wisps flew directly into the great space, joining a sea of other such creatures that made the cavern glow. The ceiling was covered with strange, winding formations that could have been the veins in any beast's heart. Of course, this was the heart of the world.

Jo suddenly felt the presence of another in the chamber. It did not enter from one of the many corridors that opened along the walls, floor, and ceiling. One moment it wasn't there, and the next it waited in the center of the chamber. The sloping, uneven walls began to glow more brightly, like dawn breaking through a drawn curtain. Jo stepped into the room and assumed a full defensive posture, Peace held out before her in both hands, her right foot in front of her left.

Teryl Auroch appeared, standing, in the center of the room. His body grew more corporeal with the increasing light. He materialized beside a huge red stone that Jo imagined was a ruby, a gem imbedded in the fleshy floor of the cavern and rising to the height of a giant. The stone was larger than Auroch, with a rough shape oddly familiar to Jo. Once Auroch was fully solid, Jo saw that his form was much younger and much more vital than it had been in Penhaligon. Many of the magical, glowing creatures swarmed around him, their bodies dissolving away into his young skin.

The light continued to grow. Jo now saw that Auroch's feet were rooted into the floor with ropelike veins that encased his legs and led back to the huge stone itself. She was repulsed.

"You are the one who brings Peace," the sorcerer said rhetorically.

Jo gave no reply. She took a single cautious step forward, shuffling her left foot up to her right, then broke into a full run. She yelled her rage as she charged the heart of this evil world. Her steps echoed softly in the chamber.

Auroch motioned casually with his hand, and a ball of flame appeared in the air before him. When she was within twenty paces, the fiery sphere sped directly toward Jo. Without thinking, Jo swung Peace in a tight arc, the blade impacting the flaming missile. The air exploded in a flash, instantly engulfing Jo in heat and flame. There was no sound.

The flames arced around Jo, pushed away by a sphere of power. They disappeared within a few moments, leaving Jo standing unharmed, but stopped and short of breath.

Jo stared into Auroch's eyes, feeling her heart race and her blood flow hot. She focused her thoughts on him.

"You are dead, Auroch," Jo hissed through her teeth.

"You are in my world, in my land, in my heart chamber now, girl," the mage replied evenly, returning Jo's dark stare. "This place is the heart of all things. I cannot be killed here."

Jo realized that the amorphous shape of the ruby was almost like that of a heart. Wiping her hands on her indigo tunic, Jo checked her grip and stalked forward again.

With another wave of his hand, Auroch sent a second ball of flame across the chamber toward Jo. The fires raged around the sphere of power surrounding her, bathing her face in their heat. She still was not harmed.

"Do not bother with your spells, Auroch. I am going to kill you."

"We shall see, Johauna Menhir," the magician replied. He motioned again, sending a third fireball, then a fourth.

Jo did not swing as she had against the first attack. She

began to stagger slightly from the force of the flames against her protective sphere. The fire grew hotter and seemed to press in closer than before. She ignored the pain and forced herself to move forward.

Ten paces away, Jo was turning red from the heat, and it was blistering. The air around her had grown difficult to breathe, and her lungs labored hard and deep. Her tabard and undershirt were beginning to smoulder, and she could not smell anything except the scent of ash and flame. The sudden memory of Armstead gave her strength to walk forward. She held Peace in both hands, pointed toward Teryl Auroch's throat.

The sorcerer made a different gesture with his hands, and a lance of white light splayed out against Peace's sphere of protection. Jo closed her eyes and shielded her face from the attack, staggering backward a step. She was forced to plant her feet on the soft floor of the chamber and lean into the tidal force of the spell, pushing against it with her strong legs.

Lances of cold and lightning sparked around her barrier, seeping through and striking Jo in the shoulder and back. The pain was greater than that caused by the spheres of flame. She gritted her teeth and attempted not to yell, not to show the sorcerer any sign of weakness or pain. The sphere around her was losing its strength and decreasing in size. With dogged determination, Jo pressed again toward the mage. She wondered how long Teryl Auroch could maintain his attacks, and she hoped that Peace could resist longer.

"There is something you should know, Johauna," Teryl Auroch said, his voice resounding within Jo's agony.

At first, Jo was not going to answer, not allow herself to be baited by the mage's words. She gritted her teeth harder and attempted to breathe in the cracking air. The only word she managed was, "Yes?"

"I have destroyed the Castle of the Three Suns and all who lived there," the sorcerer replied. A detached statement of fact.

"Even if that is true," Jo spat, pressing into the light and force, "you will die just the same."

"Unlike Verdilith, I am not going to toy with you," Auroch said blithely. "Neither you nor the agent of the immortals can succeed."

The white light from his spell redoubled, filling Jo's ears with a dull roar that drowned out all other sound, all other sensation.

She suddenly realized that her body was weakening, dying.

Jo fell to the floor, three paces away from Auroch. Writhing. The sorcerer's spell dissipated.

Jo clutched tightly to Peace and caught a momentary glimpse of the final rune carved on the flat of the blade— the rune that had given the sword its name, that had shown her the true path of knighthood and all it represented. She knew it all meant nothing now. She was wounded to the point of death.

Teryl Auroch glided forward on his venous legs and towered over Jo. Through her haze of agony, she saw that the sorcerer now looked even younger than he had appeared before. His body was covered with the strange, pulsing veins, joining him to the floor and the huge stone.

Teryl Auroch produced a long dagger of black metal and held it over Jo's heart.

"All you have left now is hope."

Chapter XX

"It is time to leave, Braddoc," Flinn said, standing. The dwarf leaped up, his heart beating hard in his chest. He knew that this final journey would mean the salvation or destruction of the world.

"Where are we going?" Braddoc asked, dusting himself off and replacing his pipe as quickly as he could manage.

Flinn shook his head. "*We* are not going. It would mean your death."

"What are you talking about?" the dwarf demanded, stepping forward. "Of course I'm going!"

Braddoc saw the fires in his friend's eyes flare and then die down, and the man turned away and stared off into the distance. The dwarf cocked his head in confusion; there was an expression on Flinn's face he had rarely witnessed.

"Yes, Braddoc Briarblood, I am crying. And what of it? I know almost everything I knew as a man, and more now that I am immortal." Flinn turned back to face Braddoc and wiped his forearm over his face to clear his eyes. "There is only one thing missing."

"I could tell you," Braddoc murmured, turning away.

"No! No. It would have no meaning to me. But you cannot go along on this last quest, because I must enter the abaton. I must travel to the abelaat world."

Braddoc's wondering as to why the *Denwail* of humanity was not on Mystara was immediately swept away by a profound realization. He staggered back, away from his friend, and raised his hand to his forehead with disbelief.

"You're leaving. Not coming back," the dwarf said softly.

"I must. It is my reason for returning."

Braddoc lowered his hand and placed it over his heart, clutching at his flesh. He had lived over five hundred years, known sorrows deeper than any mortal, but he knew that this time he would not recover from the pain. Flinn, his friend, had come back from the Land of the Dead to rescue Mystara, and Braddoc had been there for the man's rebirth and all of his reaffirmations. Braddoc had known through the voice of his ancestors that Flinn the Mighty would return. But the voices were damnably silent now about the fate of Flinn. Braddoc could not bear the pain of this final passing.

"Take me with you, Flinn," Braddoc said without peering up. "I am too old for this world."

"If I were to take you with me, I might as well kill you now," the immortal replied. "You must stay and guide the dwarves of Rockhome."

"No!" Braddoc spat, standing straight and stepping forward. "I must stay with you, no matter the cost!" After a moment he added, "My ancestors said I must."

Flinn stepped back, surprising Braddoc and making him realize that his own foolish anger had meant something to Flinn the man, Flinn his friend. The immortal ran his hand through his hair in obvious frustration. After a moment he said, "You cannot go."

"Then take me as far as the abaton. I can defend myself against its power," Braddoc replied.

"You were far away from the pillar of light when you found me in Armstead," Flinn said. "I doubt even your ocular could save you now."

"It can and it will. We are wasting time," the dwarf answered, pushing Flinn and turning the man around.

Flinn dug his feet into the ground and turned to face his friend. Tears remained in his eyes, and he hugged the dwarf tightly. Braddoc returned the gesture, the only time he remembered Flinn showing any outward affection.

By means of a power Braddoc did not even know the ocular had, he could now see the dwarven ancestors that surrounded Flinn and himself. Braddoc continued to hold Flinn as he looked to each spirit in turn. They, one by one, closed their eyes and bowed deeply. When the last ancestor had honored the dwarf, Braddoc released Flinn, closed his eyes, and bowed in return.

Wind tore at Braddoc's clothes and hair, howling in his ears. When he opened his eyes, he found that they no longer stood in the rocky cleft. They were poised now before the pillar of light. Braddoc felt the life leaving his body, but he raised his left hand to the ocular, invoking its power for what he knew would be the last time.

"Oh, great lord Kagyar, Kagyar the Artisan, Kagyar Flasheyes, I, Braddoc Briarblood, your humble servant, thank you for blessing us with this, your power. May it save our lives and the life of this world." Braddoc paused as he looked to his friend.

The pain of the ocular resounded through Braddoc's body as he felt his flesh begin the transformation to stone.

The dwarf saw Flinn's mouth twitch in sympathy, and he realized that the man had become more than he was when only a man, more caring and able to show that caring. According to the spirits of the dwarven ancestors, that was the greatest strength of all.

"Return quickly," Braddoc said to his friend.

"Good-bye, Braddoc."

❧ ❧ ❧ ❧ ❧

Jo could not move; her body would not respond. She felt horrible pains from within; somehow she knew that her blood, sick with the taint of the abelaats, was flowing without natural direction in her frame. She felt her life-force seeping out from between her clenched teeth and imagined she could taste the poison.

"There are no great words for this," Teryl Auroch said, placing the dagger against her indigo tabard. Jo felt the tip of the black blade penetrate the perfection of her elven armor, cutting deeply, killing her heart.

"My world will live again."

≈ ≈ ≈ ≈ ≈

Dayin allowed Flinn passage, knowing he could have stopped the immortal if the man had attempted to harm the abaton. The beautiful young man's soul had become the power of the abaton, the bridge between worlds. It was as his father had planned from the beginning. It was necessary. It was good. With his eyes closed, he would guard the abaton with his final essence. If the abaton were destroyed, he also would die.

Flinn said nothing and made no affirmation of Dayin's existence as he left one world and entered the next. Dayin watched as the immortal stood behind a woman who had fallen to his father's magics.

Johauna.

Dayin remembered Johauna, who had opened his dead, white eyes in a dream. When his father had forced him to forget everything and become the embodiment of the abaton, the savior of their world, he had not been able to remove the thought of Johauna, the true hero, the vision. And she had returned and reminded him again that she was alive, still a hero, a vision.

But now Johauna was dead. Teryl Auroch leaned against the ruby heart, the seat of his power, blood raining down from the tip of the black dagger. Flinn, perfect, filled with power and fire and inspiration, pushed away the firefly lights with his entrance, his steps burning pure holes into the living floor. Without glancing at Auroch, he stood over Johauna's body, then kneeled down, touching her with his hands.

A tear came to Dayin's tightly closed eyes.

Flinn was remembering the woman he loved. Dayin
had loved her as well before the life of the worlds flowed
through him, and in his heart he knew he could love her
again. In his hidden heart were all the memories of
everything he had been as a child. Suspended between
the worlds, Dayin saw the lives of Johauna and Flinn
touch a last time, both releasing the pain of the other in
their love and remembrance. Dayin watched joyfully as
Flinn drew in her essence and died, his form fading and
unweaving itself into life and flames, his spirit entering
the place between the worlds.

And beneath his immortal touch, Johauna drew in his
essence and was reborn in a halo of golden light, the hope
of her world. Inspiration. Her flesh restored.

⁂ ⁂ ⁂ ⁂ ⁂

Jo wept.

Teryl Auroch lurched forward, his body blackening and
charring, losing its shape. He held the dagger above his
head and ran toward her, his venous legs lifting from the
floor, parting with the life of the world. Jo swept Peace in
a tight arc and struck Teryl Auroch. The sorcerer clutched
at his wound with a bloody hand but did not stop, forcing
himself onward.

Without a sound, Jo stepped back and stabbed again
with Peace, piercing the mage's chest. She pressed the
blade through his soft flesh, feeling the ground tremble
beneath her feet, every inch of the metal's downward
journey intensifying the tremors. The sorcerer's eyes
rolled back, and his face collapsed in on itself. His black

dagger fell from his hands and disappeared into the soft floor, his body melting out from around Peace. The tremors continued until the mage's flesh had drained away like water into soil.

Johauna stood up, panting, gasping. Her eyes were wide with disbelief and amazement. She stood, silent, unthinking. The ruby heart began to melt, and the walls of the chamber lost their vitality and light, slowly dying.

Johauna released the blade and fell backward, letting herself tumble, sobbing, to the trembling ground.

ва ва ва ва ва

Flinn arose in the pillar of light, reborn for what he knew was the last time. He knew Braddoc waited for him outside the coruscating power and light of the abaton, and he wished the dwarf would live. And, with the strength of the world, he hoped that Johauna would find her way back.

Dayin lashed out, blind, and took hold of Flinn's neck. Flinn reached out with hope and fire and love and returned the hold, staring into Dayin's beautiful, dead eyes, fully open now.

From the other side of the abaton, Johauna's cries reached the ears of Flinn and Dayin. The young man nodded once to Flinn, and Flinn returned the nod in understanding. Johauna needed to return home.

With trust and the love they both felt, Dayin released his grip and let the power of the abaton flow once more. Both men silently watched as Johauna was taken from the world of the abelaat to her home of Mystara. Then both of the immortals resumed the struggle that would last for eternity for the abaton to remain closed.

ર ર ર ર ર

Braddoc stood in silent counsel with the spirits of the dwarven ancestors. They had no voices other than the sounds in his soul, but these sounds made his heart unwilling.

Lowering his left hand, Braddoc asked Kagyar for a last favor. The ocular erupted with a power that had once saved Mystara by saving Flinn from the life of *Denwarf* in the caves of Rockhome; now the power would ensure that the abaton would stay closed as long as Flinn and Dayin wrestled between the worlds. The red light from the ocular bathed the abaton in its glow, swallowing the pillar, slamming the puzzle-box's lid, forcing a final scream to be ripped from the dwarf's throat as his flesh was turned forever to stone.

Chapter XXI

eryl Auroch had not lied. The Castle of the Three Suns had been destroyed. The glory of the knighthood was gone.

There was very little left of the castle and the surrounding town. Jo picked through the ruins. The towers of the castle had fallen to rubble, and the walls had been smashed by the siege engines she had seen in her vision. The portcullis of the main gate was several feet away from the gate itself, its black iron bars twisted and rent. The gate houses were leveled to a few remaining stones. Jo stepped across the threshold, forcing away the fond memories of the first time she had entered the castle.

She hoped that the people had made their escape before the enemy had arrived at their doors. Perhaps even some of her friends escaped: Arteris, Colyn Madcomb . . .

Graybow. . . . Perhaps Auroch had lied about that fact.

Jo stopped herself from feeling the love that she had held for her friends, the love she had shared with Flinn, from Dayin. She was alone now, as she knew she must be when she began the journey. The loss of Flinn a second time was too much for her to bear. Jo rubbed the place where the dagger had pierced her heart.

Walking through the devastation, Jo attempted to find the remains of Sir Graybow's chambers, but she could not find anything recognizable. Even the rose-colored granite from the courtyard was torn up and shattered.

She sighed and stopped walking, sitting on a rock and holding Peace up to her eyes. All but the last rune on the blade distorted her reflection. She wondered if this were some message from the immortals, but did not allow herself to care. The devastation of her life was too great to hold within her heart. She knew that only through the greatest effort and will would she be able to restore peace within her soul.

The first thing she needed was food. If she were going to travel, or rebuild, or live, she had to eat. Glancing around, she hoped to find something, even some water in a jug. She turned and reached down into a pile of rubble, pulling out a piece of dark cloth.

It was the tunic of a knight of the Castle of the Three Suns. The new sun's light threw golden rays off the cloth's fine embroidery.

Tears welled up in Jo's eyes, running down her face and staining her tabard. She cried now for everything she had known and loved.

❧ ❧ ❧ ❧ ❧

"You will never understand, Braddoc Briarblood."

Braddoc scowled from beneath his hair, his broad arms crossed over his chest. His spirit stood in Armstead near his stony body. He did not like being told he did not understand, especially now.

"What does this all mean, then?" the dwarf demanded, maintaining his pose. "I suppose you had all this planned from the beginning."

"Don't be foolish. The world is a bigger place than you know, and there are many things planned from the beginning. However, now that you are one of us, I suppose it won't harm you to know that you guessed correctly. You always were a personal favorite."

Braddoc dropped his arms and sighed loudly. He asked, "What happens now? Do I have to remain with you for all eternity?"

"For all eternity, Watcher, or until you must awake again."

"And Flinn?" Braddoc wondered softly.

"He, too, is trapped by eternity."

"That's just great," the dwarf mumbled through his beard. "Eternity with you great lord Kagyar, Kagyar the Artisan, Kagyar Flasheyes."

"Enough!" the immortal commanded.

Braddoc did not feel compelled to obey his patron's order and gave himself the pleasure of a smile. "Don't try your immortal tricks with *me*, Lord Kagyar," Braddoc replied smugly. "We both have a lot to understand."

Braddoc let his gaze linger over his body, turned to

stone and keeping silent vigil over the abaton. He glanced around at the mortal plane, wondering if ever he would return.

He sighed a last time before he was taken with Kagyar to the land of the immortals.

Epilogue

o awoke in the middle of the night, her light sleep broken by the sound of footsteps. She quietly drew Peace from the leather sheath she had made and stepped to the door of her hovel, built among the ruins of the Castle of the Three Suns.

The sound was definitely caused by three people, two of them men, one a woman. Jo was glad that she had drawn the curtains of her little house shut; the intruders would not be able to see inside.

"Hello!" one of the men cried out.

Jo said nothing.

"Is anyone there?" the woman asked. She did not sound to Jo like a hardened brigand.

"We mean you no harm. We have come from Bywater, Specularum, and Threshold," the last man said.

"What do you want?" Jo demanded.

"Nothing more than a place to rest," the woman replied. "We have traveled a great distance and seek the Castle of the Three Suns."

Jo opened the door and faced her three visitors. They were young—younger than she—and covered with dust from the road. She saw that the arms and armor they carried were reasonably new, though scarred with some use. As she stepped out and held Peace up in defense, the three retreated, one of the men putting his hand on his sheathed sword.

"This," Jo replied leadenly with a nod of her head, "is the Castle of the Three Suns."

The strangers glanced at each other, Jo seeing disappointment in their eyes.

"I have been here many months and you are the first to come seeking the castle," Jo said, lowering her red-silver blade.

The woman nodded. "I wouldn't doubt that we are among the first to begin traveling the roads again. Those creatures were everywhere, destroying villages and towns."

"You might as well go back home," Jo answered. "There is no more castle, no more glory. No more knighthood."

"But you wear the tunic of the order. Aren't you a knight?" the first man asked.

Jo stared down at her tunic, the three golden suns of the knighthood sewn into its indigo cloth. She remembered the time when Flinn had used some of his tabard as a bandage. She had resewn it, good as new.

Staring up into the faces of the three travelers, Jo felt very much like she guessed Flinn must have felt when she had arrived at the door of his home in the forest. She had learned much from him, but the greatest lesson was learning from the past and using that lesson wisely.

"Please, come inside," Jo said. "We can speak of knighthood while we eat."

D. J. Heinrich is a pseudonym used in collaboration for the Penhaligon Trilogy. Author, poet, and screenwriter, Kevin Stein, author of *The Fall of Magic*, has studied in both England and America.

The Penhaligon Trilogy

If you enjoyed *The Dragon's Tomb*, you'll want to read —

The Fall of Magic   Book Three
A sinister mage unleashes the power of an ancient artifact on Penhaligon, an artifact that drains the world of all magic except his own. In a final, desperate gambit, Johauna and her comrades set out on an impossible quest to stop the arcane assault and save the world of Mystara! *Available in October 1993.*

ISBN 1-56076-663-8
Sug. Retail $4.95/CAN $5.95/£3.99 U.K.

The Tainted Sword
Book One
The once-mighty knight Fain Flinn has forsaken both his pride and his legendary sword, Wyrmblight. Now Penhaligon faces a threat only he can conquer. All seems hopeless until . . . Flinn regains his magical blade. Yet even Wyrmblight may not be powerful enough to quash the dragon! *On sale now.*

ISBN 1-56076-395-7
Sug. Retail $4.95/CAN $5.95/£3.99 U.K.